HIGHLAND
FLING

Emma Baird

Pink Glitter Publishing

First published 2019
PRINT ISBN: 978-1-9997738-3-0
Copyright © Emma Baird 2019

Cover design by Enni Tuomisalo of *https://yummybookcovers.com*
Published by Pink Glitter Publishing.
https://emmabaird.com

To Sandy, the keeper of my own Highland heart.

CHAPTER ONE

"I didn't mean to smash his heart into smithereens—and they were his words not mine—but if you want to make an omelette you have to break a few eggs, don't you?"

"Stop right there!" My best friend excels at bossiness. She gets up from the sofa and holds a hand out, traffic cop style.

"Do NOT mix metaphors like that," she begs. "Please. You're hurting my ears."

She's a copywriter and very fussy about what people say in front of her. If you ever dare utter, *you know?* at the end of a sentence, she jumps down your throat. No, I don't know. That's why you're telling me. I cut that habit out after about the hundredth time she said it.

"Katya!" I too am on the sofa in my soon to be vacated home. I love this sofa. It took me five visits to the Sofas-

1

RUs (and all on the days when there were sofa sales, so I wasted a lot of bank holidays) to find my perfect one. This is it. Dark red velvet, super squishy and big enough to fit four people, five if you know each other well.

And tomorrow I say goodbye to this sofa. Just like I wave farewell to the coffee table I rescued from a junk yard, sanded down and varnished myself, the bookshelves I built from flat packs accompanied by a lot of cursing, the laminated floorboards I laid one hot and sweaty weekend, the curtains…

Gabrielle Amelia Richardson! My mother's voice. *This moping will not do.* Katya backs her up. Not in real life, but in my head; the two of them competing to see who can order me around the most.

Katya rummages through her handbag, and her hand emerges with a large bar of chocolate that she waves in front of me.

"Okay," she says, "if you promise not to mix any more metaphors and refrain from terrible clichés, I will break this bar in two and give you half." She inspects the bar, checking the label. It's the Oreo cookie one, tiny bits of biscuit crumb encased in thick slabs of chocolate, and it snaps with a satisfying crack.

"The much smaller half."

I am not having that. I lurch forward and grab the bigger bit from her hands, dancing away from her as she shrieks and tries to get it back. My fingers move fast, ripping through purple foil while Katya howls, "No, no, no!" I jam it into my mouth, bite off a quarter and hand it back to her, tooth marks and all.

All's fair in love and war, or love and chocolate, right?

"You pig," she says, but bites off her own bit anyway, and sinks back into the sofa. I do too, seeing as me and this comfy hunk of red velvet are on the brink of a split. Best I make the most of it.

We finish the bar between us. Katya holds chocolate-y fingers in the air and wiggles them. I raise my eyebrows, and she lifts the cushion underneath her and wipes them clean on it.

Not my cleaning problem any more.

"It's so selfish of you to move to the ends of the earth," she pipes up.

"Hardly," I say. "They do have public transport in Scotland, you kno- I mean, yes you can get there by train and bus, even plane if you want to."

"Not the same," she says, and she is right. We have lived not more than fifteen minutes from each other ever since we were kids. Even when we went to university, we chose the same city.

"You're the one who cheered at the engagement party," I add, sticking my ring-less hand out so I can place it on her knee. "Or rather, the not engagement."

"And I would cheer again. Every single time. I just didn't think you would do something this drastic."

But I don't have a choice. Not really. Ryan is still at his family's place in France and he made it clear I was to be gone by the time he returned. He's got a point too.

Despite the lavish sofa and the hand sanded coffee table, this is his house. Ryan works in his family's garage and car sales company. They had a few rough years during the recession, but car sales have peaked once more. He is fantastically rich, and he owns this house outright. I am a tenant the landlord now wants rid of. Fast.

Katya gets her phone out and scrolls through the pictures I sent her. She moans about what I am about to do, but it was her idea.

One week ago when I was still a teary, snotty mess, she marched round to the house, whipped out her laptop and put it in front of me.

"Cat sitting!" she announced. "I wrote five articles for a website some months ago. You live in a strange person's house and look after their beloved cat in exchange for free bed and boarding."

"But, but, but." I had plenty of objections. One, you don't get paid for it. Free lodgings are all well and good but not much fun if you can't afford to eat. And two, I am, whisper it, not much of a cat fan. Please don't hate me. I know cat lovers make up a decent percentage of the population and they could tell me plenty of reasons why I'm misguided or deserve to die because of my misguided opinions.

Katya waved my concerns aside. If I spoke nicely to my boss, Katya said, she might let me work from home or remotely. I am a graphic designer, so I don't 'need' an office only an iMac and an internet connection. And cats, Katya claims, are dead easy to care for. You feed them twice a day and that's it. At least you don't need to take them for walks. Or do the dreaded pick up poo after them.

"And people let you stay in their homes, total strangers, all because they can't bear the thought of their cat being on its own?" I asked.

Katya nodded solemnly. She spoke to the people who run the cat sitting agency's website. Cat owners, it seems, are a devoted bunch. Nothing is too much for dear kitty. They hate the thought of the little beast thinking it's all on its lonesome. All I needed were references from reputable people—my boss and the minister from our local church who would happily add hers, even though I'm her least regular audience member.

Neither of us expected my first search to be so successful. I uploaded a pic, wrote a bit about myself and told only a few white lies. *I love cats. I have been looking after cats all my life* and bam! A few hours later, my phone beeps. You have a new message.

Hey Gaby, my name is Kirsty. I am 26 years old and I have just split up from my boyfriend and need to get away. The only thing stopping me leaving immediately is my adorable little cat, Mena. She loves our cosy home, so I don't want to uproot her. Can you help?

"Fate," I said to Katya. "She's my age, and she's also just split up from someone and needs to get away. It's like my all-time favourite film, *The Holiday*, where Cameron Diaz and Kate Winslet swap homes because they are desperate to escape their ex's."

My butterfly mind skipped ahead to the Jude Law bit where the Cameron Diaz character realises her house swap's brother is this delightful dude. Could Kirsty have such fabulous relations? Then, I ticked myself off. Getting over Ryan, remember?

Katya rolled her eyes at *The Holiday* reference. She isn't a fan of that movie. "Okay then," she said, "where does 'Kirsty just split from my boyfriend' live?" She zoomed in on Kirsty's profile.

"Whaattt! I've never heard of this place—Lochalshie. It's zillions of miles away!"

"Zillions," I said. "That's not a proper word is it?"

Actually, the idea of moving miles away excited me so much I didn't bother with any of the other responses. Talk about a fresh start. I've lived in Norfolk all my life, and Katya, and I proved what homebodies we are when we both ended up at uni in Norwich. My new 'job' would mean not only leaving my county but my country. I was about to ask Katya if she thought I needed a passport to cross the border when I zipped it. I have a habit of letting my mouth work before my brain engages. If that question had ever seen the light of day, Katya would never have let me live it down.

When someone says Scotland to me, I imagine wild hills and mountains, lochs and out of the way beaches where waves crash against the shore. And I'm a quarter Scottish. Maybe I'll find cousins up there, a mad, friendly bunch who drink tonnes of whisky and welcome me with open arms.

I am reluctant to leave my friend, but I promise her we'll Skype, WhatsApp, FaceTime and everything else that is available to the modern gal. Katya mutters I might be lucky to get internet access in the middle of nowhere, but I dismiss her fears. Blimey, you spot masts left, right and centre these days. We'll be able to do our daily catch-ups no probs.

It. Will. Be. Fine.

She goes quiet, her face focusing on her phone screen.

I snuggle up closer and check out what she's looking at. It appears to be the town's website—stuff to do, places to eat, and all that. She clicks on a link to the gallery and we scroll through pics of last year's Highland Games.

"Stop!" I shout before she fingers one of the pictures out of the way. "That one!" She flicks the picture back and blows it up. Who IS this vision? The photo shows a young guy in a dark green and black kilt standing in a field next to a giant log, his hands on his hips and a massive grin on his face. He's got dark red hair, curls that touch his shoulders and a broad torso expertly displayed in a black, tight tee shirt.

"That's Jamie Fraser," Katya twists her head so she can spot what my face is doing. The same as hers, I suspect—slack-jawed and wide-eyed in astonishment. We are big… No, scrap that. We are Outlander's number one fans. We've read all the books and watched seasons one, two and three together on Amazon Prime, pausing it every time Jamie's bare-chested. Ryan wasn't around those evenings.

I take the phone from her and peer at it closely. "No, it's not Jamie," I say eventually, reluctantly. "But pretty darn close." I squint at the caption. "Says here he's local resident Jack McAllan, and he's just won the annual tossing the caber competition."

Katya's eyebrows shoot so high at that I worry she's about to experience the first non-surgical facelift. They revert to normal, and a grin spreads its way across her face.

"So, my newly single friend. Off to the wilds of Scotland; where Jamie Fraser's doppelgänger lives, a dude who is a strong man too. Do you think Kirsty would prefer two cat sitters to look after her precious Mena?!"

CHAPTER TWO

"You're late."

Oof. That's not friendly, is it? A pity too as when I saw who was waiting for me outside Kirsty's home, I sent prayers heaven-wards. Katya, guess what? I imagined how the conversation I'd promised her as soon as I arrived would start. Only Jamie bloomin' Fraser was waiting to greet me in the village. Kirsty had said one of her friends would be waiting with the keys, but she mentioned no names.

And darn, if he isn't even better looking than the pictures we saw of him on the town website. In those, he grinned at the camera and his dark-red curls touched his shoulder. Now, his hair's been cut buzz-cut short. I'm not always a fan of hair you can't run your fingers through, but the short length of it shows off his razor-sharp cheekbones and a jaw that is at this moment clenched tight. You can see his eyes better too, and they are so dark brown they are almost black. They flash with irritation, instead of laughter and immediately I'm reminded of school and the chemistry teacher who took a dislike to me after I blew up a lab.

[Hey. You give teenage girls the means to create chemical combinations that are highly flammable and what do you expect to happen?]

Jack's dressed in combats too. Perhaps he really is a soldier. The cargo pants mould to his shape, and it looks like he's giving that black tee shirt from the caber toss win another airing. His foot taps in irritation.

"You told Kirsty you'd be here at two o'clock. It's now half-past four," he says, the eyes turning from annoyance to a full-on basilisk glare. I want to poke my tongue out at him, but I sense such an immature response would only inflame him further.

"I stopped at Glencoe," I say. "Isn't it obligatory?"

When preparing for my move to Scotland, I read lots of travel blogs. All of them told drivers heading northwest to stop at Glencoe. The A82 road took me that way, anyway. My journey started at eight thirty this morning—half-an-hour later than planned because my farewell to my mum and Katya proved more tearful than any of us had expected. Despite Katya's jokey promise that she'd be coming too so she could check out Jamie Fraser, in the end, I was the only one to say goodbye to Great Yarmouth. I stuffed my tiny Toyota Yaris with everything I thought

I might need—my iMac, my clothes, Wellington boots and a lot of toiletries and food as Mum and Katya both insisted that Scottish villages in the middle of nowhere have no shops—and set off. The minute I reached the Scottish border, the heavens did what everyone tells you always happens in Scotland. They opened and let it all out. Honestly, every cloud reminded me of me, post the engagement party and coming to terms with the non-Ryan future that now beckoned me.

I made slow progress. Scottish drivers, I decided as I hunched over the steering wheel and peered through the windscreen wipers swishing back and forth, must develop specialist driving skills that make them good at this kind of thing. Unfortunately, I couldn't master it at all as the occasional angry honk of the horn proved. "Yes, yes," I muttered at the other cars on the road. "I know you're allowed to go 60 miles per hour here, but 40 is fine in these conditions isn't it? Learn some patience."

Something miraculous happened as soon as I got to Glencoe though. The travel bloggers all said the same thing. "Glencoe," they announced, "is *the* most magnificent sight you will see. The problem is seeing it. Expect shyness from this glorious glen and its surrounding mountains. It rarely likes to peep out from behind the clouds." Not so for me. A few miles before my car drove through, the rain stopped and the clouds cleared away. Honestly, it was like someone had taken a duster to the skies, rubbed hard and revealed a light polished blue and a bright sun that sent rays down to spots where it lit the whole place up. I had to stop.

And the minute I did so, I got caught up with two coach loads of tourists, giddy with excitement. The first load had spent a week on the roads, and the rain hadn't stopped once. They'd travelled to castles, cliff tops, ancient battlefields and more, accompanied all the time by rain or at least drizzle. Like me, they clung onto the bar at the viewpoint and stared in wonder at the purple-topped mountains glistening in the sunlight. As they were Japanese, most of them had those top-of-the-range cameras and they shoved them at me. "Please, can you take our photos?"

I don't get asked that question often as most people use their phones or selfie sticks. It felt like a huge responsibility, so I had to take a lot of photographs. I wanted to make sure when the tourists got home and raved about Glencoe to their friends and families, they didn't pull up a picture where I'd cut off the tops of their heads or made them so blurry it looked like an alcoholic going through detox had taken the shot. (That might also confirm stereotypes of Scots, my one-quarter only status notwithstanding.)

Then, the other coach load moved in and didn't they turn out to be American? I heard one woman excitedly tell her friend that they'd filmed part of Outlander here, and I had to butt in. Katya and I count ourselves as the number one fans of everything Jamie Fraser related, but the woman on this coach tour who introduced herself as Darcy had Wikipedia style knowledge of everything Outlander. She pointed at a particular bit of ground and swore that was where Jamie and Claire had galloped over in series one, episode four. I stared long and hard at it until she pointed out a stone and its proximity to a small stream of water. "That bit there," she yelped. "Claire got off her horse and bent at the water to drink a little." I took her word for it. After that, we had to compare our viewing experiences to the book. There, we were in agreement.

"I love a good book," my new friend Darcy said. "But Sam Heughan who plays Jamie is exactly how I imagined! Don't you think?"

And we were off again. I was on the verge of inviting her to come on a detour to Lochalshie with me when the coach tooted its horn, and a cross-looking tour guide emerged. Darcy's chat with me had held them up for half-an-hour, and they were eager to get on their way so they could make the next stop on their tour.

"A haggis factory," Darcy whispered to me as she hastily gathered up her bag and coat. "Do you know what it's made from? I guess they're gonna make us eat samples."

"Oh, it's delicious!" I said on behalf of the tourist board in my new land. "It's just like chicken."

So, that's why I was late. Common sense warns me now I'm at my destination that repeating the photos, the Outlander stories and the haggis explanation will not go down well.

"Tourists," he mutters, and the temptation to not only poke my tongue out but blow a gigantic raspberry returns. Instead, and bearing in mind this is my new home for the next three months, I opt for stating the obvious.

"This is Kirsty's house then?" I say brightly, the sat nav having delivered me to the location. The sun disappeared again fifteen minutes after leaving Glencoe, but the rain kept away. Lochalshie highlighted its location with a bright sign, *Welcome to Lochalshie! We love careful drivers.* And then something in an incomprehensible language I took to be Gaelic. The village comprised a long high street in front of a lake, or a loch I should call it now I'm in Scotland. Clouds gathered at the far side of the loch in front of more heather-clad hills, but otherwise, it was picture-book pretty—enchanting little houses with well-cared for gardens lining the street, one small shop that promised it sold everything and two hotels book-ending the place. One had pride of place at the far end, a huge Victorian edifice that towered over the loch as if daring the waters to rise, and the other appearing much more up to date, three floors and a large garden studded with tables and benches, all occupied by people enjoying an early evening pint.

Kirsty's house astonishes me. It is next to the pleasanter hotel (the Lochside Welcome) and sits forward, so its garden runs onto the loch shore. I spot a barbecue, sun loungers and a swing ball which makes me jump for joy. As a kid, I was Great Yarmouth's best swing ball player as even Katya would grudgingly admit. Next to the house is a lean-to garage up a neat gravel pathway. The Toyota Yaris seldom gets to sleep inside, and I gave the old girl a little pat as I got out. "Sleep well, tonight sweetheart. Not often you escape the elements at night."

A good job, I reflected now, that Jamie Fraser aka Jack McAllan didn't overhear me saying that as I got out of my car. As it was, he appeared minutes after I'd driven up, marching from the pub and making bad-tempered comments on my timing.

"Should I…" I gesture at the loaded-up Yaris, but Jack shakes his head and mutters something about already being way behind schedule. Chastened, I follow him into the house, the front door opening into a well-lit hallway.

Good grief. I don't know about most people my age, but we don't tend to live in these kinds of places. Our lot is either to live with our mums and dads, in which case we do live in homes like this depending on our luck at birth. Or we're more likely to live in grotty rented bottom of the barrel dwellings. Katya shares a flat with four others, the place originally intended to house three. Mould on the walls in the bathroom and kitchen are among its delights, and Katya and her house-mates fight a losing battle with the cockroaches. And I might have left my plush red sofa and hand-sanded furniture behind, but the house Ryan and I shared was nothing like this. There's an atrium—an atrium for goodness sakes—above me as the house is open plan. The hallway is really a living cum dining area fronted by full-length windows where you can sit on grey, sink into 'em sofas and chairs and stare at the gently rippling waters of the loch. The kitchen space is to the right, all Shaker units and walls festooned with hanging copper pots and pans, and above me are mezzanine floors. It looks like two bedrooms take up most of the space up there, the master of which is above the seating area so it must share that same full-length window looking out over the water.

Unless house prices are vastly different in Scotland, how on earth did a 26-year-old afford it?

I'm still staring at it all wide-eyed when Jack clears his throat impatiently. He pulls out a sheet of neatly typed paper and thrusts it at me.

"Here's the extra info you need," he says, words abrupt and clipped. "Wi-Fi password, where Kirsty stores Mena's food, the phone number for the vet etcetera. I take it you don't need anything else?"

He's not said that much to me, but the Scottish accent is kind of killer. He rolls his r's—numburrr, etceterrra. I've always had a thing for accents, and since Katya and I started watching Outlander, my love for the Scottish one has only increased tenfold. If only the present speaker of it wasn't so grumpy.

I take the piece of paper and glance at it. My mistake. Not a piece of paper; five of them with instructions typed on both sides. I skim the first—*Mena likes lightly boiled chicken chopped into small pieces*—and decide it can wait till later. Then it strikes me. I've yet to clap eyes on this pampered puss.

"Where's Mena?" I ask, and Jack... smirks, I decide after a few seconds of trying to work out what the tiny upturn to his mouth means.

"Sleeping, probably. You'll ken when Miss Mena wants your attention."

And with that, he's gone throwing a hasty goodbye over his shoulder as he leaves. "Not even a bloomin' offer to help me unload my stuffed to bursting car," I tell Katya in my head and nod along with her when she says she's outraged.

"Too right, Katya," I answer back. "He might look like Jamie Fraser, but I promise you looks are the only thing he has in common with our favourite fictional man. He's awful!"

CHAPTER THREE

A-CHOO!

One's a wish, two's a kiss, three's a disappointment…

And what does twelve mean, or is it twenty by now? When I was a child, my nanna used to tell me what the number of sneezes signified. I can't remember what she said for twenty, but it can't mean anything good. Death, perhaps. Sneezing on this scale is not fun.

It started precisely three minutes after Jamie Fraser / Jack McAllan left me to unpack all by myself. I heaved the first lot of bags and rucksacks into the house and felt my nose tingle and my eyes water before the sneeze exploded out of me, and I dropped the box of food I was holding. Food packets, tins and boxes rolled everywhere. "Must be a summer cold," I said to myself as I sneezed again two seconds later. By the fourth time, I knew it wasn't a cold. The itchy eyes gave it away, and the guilty culprit herself wandered into the room—Ms Mena, a fat little brown and white creature. It appears I'm severely allergic to cats. I've just accepted a three-month job as a cat sitter, having lied about my years of experience of cat sitting and the wretched little beast turns me into a snivelling, snotty mess just by walking into the same room.

Ms Mena watches me coolly as I attempt to blow my nose. She jumps onto the coffee table and licks a paw, her tongue delicate and precise as it flicks back and forth. I suspect she's doing a *ya boo sucks to you* human gesture at me. Her furry little body radiates nothing in the way of apology or sympathy. Having completed a thorough cleaning job that covered ears, paws, tail, stomach and… urgh, bottom, she yowls at me. I thought cats miaowed. This one cries like a baby.

Kirsty's instructions said the food bowl was in the kitchen area. My mum sent me up to Lochalshie with a tray of Asda's own brand cat food she told me she'd got at a bargain basement price. I open a tin of it, try not to retch (the smell is overwhelming) and shovel out half of it as quickly as possible. Little Ms Mena sniffs it, lifts her head and yowls once more. Disapproval, I guess. I back away; the closer I get to her, the itchier my eyes get, and the more I sneeze. The beginnings of a headache tightens my temples.

As an experiment, I try going upstairs to see if the effects well lessen the farther away I get from her. No such luck. Mena follows me, the yowling still at full pitch. What if one of Kirsty's neighbours hear her and thinks her new cat sitter is a psycho cat killer in disguise? Distracted as I am, I can't help noticing the house's upper interior is as sumptuous as the bottom half. The master bedroom, as I'd guessed, shares that same full-length window, and the view is even better up here, thanks to the extra four metres of height. Light shimmers on the gently rippling waves and a boat makes its way slowly across the loch. Kirsty's bed looks so comfortable and inviting I'm almost tempted to dive straight on it until I notice the light covering of cream and brown fur on the pillow on the right-hand side. Great. She shared the bed with the cat. I'll need to sleep in the spare room.

Naturally, the master bedroom has an en suite bathroom, complete with a sunken bath, a marble sink and a toilet so luxurious looking, I know I'll have trouble sitting on it. Something so beautiful shouldn't be soiled, right? And still the sneezing goes on, my A-choos punctuated by Mena's yowls. What am I going to do? Fair enough, I'd not looked after cats before but an allergy to them? Why hadn't I noticed it before, I should have realised when I went round to visit friends who had cats, the sneezing when one of them came near me would have given it—

Oh, right enough. None of my friends have cats. I haven't encountered too many of them in my life. I whip out my phone, deciding that when it comes to one to ten emergencies, this comes out at the top end. I need to talk to the fifth emergency service—Katya. I hold the phone to my ear and will my friend to pick up ASAP. When the time between dialling and the phone making the connection stretches out too long, the screen tells me I'm not getting a signal. As Katya warned, Lochalshie doesn't seem to have the same number of phone masts as we have down south. Again, what am I going to do? Panic mounts, making my breath come in panicky gasps. I bolt outside holding the phone in front of me watching as the bars move from one to two. Poor, but better than nothing and enough to get me through to my friend.

"So, what's it like?" she answers, her words coming in bits and pieces. Katya always has her phone close to hand so I must have caught her at her spin class. It's one of my best friend's most marvellous achievements that she can talk during a spin class. I tried the class with her once and panted so hard you could hear me above the hard-core rave music they played at eardrum-bursting volume. "And the caber tosser. Is-he-as-dreamy-as-the-real-Jamie-Fraser?"

I hold the phone away so she wouldn't have to listen to me do yet another explosive sneeze, enhanced by my snort at her remark about Jamie aka Jack.

"No," I said. "He's the rudest man I've ever met. He didn't even say 'hello'. Just told me off for being late. Then, he didn't offer to help me carry my stuff in, and you saw how much was loaded in the Yaris."

"How-late-were-you?"

"Two and a half hours," I announce airily, or as airily as you can manage when you're trying to hold back what might be your millionth sneeze. I'm in danger of stealing that woman from the Guinness Book of Records award for the highest number of sneezes in one day. Katya's reply is indistinct, partly because the class instructor in the background yells at her that she can't be working hard enough if she can manage a phone conversation at the same time. She says sorry but doesn't hang up.

"I've got this problem," I say, and this time don't bother covering the phone while I let out yet another a-choo.

"OMG! Are you allergic to cats?"

In response, I flick my phone to Face Time mode so she can see me, red-faced and eyed, and a thin line of snot running down my face. It's a good job we are such close friends. Other people might shriek in fright if they saw me now.

She laughs. (Yet another remarkable achievement—being able to laugh while some Lycra-clad sadist walks around a spin class and tightens the resistance on bikes of participants he doesn't think are working hard enough.)

"Only you, Gaby. Only you."

"But what am I going to do?" I cry. "I feel hot and sweaty and horrible. But I've promised I'll do this job for three months and I've got nowhere else to live!"

The last few words are more like a wail. Now, I sound like Mena—a tantrum-like two-year-old stamping her feet and screaming.

On the plus side, Katya stops laughing. "Soon as I'm out of this class, I'll research it," she says. "Maybe you can take Vitamin C or something, and that'll help?" A few years ago, Katya wrote the content for a health store's website and now believes that Vitamin C is the cure for everything. I rack my brains to try to remember if my mum's food package included orange juice.

"Okay," I say. "And phone me back as soon as, promise?"

She does, but it's only when I step back inside the house I remember there's no signal inside. I'll need to keep popping out every ten minutes to check if she's tried to ring me. Great, great, double great.

Little Ms Mena hasn't let up on the yowling either. When I open the door, she sashays her way towards me, plonks herself in front of me and starts afresh. I gather up some of the food items that spilt from the box earlier and find a tin of tuna—one of the posh ones in olive oil too, and I open it.

"Try this, you thoroughly spoiled moggie," I say, scooping it out into her newly emptied dish. No, not good enough either. She bends her head, takes one cautionary lick and glares at me. That blasted tuna is three times the price of the bog-standard stuff in brine.

Another thought occurs to me which once again sends me hurtling outdoors. I retrieve my iMac from the back of the car and carry it into the house, attaching it as quickly as I can and firing it up. Kirsty's left the Wi-Fi password in her instructions, and I type it in as fast as I can. Nada. No connection. I stare at the screen in disbelief, tempted for a few seconds to bang my head on the table in front of me. No Wi-Fi means I can't work, as I need the connection to keep in touch with people and exchange documents. Did I say that loudly enough? NO Wi-Fi MEANS I CAN'T DO ANY WORK.

My boss, Melissa, took some persuading when I approached her with my idea. "Melissa," I said, "I've thought this all through. You don't need me in the office. I can be one of those digital nomads, can't I? Have internet connection, will travel! And what about those new clients you've just landed in Glasgow? I can be your on-the-ground girl there."

That sold the idea to Melissa. Last year, she decided she wanted to make her graphic design company UK-wide instead of just county-wide. Her employees were relieved. Truth to tell, designing fliers for the Norfolk show and websites for farmers had lost its appeal. We wanted exciting jobs—online fashion sites, say, or just anything that didn't involve agriculture and top of show awards for Friesian bulls. In January, Melissa landed our most exciting client. An American make-up and skin care brand decided it was time to conquer Britain, and they needed a UK-specific website, animated videos, materials for a Facebook page and more to make their presence felt. Trouble was, they'd made Glasgow their base, reasoning it was a lot cheaper to headquarter their staff and warehouse there than anywhere down south. And now here I was, about to move to Scotland albeit on a temporary basis. Their demands had grown steadily since January. If I was close by, I could liaise and ensure our biggest payers to date stayed happy, which meant they would stick with Bespoke Design.

Except… except… And this was another thing. I'd spotted the signs to Glasgow on my way up here. Alarm mounted as the sign disappeared behind the car, zooming away at a terrific rate. When I'd looked at it on Google Maps, the city hadn't seemed that far. A few centimetres or so, give or take. Now I was here, I realised the truth of Katya's words. Lochalshie was a gazillion miles away from anything. I'd imagined myself hopping on the local bus, chatting and laughing with the locals as it took us to Glasgow in… oh, twenty minutes. I'd now worked out that journey was closer to three hours or so.

Mena hasn't given up the plaintive cries, and I resort to searching the cool-bag Mum also pushed on me. In it, she'd included a freshly made kale smoothie, which will go straight down the sink, some eggs and a packet of smoked salmon. "Bit like taking coals to Newcastle," she said to me when she packed the bag, "seeing as Scotland is the home of smoked salmon. But it might be nice as a treat with some scrambled eggs for your first breakfast."

Mena leaps up on the kitchen counter the minute I pull the smoked salmon out of the bag, not even flinching when her proximity triggers off a fresh bout of sneezing. Her tail goes up, and she looks at me expectantly.

"You have got to be joking," I say, fixing her with my best stern stare. I'm in the presence of a master though. This one fixes me back with her best 'give me the smoked salmon now' look, and we lock eyes. Hers are large, liquid gold surrounding big black pupils. Mine are ten times smaller than usual thanks to swelling, green and red-rimmed. We are not an equal match.

I rip open the packet and hastily pull it back as Ms Mena tries to eat the first slice before I've got it out. I don't manage to drop it before she gobbles the slice up. And the one after that, and the next and the next. My scrambled egg and smoked salmon breakfast tomorrow will be missing one crucial ingredient.

I wander back outside, debating whether it's worth unpacking. My mind runs through all the things I'll need to do. Phone Kirsty. Apologise profusely and promise to stay as long as it takes her to find another, better qualified cat sitter. Grovel to Melissa and beg her to allow me to work in the office once more, promising I'll travel up to Glasgow ten times a week (or whatever) so I can be super friendly to our new clients. Write an email to Ryan where I say, 'okay so I told you I was moving out and I may have been a little too descriptive when I told you how I imagined the rest of your sorry life would work out, but is there any chance I can move back into the flat, perhaps you're right and we should…'

No. It's too much. I can't, can't, can't go back. On cue, my phone rings and I dart to the front of the garden next to the Lochside Welcome where the signal is most reliable.

"Katya!" I say, and it all comes out, the terrible allergy, the lack of signal and internet connection and the village being miles and miles from anywhere. "I've made a ginormous mistake," I wail, not caring that by now the happy-go-lucky pint drinkers in the pub garden are staring at me, transfixed. Katya murmurs shushing noises and then pauses.

"Ah," her voice too breezy. "I've been doing a little research. Um, so the site Ts & Cs. Once you sign up, you have to go through with it unless you've got something life-threatening. Or you die. You agreed to them, didn't you?"

"No-one ever reads the T&Cs!" I exclaim, and two of my pint-drinking audience nod their heads sagely.

"But the good news is!"

I brace myself. People always do that when they are about to deliver not-so-good news.

"You can take anti-histamines. They'll help with the cat allergy. And Vitamin C too."

"Where do I get anti-histamines from?" My pint drinking audience leans forward. Katya's answer must interest them too.

"A GP can prescribe them for you. Take a couple, and you'll be right as rain. And I will come to visit you as soon as. Gotta go, bye!"

One of the pint drinkers—a heavy-set guy whose shaggy hairstyle matches the dog sitting at his table—gets to his feet. "Aye, lass," he shouts at me. "Anti-histamines will sort out the cat allergy nae problem. Get the strongest ones ye can. When ah first got wee Scottie here, ah used to sneeze something terrible. And look at me now!"

He points a finger at his chest and grins. I'm not one hundred percent sure he is the picture of health he supposes. He's scarlet-faced, and that pint of beer went down in record time.

"Where's the GP surgery?" I ask, and he grins.

"Just doon the High Street. Ask for Doctor McLatchie. She'll sort you oot."

I wave thanks at him and open the gate, turning in the direction he pointed. I've only taken four steps when the guffaws behind grind me to a halt.

"It's half five on a Friday, hen!" the words sing out. "The doctor's surgery isnae open now. But if you wait till Monday, you can see her then!"

As I stomp back into the house, the laughter continues far longer than it should. It wasn't that funny.

Inside, I shut the door, and the sneezing starts up again. How am I going to last until Monday? My mum and Katya have always said I'm too impulsive. Here's the proof. I'm stuck in the middle of nowhere, my head pounding, my nose and eyes itching furiously, no internet connection, a risk I might get sacked and no-one to talk to. And yes, I thought I was okay about Ryan—the guy I've been with for the last ten years. Ha, my silly self told my conscious. All I need to do is take myself far away from Ryan, and our lives together and I'll be fine. My subconscious mocks me now. It knew better all along.

As for Jack McAllan? That almost makes me laugh. I imagined… I know what the silly yesterday me thought. As I packed my car, I had daft dreams where I walked down the street of my new town and bumped into Jack stroke Jamie, and just like Outlander, he fell in love with me at first sight.

I couldn't be further from the truth, could I?

CHAPTER FOUR

Monday morning arrives, and I am waiting outside Dr McLatchie's surgery ten minutes before she is due to open at nine am. I'd spent the weekend sneezing, not sleeping and making tearful phone calls to Katya and my mum, all of which I had to do outside in the howling wind. Friday's fine weather had lulled me into thinking all those stories people told about how much it rained in Scotland are an exaggeration.

They aren't.

I discovered too that the more you try to flee a cat, the more they see it as a come-on. Everywhere I went, Ms Mena followed me—even into the toilet. I tried shutting doors, but she howled her head off. Have you any idea how disconcerting it is to sit on the loo while a cat watches you without blinking? I blushed as I imagined her having conversations with the other cats in the neighbourhood:

"Uses excessive amounts of toilet paper, let me tell you! And nowhere near regular enough..."

The doctor pulls up in her car outside the surgery at quarter past nine. A Volvo estate screeches to a halt in front of me, barely missing the kerb. The door is flung open, and a woman pokes her head out.

"Sorry I'm late! Sheep on the road. You know what it's like around here."

I nod, then shake my head. No, I have no idea. But she isn't listening, anyway. She pushes past me, keys jangling, and opens the door. The surgery looks nothing like any GP's surgery I've ever been in. If you'd walked up and down the street and someone said to you afterwards, "Where's the GP in Lochalshie?" you'd have said, "I haven't a clue! I just walked past a lot of houses." The surgery is one, a neatly painted door and windows and a tiny sign outside that says Dr McLatchie & Partners. I have my suspicions that the partners do not exist. When I follow her in, past the small waiting area, I spot only one room with a doctor's name on it off the hallway.

She opens the door, telling me to take a seat and fill in the form asking me general health questions. I park myself on the chair. They seem to favour informality here. There is no desk, or hard-backed chair—just two armchairs, a coffee table and a laptop, and scales in the corner.

Sheet filled in, I hand it over. The doctor prods her laptop, and it opens. She pushes herself back into her armchair, folds her arms and smiles at me, fuchsia pink lips stretching across her face in a smile that looks vaguely familiar.

"Well! I've never seen you before. Have ye come from a big city?"

I shake my head and watched her face fall. She leans forward and picks up a notepad and pen.

"Ah well, never mind! What's your problem? Have ye got…?" She takes the pen and points at my crotch. I cross my legs and shake my head furiously.

"Aw! So, no problems down below. That's a shame. I was hoping because ye were an outsider, ye'd have all kinds of—"

"No, no," I blurt, eager to stop this flight of thought, "I'm very allergic to cats. Do you have anything that can help?"

The doctor steeples her hands together and regards me seriously. Then, she bursts out laughing.

"Are ye… the wee lassie."

She laughs so much, I can barely make out a word she says. "So, you're the wee one who… ha ha ha… went tae Kirsty's hoose… wish I'd been there!… and then had tae stand outside on Friday night because her cat was making you sneeze that hard?"

When I nod, the mirth grips her so tightly it takes her five minutes to recover. I sit back, rub my eyes and let

33

out a fake but ferocious sneeze. That was a hint; less than subtle body language to say I am in pain.

"And ye've broken up from your boyfriend?"

The question is so left-field, I agree straight away. What does that have to do with anything? Great Yarmouth is hardly the Great Metropolis, but I've never experienced nosiness on this scale. And how is my previous love life connected to crazy sneezing?

"Stand on the scales!" she barks, and I obey, twisting my face to top of the room so I don't see the result. Again, the connection to an allergic reaction is lost on me, but who knows? Repeated sneezes might do funny things to your body weight.

"Ye're only 54 kilos!" I hear rustling as the doctor flicks through a book. "It says here ye're allowed to be 56-62kgs! Are ye one of those anorexics?"

"Er, no. I inherited my mother's fantastic genes. But can we get back to my real problem?"

"Aye, the sneezing. Did ye know that's where that nursery rhyme comes from—the ring a ring roses one?"

I shrug. "No."

"Sneezing was one symptom of the plague. The ring o' roses described the rash people would get, then they'd sneeze, and the bit about we all fall down is where they died. Sometimes only a day after the rash appeared. It's a pity that—"

She breaks off, quelled by the look I give her. What medical training school taught her appropriate bedside manner is to tell your patient she might have the early symptoms of Bubonic plague?

"Ah well. Too good to be true. All I deal with here are colds and the odd ankle sprain when some short-sighted farmer stands in a rabbit hole. I live in hope that something exciting will walk through my door."

She sounds so disgruntled, it almost makes me wish I had turned up with a condition more intriguing than a severe allergy. Almost. When she presses print on her computer and out pops a neat prescription for what she promises are the world's strongest anti-histamines, I have to sit on my hands to stop myself snatching it off her.

I should try to spend as much time as possible outside, the doctor adds. And it would be a good idea to vacuum the place from top to bottom every day.

Good grief. If Ryan could hear that, he'd curl his top lip and tut. One of our recurring rows was about the housework. Ryan had weird ideas that women should do all the domestic stuff, so I'd pointedly not do it a lot of the time to prove to him housekeeping wasn't an inbuilt gene.

"Anything else I can help ye with?" Dr McLatchie asks, the fevered look back on her face. "Are ye feeling suicidal because of your boyfriend dumping you?"

"I dumped him!" I say, indignant, though her question makes me pause. There might have been a lot of tears over the weekend where I wept and wailed about being on my own, but killing myself isn't on the agenda. I shake my head and marvel once more at the way her face droops when I say no. Then, I remember the work dilemma.

"Is there such a thing as an internet cafe around here?" I ask. "It's just that Kirsty's house doesn't seem to have any connection and I need the internet so I can work."

"Aye, that bit of the village has been having problems recently. Your neighbour at number 12 has complained to the phone companies endlessly about their lack of masts. The poor guy's got tae keep up his Tinder account. He cannae swipe left, right or centre if he's got nae access can he?"

"What?" I passed my new neighbour this morning out in his garden digging up weeds. He didn't look a day under ninety.

"I know," the doctor shrugs. "You'd think a plea from a helpless old man would make them sort it, wouldn't ye? But listen, you can use Jack's house. He's no' there a lot of the time, so he willnae mind. I go there when I do my Skype calls to the patients that cannae come into the surgery."

"Jack?" I say, willing there to be more than one man by that name in the village.

"Aye, Jack McAllan. He was the one who let you into Kirsty's house the other day. Even though you were more than three hours late."

"Two and a half!" Is nothing sacred around here?

She rustles around in an enormous handbag and pulls out a key attached to a tartan keyring which says 'Highland Tours'.

"Here's the spare key. If you go there now, you'll get in, and you can see where you can put your iMac."

Disregarding that she also knows what kind of hardware I have, I stutter "But, but, but.." I mean, shouldn't I ask the not very friendly, super rude Jack first if I can use his house? And did it have to be him? Isn't there someone else in the village who also has super-fast broadband?

"Off ye go," the doctor stands up, shoo-ing me out with her hands. "Ye can drop in at the pharmacy on your way to the house and then pick up your medication on the way back." At the surgery door, she points right. "The pharmacy's the second to last building and Jack's house is the one after that. Best of luck to ye."

She doesn't go back inside when I leave either, so I have no choice but to follow her instructions. The pharmacy assistant—and again, the chemist shop looked more like someone's home from the outside, the door opening into a carpeted room, armchairs and wooden shelves stocked with toiletries that I suspect are older than me—takes the prescription and tells me to come back in ten minutes.

On the street, I can't help feeling net curtains twitch in all the houses round about. And what if, please no, Jack is in? It will hardly help change his opinion if he discovers me letting myself into his home. I mean, what if he is…

Gabrielle Amelia Richardson. My mum's voice again. *Take your thoughts out of the gutter and stop imagining him coming out of his bathroom, wearing only a white towel wrapped around his lower half.* Amazing how, having never seen this impressive sight, my mind has made the image bright, colourful and very detailed. I've even given imaginary Jack a tattoo on his left arm which moves when he flexes his substantial biceps.

Thankfully—disappointingly—the house is empty as Dr McLatchie had promised. His home, a neatly terraced house, is the end building on the street, so it takes up twice the space of the others. It is on two levels, with a room added in the attic. While it doesn't sit right on the loch as Kirsty's house does, the view is better as this part of the loch nestles half in and half out of trees and mountains. I'd expected his home to feel very masculine—all black leather chairs, state-of-the-art connected speakers, laminate flooring and that kind of thing, but I am wrong. 'Cosy' is the right word instead, It's a place that makes you want to take your shoes off and snuggle up in a chair as soon as you come in. Thick, woolly carpet in a moss green shade covers the hallway and the living room, while wallpapered walls in blue, grey and silver remind you of the sea. He has a lot of paintings too, oil landscapes that feature lochs, glens and hills I assume are inspired by the surrounding area.

All the furniture in his front room, including a large sofa that allowed its occupants to stare out of the window, faces towards the front of the house, He's also put a desk close by, which will make the ideal spot for my iMac if I can discipline myself not to spend my entire day gazing at the loch. Working potential assessed, my nosiness instinct (perhaps triggered by the doctor's own rampant curiosity) kicks in. Shouldn't I have a little look around to try to work this guy out? You know, check out what he has in his fridge and if any photos are hanging in the kitchen? Pictures that might show him arm-in-arm with a woman? Or a man. I am open-minded.

The fridge check proves frustrating. I find people's food choices revealing. If he had margarine rather than butter, I'd go off him for sure. Or suppose a bar of chocolate lurked in in there with only one or two squares missing? Proof positive he and I are incompatible. Friday's brief conversation showed we already are, but people who have the willpower to eat one bit of chocolate at a time—who are these alien-beings?

In the upstairs hallway, however, I find a far more thought provoking oil painting. Every other picture is a landscape. This one is a portrait of a young woman. My age, I guess. She looks over her shoulder in an 'oh you surprised me' way. The artist has used tiny splodges of the thick paint to create the sitter's skin tone. The artists has done it so skilfully, the skin appears uniform and alive with colour and life. Light blue eyes dance and sparkle and thick blonde hair ripple from a perfect widow's peak down past her shoulders and reaching almost to her waist. An ex-girlfriend, perhaps? I snap a photo of it on my phone, deciding I'll send the picture to Katya. Between us, we'll be able to find out who the mystery woman is.

Back at the chemist shop, the pharmacy assistant taps her watch as soon as I walk in. "That was twenty minutes, no' ten. Did you enjoy your wee nosey around his house then?"

"No! I was trying to work out the best position for my iMac so I could avoid the glare of sunlight." Honestly. Is there nothing these people don't know about me? I add, *Remember. They are always watching you. Take care,* to the ever-growing pile of notes to self.

"Aye? If you say so." She hands over my paper bag, and I snap it from her fingers and walk out with my nose in the air. My gesture goes wrong anyway. I trip over the raised edge of the door frame on the way out, and the pharmacist assistant's guffaws follow me all the way back to Kirsty's house.

Luckily, the antihistamines work their magic in no time. By Monday afternoon, I've stopped sneezing and feel well enough to set up the iMac in Jack's house. I open the door warily, worried again that he might be in and will object to a stranger letting herself into his home and setting up her computer quite the thing. But once more, the place is empty. When I switch the iMac on and type in the Wi-Fi password, I am able to connect to Bespoke Design's remote access desktop straight away, and I email Melissa promising her I'll start on the website product page template Blissful Beauty needs tomorrow. At least something works.

I drop in on the local shop after I leave. I'd made its acquaintance over the weekend when I'd stocked up on orange juice as per Katya's recommendations and blasted smoked salmon. Little Ms Mena now refuses to eat anything else, even though Kirsty's instructions promised she isn't a fussy eater. Not only that, the little shop stocks two different brands of smoked salmon, one expensive and the other you've got to be kidding pricey. Guess which one the little furry wretch prefers?

"How are ye, Gaby?" Lochalshie General Store's manager now thinks himself on first-name terms with me, which isn't surprising given how much money I've now spent in there. And as advertised, there is nothing this shop doesn't sell. The building has a high ceiling of which the manager has taken advantage by putting shelves all the way to the top. You can buy clothes, mainly raincoats and wellie boots, fishing gear, buckets and spades, deck chairs, insect repellent, every single foodstuff known to man and woman, wine, beer and champagne, make-up, books, bakery and more. When more than one person is in the store, the space closes in you as the aisles in the shop are only wide enough for one.

"Fine," I say, "orange juice and another two packets of this stuff please."

The manager, Jamal, moves to the fridge and pulls out a packet of chicken breasts. "Try these instead," he says. "They're a lot cheaper. You dinnae want that cat getting ideas above her station."

Too late for that, but I take them anyway. They come in at five pence cheaper than the expensive smoked salmon. When I stare at him, wondering if chicken has suddenly developed rare breed status, Jamal tells me they come from the farm next to the village, so they're free-range and organic. I'd have preferred the chlorinated, mass-produced variety for the cat, thank you very much.

Back in the house and Ms Mena fed, I jump out of my skin when a shrill bell sounds out before working out it's the 1930s style phone on the table next to the kitchen area. I pick up the receiver warily. I knew no one who had a landline any more.

"Hello… Gaby?"

The voice is soft, the trace of a Scottish accent but not much of one from what I can work out from two words. She also sounds breathy, just like Marilyn Monroe when she sang 'Happy Birthday' to the president. Mena, who is making her way upstairs where no doubt she's about to settle on the super-big, super-comfy bed, pauses and yowls.

"Oh, little Mena! I miss you so!"

Aha. My superior detection skills tell me this is Kirsty, said owner of deluxe house—how, how, how can she afford it at her age?—and spoiler of Mena. We've never spoken, exchanging all the relevant information we needed to do on the cat sitter website. She asks me if Mena is okay or if she seems to pine after her, and I promise her that yes, Mena misses her mistress, but I'm an okay second-best substitute. Mena flicks her tail and proceeds back upstairs, the picture of pining sorrow. Not.

"The Wi-Fi," I begin, and I hear the sound of someone gathering their thoughts. I told a white lie or two to get this job. Kirsty was less than truthful too when she promised me online that Lochalshie wasn't that far from Glasgow, the internet worked fine, and her cat isn't the world's fussiest moggie.

"Ah, yes, um… Bit of a problem there the last few months, but there are ways round it. If you log on at two in the morning, it works perfectly. Fewer people using it, I guess."

As. If.

"The doctor here told to use Jack's house. Brilliant Wi-Fi there," I reply and hear a sharp intake of breath.

"Jack!" she says. This time the breathlessness is accompanied by a tiny sob. "He smashed my heart into smithereens!"

Wow, my own words only a few weeks ago. When someone else says it, I conjure up the image of a man with a gigantic hammer, whacking it up and down on top of a red blob, droplets and bits splattering everywhere. Urgh.

"Was he the boyfriend you've just split up from then?" I say, anxious to move on from barbaric heart destructions. And never let it be said that Gabrielle Richardson is slow on the uptake. The Jack connection also explains why Jack still had her house keys.

"Yes! Gaby, it's my duty to warn you! Please, please promise me you won't get involved with him! I know he's super lush, but the man is a commitment-phobe through and through! He will break your heart into tiny pieces and won't care in the slightest!"

More images of Jack, back in the tight black tee shirt, grunting as he hauls the hammer way above his head and brings it smashing down on the red blob. How disgusting… And er, goodness me, he handles that hammer like a PRO.

43

"In the slightest, Gaby!" Kirsty says again, my attention having wandered too far into men with hammer expertise territory. Everything she says sounds as if it comes with an exclamation mark. Katya would hate her.

"Um, no I won't then," I say. "I don't think he likes me very much, anyway."

"Oh? Doesn't he?" She perks up a bit at that. "Anyway, the reason I'm phoning is this! I have something to beg of you! I know you're such a kind and helpful person, Gaby," I am? "and you won't hesitate. The thing is…"

The last few words come out in a rush. Kirsty is down south working on something big, no huge, she can't tell me about, it so she needs to stay there for longer than she thought. Six months, not three, and am I able to cover the Mena sitting for her?

I look around me. It's another 'dreich' day. I picked up the word from Jamal, and it's an excellent one conveying wind, rain and grey skies. The water on the loch's choppy. I've only just managed to spend three hours without sneezing. Glasgow and the promise I made my boss about visits there seems impossible. The locals laugh at me. That is, when they aren't actively hating me as Jack seems to. An extra three months here? No, I don't think—

"Pleasy-weasy dear darling Gaby! I'll write you a super-duper review, and everyone will want you to cat sit for them! Imagine! Your next job could be somewhere really exotic like Las Vegas or something!"

"Oh. Okay," I say. I am, as I pointed out to Katya, homeless anyway. Maybe I'll be able to save up enough money for a deposit while I'm up here. I won't be spending money on a busy, packed social life, will I?

Kirsty hangs up indecently quickly as soon as I say yes, and I mull over what she told me about Jack. Darn it, she meant to put me off with her description of him as a commitment-phobe. Unfortunately, the perverse bit of me now adds that to my little stock of information. Together with the imaginary encounter I had with him where he wore only a towel, and the expert hammer wielding, he's now a glittering, glorious specimen of masculinity that sets off every tick on the list of types I fancy.

What a pity he doesn't like me at all.

CHAPTER FIVE

"Good morning Gaby! Are ye off to Jack's to do your design-y stuff?"

After only a few days of making my way along the main street to Jack's house, all and sundry now know my routine. As they do my name and occupation. This morning's questioner is the guy I saw in the Lochside Welcome's beer garden the first day arrived, the one who told me to go to Dr McLatchie's and get myself antihistamines to deal with the cat allergy. He walks his dog along by the water twice a day and has decided our shared pet care responsibilities make us the best of buddies.

"Yes," I say, and he falls in step beside me. Scottie, the imaginatively named West Highland white terrier, barks enthusiastically and runs round my legs, trapping me with his lead.

"Er…" Everyone knows who I am, but I've noticed the villagers have a weird habit of never introducing themselves, so I've no idea what the once-allergic pint-drinking dog owner is called.

"Oh, aye. Wait there a sec and I'll de-tangle ye."

He gets down on his hands and knees and crawls around me to free my legs. It would be one hundred percent more efficient if he just released the lead and unwound the dog, and I dread to think what this looks like to anyone who is watching—a shaggy-haired, long-bearded bear of a man whose head is level with my crotch at the moment moving around in front of me. Jamal from the General Store is putting out his baskets full of buckets, spades and sun hats (optimistic), and he stops what's he's doing to stare, hands on hips and eyes squinting in disbelief.

"Um." I draw back and only manage to get myself more tightly tied up. My neighbour appears—the ninety-year-old Tinder user—opening his back gate and stopping abruptly next to us.

He does an abrupt U-turn, heading back the way he came. "Ah can see youse are busy. Must be one o' they new ways folks hae to—

"No!" I yelp. My neighbour's Scottish accent is stronger than most of the people here, but I can make out the gist of what he says. "The dog's lead has got itself tangled up around my legs."

"Och, aye well here's whit tae dae." My neighbour does what was obvious all along, neatly un-clipping Scottie's lead from his collar. The dog continues running his wild circles around me, tail wagging furiously. When his owner tries to unwind the lead from my legs, I tap his hand smartly. I'll manage that bit myself thank you very much.

Lead handed back, and hasty goodbyes muttered, I head towards Jack's house, hood pulled up against the rain. Yes, the rain hasn't let up since I arrived at Lochalshie. Every evening, the BBC weather woman smiles at me from her warm, cosy studio, her arm moving behind her as she points out that yet again the north-west of Scotland will experience wind and rain. She promises that it's unusual for this time of year. May is often the best month for sunshine and warm temperatures in this part of the world. I'm tempted to take to Twitter or Instagram with all the photos that prove her wrong. Hashtag BBClies.

Dr McLatchie adds her good wishes as her Volvo bumps onto the kerb on the pavement next to the surgery as it does every morning and she throws open the door, complaining about cows on the road.

In comparison, Jack's house is a haven of peace and calm. I let myself in, shut the door, lock it, and lean back on it taking deep breaths. The carpet, paintings and wallpaper work their soothing magic. I can't see much of the loch thanks to the grey skies, but the lack of cars around here makes the distant lapping of the water just audible. I've established my working routine—four hours in the morning, home for lunch and to feed Little Ms Mena who has decided twice a day is nowhere near as good as four times, then another four hours in the afternoon.

Now I no longer have office colleagues,, my productivity has soared. I rattle through cut-outs, templates and more. Who knew? I always thought I was a hard worker, but it turns out I used to spend a lot of my day chatting with my colleagues and offering to do the coffee and tea runs. When you make coffee just for yourself, and you take it black without sugar, it only takes a minute.

I've yet to meet Jack again. I asked the doctor if I should phone him to double check if it is okay for me to use his house, but she promised it was fine. He's away on business this week, she says, and won't be home until tomorrow.

This morning, there's an email from Melissa. I'm to catch up with her in Glasgow on Monday to meet with Dexter Carlton, Blissful Beauty's head of marketing. He needs to discuss their product-page templates and other ideas he has for the big launch. Can I get there for 9am? Yes, I type back and decide to worry about it later. I have a car. It won't be a problem though it will mean an early start.

As I scroll through Blissful Beauty's picture library for suitable images, I remember the woman upstairs, and my curiosity resurfaces. If you're a man you don't keep such a stunning picture of a woman in your house unless she means something to you, do you? Kirsty said she'd dated him, but would he still have her portrait up if he'd finished with her? I've no idea what Kirsty looks like. On the cat sitter website, her avatar was a picture of Mena. A far too flattering one if you ask me. My professional experience told me she'd used filters to make Mena slimmer and her fur appear glossier than it really is.

I send the picture of the woman to Katya, who is up to date with all the latest happenings in my life. After the phone call from Kirsty the other day during which she asked me to stay on beyond three months, I phoned Katya immediately afterwards. "This place is so awful!" I sobbed. "How am I going to last that long? And I miss you. I hate not being able to see you every day." Katya went into full buck up mode, her voice artificially bright. She'd visit as soon as, though when I tried to pin her down on a date, she wouldn't commit. She'd just landed a job as a ghost-writer where she was to write some celebrity's self-help book for them. "Who?" I asked, diverted enough to wonder at all the possibilities.

"It's hush-hush," she said. "I've had to sign a very scary non-disclosure agreement promising never to reveal I've written a book for someone who passed it off as all their own words."

"But-but," I protested. "Everyone knows the truth of NDAs. They have two sentences buried down the bottom in tiny print that say, 'We expect you'll tell your best friend. Just make sure she keeps her gob shut.'"

What was the definition of best friendship after all? It's where you have someone who knows your every secret. A poncy legal document can't get in the way of that.

"Gaby," Katya's voice was sorrowful. "You're right about the sentences they bury in the legalese. But what about the second one?"

Huh. Harsh but fair, if I'm honest.

"We'll speak every day," she promised. "And think what all the fresh air will do for your complexion. You've no need to worry about future wrinkles because there's no sun up there. Brilliant, eh?" Katya was also working on the Blissful Beauty account writing copy about the golden rules of skin care. She'd now added SPF30 to the Vitamin C promise as the cure for everything.

Ten minutes after sending the woman in the painting pic, my phone vibrates. Katya.

"Do you know who that is?" Her tone is one of awe and wonder.

"No?"

"That's Christina the Dating Guru. Haven't you heard of her?"

Well, no. But then I haven't needed dating advice for a long time. Ryan and I got together while we were still at school and we were together ten years so I'm bound not to be familiar with a dating guru. And what does that even mean?

"Have you used her advice, then?" I ask, "and if so, does it work?"

"Nope. I've just heard of her. An influencer and all that, and you're not going to believe the weird co-inci… Oh, never mind. Her website address is datemate dot com. Look it up."

And with that she hangs up. I tap out the name on my keyboard. Wow. This woman is all over the internet. She's got a blog, podcasts, YouTube tutorials and everything. Curiosity piqued, I read through some of them. They include guides to using dating apps, what to do the first time you go out with someone so that they ring you back (guaranteed), the best profile pics to use and what make-up you should wear for a first date. There's nothing she doesn't cover. I'm half-way through an article about what will make you a sparkling conversationalist capable of capturing his attention and keeping it when someone clears their throat behind me.

"Ahem. Not interrupting anything am I?"

I whirl around on my chair so quickly, I fall off and land in an undignified heap at his feet. I had no time to minimise the screen either, and the site's header—a riot of hearts and stars complete with the tag line, *How to Go from Dating Loser to Loved Up*, flashes there. I'm about to get up when another thought strikes me—*he's got the Dating Guru's portrait upstairs, and he's caught me looking at her website! I've just signalled loud and clear that I sneaked upstairs and had a good nosey.* I might stay here, face down on the floor and praying the ground will swallow me until he goes away.

"Do you want a hand up?"

"No, no!" I straighten up slowly, keeping my eyes on that calming moss-green carpet until the last minute. Heavens, I'd forgotten just how... *divine* Jack is. Last week, his hair was army buzz cut, and now it's grown in a little. Still short enough to show off those eyes and cheekbones but the extra millimetre of length emphasises its bright copper colour. The eyes regard me with amusement. Or perhaps it's irritation. I'd better check with him that it's okay for me to use his office.

"Er… I wasn't expecting you until tomorrow. Doctor McLatchie said I could use your house as the broadband connection is much better here," I say, dismayed when he rolls his eyes and says, "She would". Oh heck, didn't the blasted woman warn him? And what right does she have to offer strangers the use of someone else's home? I should have asked her to find me somewhere else to work.

He heads for the kitchen, asking me if I want another coffee.

"Yes please," I follow him through. "Though I can make them, least I can do…" I trail off. He hasn't actually confirmed I can use his house as my office.

In the kitchen, sunlight makes a brave attempt at cutting through the grey clouds to bounce off the redness of his hair. He leans against the kitchen counter, one foot up and his arms folded—one of those guys whose face gives nothing away. Does he ever crack a smile? I remember that photo Katya and I saw of him online when he'd worn this wide grin, the upturned mouth creating a dimple on one cheek, and how lush the smile made him seem. Now though, those dark eyes remind me of the stand-offs I have with Little Ms Mena when she and I argue over how much smoked salmon she's going to eat. Who will blink first? My wretched imagination peels clothes off him. He lifts his arms above his head and the tee shirt disappears. Before I know it he's in front of me wearing only that

54

white towel, neatly knotted over a perfect six-pack torso. I blink twice to dislodge the image.

The face in front of me cracks, a tiny upturn to the corners of the mouth signalling amusement. The change in expression is welcome but (ye gods) did he just read my mind? Flippin' heck, I hope not…

"It's fine," he says. "She told me she'd given my spare keys to the new-comer. So, apart from researching what to do on a first date what do you do?"

I curse Christina the Dating Guru and Katya. My current toe-curlingly awful predicament is all their fault.

"I'm a graphic designer," emphasis on the words so I sound like the consummate professional. "I persuaded my boss I'd be able to work remotely when I came here, but when I turned up, I realised the signal doesn't work in Kirsty's house."

"No," he says, turning away to fill the cafetière with boiling water. I don't bother with the fancy stuff myself. It's instant all the way. "She used to do a lot of work here too."

Curiouser and curiouser. And thanks for the heads-up Kirsty. Not.

"Why did you come here, Gaby?" All we need now is a too bright light overhead to reinforce the interrogation-style questions, but something about those dark, flashing eyes compels me to answer. And if I do, doesn't that entitle me to a few questions of my own?

"I split up from someone," I say and regret the words as soon as they're out of my mouth. That's going to make what I was doing earlier seem even sadder. "Plus, I've always wanted to be a cat sitter! Yes. The perfect job, isn't it, travelling up and down the country looking after delightful pussies? What could be better?"

Gaby! Be quiet. Katya's voice this time. *You are making a total fool of yourself.*

Jack's expression signals agreement with Katya loud and clear. He pushes down the cafetiere's plunger and pours coffee into two mugs, one of which he hands to me.

"How do you take it?" he asks, the eyebrow waggling. "Sugar? Cream?"

Crrreammm. Oh heck, again. Are we in double entendre territory?

"Black, no sugar," I bleat, then fret that my coffee choices signal I'm no fun loud and clear. Personal questions about Jack feel like a better idea.

"And you? What do you do?"

"I run mini-bus tours," he says. "American and Asian tourists in the main. That's why I'm not here often."

"Yoo-hoo! Jack? Gaby? You in?"

Jack gives another eye roll and shouts back, "In the kitchen," and Dr McLatchie sticks her head around the door, waving a hello to me.

"Ah good! I'll have a coffee too. And have ye any shortbread on the go?"

Good lord, she's familiar, isn't she? Bursting into someone's home without knocking and ordering the occupant to make her a coffee and get her some biscuits to go along with it.

Jack pulls a tin out of a cupboard, takes the lid off and holds it out to me first. I help myself to two bits, seeing as breakfast these days is one slice of toast so I can afford to feed Ms Mena her smoked salmon and poached organic, free-range chicken breast.

"I've got to do a Skype consultation in ten minutes time," the doctor says. "Can ye both stay out of the way while I do it? People prefer not to have strangers listening in when I do my consultations, though Jonah Ross's got nothing to hide, apart from the occasional trouble with his piles, which is mair the pity because—"

"Okay, okay Mum. I'll stop you right there before you break the Hippocratic oath."

That makes my head swivel between the two of them. Dr McLatchie said nothing about Jack being her son. They don't share the same surname, and the resemblance isn't clear though as I study them both, I can see Dr McLatchie's got her son's eyes and razor-sharp cheekbones. Jack notices me doing the checking them both out thing, and he smirks. Neither seems inclined to offer me any further explanation, such as the reason behind their different names or why the doctor couldn't have said right at the beginning she was Jack's mum. It explains the familiarity.

Jack finishes his coffee in record time—does he have an asbestos mouth, that stuff was boiling hot—and tells us he needs to go. As he leaves, keys jangling in his left hand, he brushes close past me, and unwittingly I take a deep breath in—washing powder, pine needles and warm skin. It's intoxicating, and the temptation to fall on him and sniff harder than a police drugs dog seeking out illegal stuff is overwhelming. When he shuts the door behind him, I'm left hanging in mid-air, face and nose forward sniffing an empty space.

In the kitchen, Dr McLatchie helps herself to five pieces of shortbread, telling me she can only tackle Jonah Ross when she's overloaded with sugar and heads back to the living room.

"Knock on the door hard when ten minutes are up, will ye Gaby? Then I can pretend there's an emergency car crash. Good lass."

And I'm alone once more. I bite the shortbread and realise it must be home-made. It's crisp, buttery and melt-on-the-tongue delicious. No wonder the doctor eats so much of it. I'm left with plenty of food for thought. (Katya would hate me using that analogy so close to musings about actual food.) To add to my stock of information about Jamie stroke Jack, I can confirm his mum's a doctor, he drinks his coffee the way I do, he runs coach tours and…

And that's the meagre amount of it.

Later that afternoon once I've finished my work for the day, I can't resist the temptation to look at the Dating Guru's website again. Maybe there will be clues there why Jack has her picture in his house, as that seems weird. Does he know her? Before I look this time, I check the window to ensure no-one walking past can see my screen and that there's no sign of Jack. A new post has gone up since this morning, an article titled *How to Find Love After a Long-Term Relationship Ends,* which seems apt.

I was with Ryan for ten years. We got together when we were in high school just before my sixteenth birthday. He's the reason I didn't go further afield to university. Katya and I had grand ideas about going to London. St Martin's College for me and the London School of Economics for her, but Ryan begged me not to. He went straight from school into his parents' garage and car sales company, and when I mentioned London, he freaked out. He knew all about students, he said. They spent their weekends boozing and… At that, he shook his head, and I was left to come up with the rest of the sentence. Did he mean having fun? When I ended up with an acceptance for the Norwich University of the Arts, I begged Katya to go to the University of East Anglia in the same city so at least there would be the two of us trying to recreate the full student experience even though we were only sixteen miles from home.

Katya never liked Ryan that much though she didn't go on about it. Heroic really, when you consider how frank my friend is about everything else in my life. From time to time if she'd had one Red Bull and vodka too many, she would say something. "Ryan's not the only man out there." Or, "Gaby, have you ever wondered if Ryan appreciates how wonderful you are?" When I told her we were engaged, she swallowed hard, took a deep breath and plastered a huge smile on her face. "That's brilliant, Gaby." Then, two seconds later. "Are you sure?"

I wasn't sure at all. No-one else my age was getting engaged. Other Millennials were too busy having portfolio careers (and again, I'd gone straight from graduation to Bespoke Design. I couldn't do that social media profile thing where I added in endless slashes to show that I wasn't just a designer), leading activist campaigns, doing micro-brewing or creating YouTube channels where they promoted plant-based lifestyles and slagged off anyone who wasn't a vegan. Those Millennials were far too busy to get engaged and then married.

But Ryan had done the whole romantic thing. I suspected he'd relied on Google to tell him how to propose and then copied the advice. It wasn't personalised to me. We headed out for a meal to a fine dining restaurant in Norwich where they served small portions on slates and charged you a fortune. After we'd eaten our mains, a waiter appeared with a trio of chocolate desserts. I tucked in with gusto. That main course had been nowhere near filling enough and Ryan was forced to tell me to slow down. When I got to the third bit of dessert, I bit down on the honeycomb mousse and cracked my front tooth.

"Yeowch!"

A tiny object flew across the room, and Ryan leapt from his seat and flew after it. The other diners watched us, astonished. Having retrieved the object, Ryan dashed back and fell onto his hands and knees in front of me. He pushed himself up onto one knee. I got it at that point and my heart sank to the floor. Oh heck no…

"Gabrielle Amelia Richardson, will you make me the happiest man in the world?"

Our audience stared at us. I heard the collective intake of breath. There was only one answer I could give.

"Er… yes?"

Cheers erupted around us. Waiters materialised, bearing champagne, two glasses and mobile phones asking us if they could take our photos and put it on the restaurant's Twitter and Instagram accounts. Hashtags #CafeFrancaise #love! #idealplacetogetengaged.

A week later, we held the engagement party. And at that point, everything imploded.

CHAPTER SIX

FIVE WEEKS EARLIER

"Is that what you're wearing? Seriously?"

Katya eyed me sternly, and I held out my arms. "What's wrong with it?"

"Nothing. If you were about to celebrate your eight-ieth birthday, I'd give you a round of applause and say 'great outfit choice'. As you've got another fifty-four years to go until that day, go back to your bedroom and choose something else."

Rude. I'd picked the dress up at a charity shop. Now that Ryan and I were getting m-m-married (even in my head I wasn't able to say the word without stuttering), I figured we should save money and therefore I couldn't justify the cost of a new outfit for my engagement party. Or, another voice whispered, perhaps you don't want a

new outfit because you can't get excited about this party…

The party hadn't been my idea or Ryan's. When we'd
gone to his parents' house the day after the proposal to
announce the happy news, Louise, his mum, clapped her
hands and told us we must celebrate. Why not have a
party at the garage? She and Ryan's dad would get cater-
ing in and book a DJ. And if the event showed off some of
the vintage cars the business specialised in, all the better.
When I said I didn't know if any of our friends could afford a vintage car, she waved a hand.

"Don't worry about that. We'll invite a few prospective
clients. Just a soft-sell kind of thing. We might as well
combine the two, don't you think?"

I nodded, my head moving automatically. If I'd
glimpsed myself in the mirror, I suspected my eyes would
look glazed. An engagement party made things much
more official, didn't it? Already, the ring on my fourth
finger dragged my left hand down, chaining it to the side
of my body.

A week later and it was clear that Louise had invited
everyone in Great Yarmouth, if not Norfolk, to the party.
She'd thrown herself into the organisation, spending six
days consulting with caterers, event planners and DJs.
The vintage cars had been polished to a high sheen, and
they'd covered the garage forecourt in bunting, banners
and balloons congratulating Ryan and me. Every time I
bumped into someone on the street, they told me how
much they were looking forward to the party. I was lucky

if I had a nodding acquaintance with any of them. And if they were looking forward to Great Yarmouth's party of the year, they had the advantage over me.

Louise ordered Ryan to the party an hour before it was due to start so she could brief him on the sales spiel which she promised would be subtle and not interfere with our enjoyment of the night. I ducked out of the early start, relieved, and said I'd come along with Katya.

"What do you wear to an engagement party?" I asked. I'd never been to one before because all my friends thought the same as me—engagement and marriage were for people in their early 30s. Katya opened the wardrobe and flicked through my tops and dresses. She is ten times more glamorous than me and always looks as if she's wearing expensive, well-designed clothes whereas I've been mistaken for a Big Issue seller.

"This is hopeless," she said, unzipping her dress.

"What are you doing?"

"We're swapping. You can wear this. It'll be too big, but there's a woven leather belt you have that'll go with it. Take your dress off."

I made a token protest and gave in. It was always better not to argue with my friend, who is the oldest of four sisters and well-versed in giving orders. Besides, the dress was fabulous—a mustard floral frill skater dress she'd matched with a deep purple and silver crochet cardigan. The belt was silver too, so as predicted it matched perfectly. I argued in favour of my Converse trainers to give my outfit a fierce edge and lost. No, she said. For such an occasion, high-heeled cork wedges were the only options. She pulled on my black velvet skinny jeans, cursing as she struggled to pull the zip up, and I wondered afresh how she made everything look so much more stylish than I did. Any time I put those trousers on, every single bit of lint, fluff and dust landed on them.

"Red lipstick too." Katya went nowhere without the full kit and caboodle—foundation, powder, eyeliner, mascara, blusher and lipstick. By the time she'd finished with me, I had to admit I looked a lot better and the prospect of the party didn't seem as grim.

No-one noticed us arrive as the place was heaving with people. Waiters circulated, all of them carrying silver trays filled with mini bits and pieces or flutes of champagne. As the average age of the guests seemed to be about fifty, I decided most of them were prospective customers rather than any of our friends. Katya aside, I'd yet to see anyone I knew.

We pushed our way to the front mainly by sliding too close to all the vintage cars, and I spotted my mum talking to Louise. My heart sank again. They'd never got on. My mum was from the rougher end of Great Yarmouth, and Louise never failed to find some way of reminding her. If it weren't for Ryan, I'd have told her to mind her manners a long time ago. I said Katya I'd speak to them and left her eyeing up the best-looking waiter. I didn't fancy his chances of escaping alive.

"Louise, hi! Mum, nice to see you."

Louise gave that tinkling laugh of hers that she saves for the garage's most affluent customers. "Gaby! And you're so glamorous."

Astonishment. Cheek.

"Mandy and I were talking about the wedding."

Mum flashed me a look I took to mean 'rescue me'. Or, 'get me out of here before I kill her'.

"We've not set a date," I said. There was another word I couldn't say in my head without it coming out w-w-wedding. "Loads of time. Mum, shall we go and—"

"Reverend Mortimer's here," Louise added. "I've told her you'll speak to her later. You need to get in quick because that church gets booked up years in advance. She's over there."

I pretended to glance in the direction she pointed and steered my mum away.

"Thank goodness, Gaby," Mum whispered as we made our way back into the throng. "If Louise told me once more 'ow lucky you were, I'd 'a done her damage. Ryan's the lucky one, that's for sure." She patted my hand and told me she was going to talk to an old school friend she'd spotted.

Where was my fiancé? I assumed he was doing his bit for the family firm. Sure enough, I picked him out a minute later engaged in serious conversation with a red-faced, Tweed-wearing man as the two of them cast loving stares at a silver Bentley Continental convertible. I sketched him a wave, and he lifted a hand, waiting till the man's head was turned away to blow me a kiss.

"And breathe, Gaby," I told myself. "Everything will be okay."

I still didn't see anyone I knew to talk to. Katya, having exchanged contact details with the waiter, returned to my side, holding a bottle of champagne.

"Look what I wangled out of the waiter. Want to find somewhere quiet to drink it?"

I jumped at the offer. It beat standing around at your own party not knowing anyone.

The prospect of escape made us giggly. We crept past everyone, keeping out of Louise's line of sight and let ourselves into the office. Even that room hadn't escaped the attention of the decorator who'd hung up yet more bunting and several helium-filled balloons.

Katya found us two plastic cups for the champagne and opened it like a pro, the cork coming out with a soft pop. I took a too-big gulp and remembered why I don't like champagne. It always goes to my head too quickly. And it's nowhere near as nice as lemonade. When I mentioned the 'm' word Louise had been talking about with my mum, Katya made me vow she'd be chief bridesmaid and I'd let her choose my dress. And she'd give me a hen night I'd remember for the rest of my life.

I burst into tears. "Katya, this is the worst mistake I've ever made. I didn't want to get engaged. Ryan asked me in a public place, and I didn't want to disappoint the crowd. And now, now…" I hiccoughed through more sentences along the same lines. "It's not that I don't love Ryan," I continued, "or don't want to be with him, it's just that I don't want all this fuss and now I'm on a runaway train that's hurtling too quickly towards a destination I didn't have in mind."

"Ooh," she said, taking a too-big gulp of champagne herself, "that's a brilliant analogy. I might use it myself. Okay, okay I'm taking you seriously I promise. Drink some more champagne, and we'll write out the pros and cons, and what to do."

Katya had been writing blogs for a life coach who strongly believed in writing personal lists and the powers of the pros and cons. I grabbed a pen and paper from Louise's desk and jotted down my list.

"Er... Katya, all I've got are cons!" I said, dismayed. I hadn't thought that's all I would turn up. When Ryan blew me a kiss earlier, didn't I find it sweet? Annoying too, though. It was our flippin' engagement party. We should have been there together, not me making my own way to the party while he chatted up prospective custom-ers.

Katya snatched the list from me and read it out loud. "I'm bored. I'm too young to get married. I don't want to stay in Great Yarmouth the rest of my life and Ryan will never move anywhere else. What if another man out there is my true soul mate? When Ryan kisses me, I fantasise he's Jamie Fraser. Louise will be the mother-in-law from hell. Everything is moving far, far too fast. Ryan watches too much golf on the TV."

That last one made her open her eyes wide with horror. "You never told me that! Golf? How old is he, 95?

69

I have nightmares sometimes where I find myself with a golf fan and he makes me do it with him. And I can't say no because he's got this little sister who will die if he doesn't play golf every day, and then I'll be responsible for her tragic death at the age of five."

Are all writers prone to weird flights of fancy? I shot her my best 'be serious' glare, and we finished our plastic glasses of champagne.

"Another one?" Katya said, and I decided I liked the stuff after all. Once you got past the nasty sour taste, those bubbles slid down easily. Outside, the DJ had started up, and the two of us groaned. This being my engagement party, it might have been reasonable for me to have a say in the music. But Louise had stipulated what was to play seeing as most of the guests were in their 50s, and Ryan was fine with it as he had terrible taste in music.

On cue, Jon Bon Jovi's voice boomed that he was half-way there. It would only get much, much worse.

Katya took out her camera, and the two of us posed for a selfie (bothie?), pulling our best duck-faced pouts and sucking in our cheeks. She tagged it #GabyEngaged and posted it. Then, she held the camera over the piece of paper where I'd listed why I didn't want to get engaged.

"Better throw this away," she said, screwing the paper up into a tiny ball and lobbing it at the waste-paper basket. "But I've taken a picture of it in case you need to reread it. Or it could make a hilarious story for your hen night."

I giggled. "Or my speech at the wedding!" The plastic glass of champagne number two had gone down more quickly than the first, and my laughter sounded hysteria tainted. I plucked at one of the 'Congratulations' balloons hanging in the office, my eyes meeting Katya's with that synchronised thought pattern we so often get as long-time friends.

"Yes!" she clapped her hands together gleefully. "Lets. I've always wanted to do that."

Neither of us was one hundred percent sure what we were doing, but it had to be easy. Release the gas from the balloon and breathe it in. I took the first gasp and Katya the second, the high-pitched hee hee hees making us howl with laughter. "I can't marry Ryan. It's too grown-up!" Saying the words in the voice of a three-year-old gave them additional weight.

"I'm going to find another balloon," Katya said. "We should try singing on the stuff."

She let herself out, and I helped myself to more champagne. My head had started to spin, and I slid down the wall. Behind me, I heard the music change from Bon Jovi to Guns N' Roses and the sound of too many middle-aged men risking their backs as they strutted their air guitars. But I also caught voices close by, a conversation just outside the office. Katya and I hadn't put on the main light when we came in. Reluctant to talk to anyone, I dived under the big desk and pulled the waste-paper basket in front of me. With any luck, it was just Louise looking for paperwork so she could sell a vintage car to one of the old men out there. I forced back a hiccough and lay as still and quietly as possible.

The door opened slowly, and I spotted an expensive pair of black Chelsea boots. Ryan. About to wriggle out and come up with a good explanation for why I was hiding under a desk in the middle of my own engagement party, I realised he was on the phone. I kept still. Maybe this was a crucial car conversation, and if I jumped out and frightened him, he'd lose the sale of the century.

There were lots of umm-hmms, and yes's and no's at his end.

"I know, mate. But what else was I supposed to do?"

Oh, not the car sales conversation then, the detective in me decided. And that he was on the phone to Josh, his best friend and someone I wouldn't pee on if he was on fire as the saying goes. When Ryan said Josh couldn't make tonight's party, I faked disappointment.

"I know you don't like her."

Yup. Josh.

"And I'm not too young," Ryan added, echoing my own concerns. "My mum and dad got married when they were twenty!"

More umm-hmms and yes and no's.

Then the killer. "Course I'm not 100 percent sure. You know the whole Kayleigh story. I never meant for it to…"

Josh interrupted, and the rest of what might have been very revealing was cut off. The Kayleigh story? I racked my brains. What, that receptionist who worked in the garage a year ago? The lady with the 'lively charms' as my nanna might put it, and who was always super friendly to me.

Evidence of hiding a guilty—

"Kayleigh got in touch with you?"

Wow. Happy voice Ryan. When I said 'yes' to that engagement, he nodded, slid the ring on my finger and wondered aloud about what Sunday breakfast tomorrow might include. The delight in his voice when he asked about Kayleigh stung, but then wasn't I the one running through a pros and cons list earlier where the balance tipped decidedly in favour of cons?

Time I revealed myself.

I shoved the waste-basket to one side and shuffled out. "Ryan."

My voice was still Minnie Mouse squeaky, but Ryan was too dismayed to notice. His hand went to his mouth, and he thrust the phone to the desk. "Gaby! I was looking for you everywhere. I was just talking to Josh about this woman he met on Tinder. Head over heels, he is."

Hmm.

"Ryan," I said. "Do you want to get married? Now? Shouldn't we wait a while?"

We faced each other in the garage office, surrounded by posters, desks and windows looking out on a back-lit forecourt with its polished cars, prices prominently displayed. On the floor lay two helium balloons deflated and sad, and a phone that kept calling out, 'what's happening?', Josh's voice tinny and echo-y. Ryan was the guy who rescued me as a sixteen-year-old from teenage hell, where you think you're the ugliest, fattest, weirdest (tick your particular box) girl in the class. A boyfriend proves that is not the case.

Ten years later, I didn't know if that was enough any more.

Ryan closed his eyes. "I don't know. You are the love of…"

"For God's sake!" The phone again. I battled the urge to throw it to the ground and stamp on it.

"Let's just go back to living together," I said, "and worrying about what's for breakfast instead of all the fuss of a stupid wedding." Knowing Louise, we'd be dragged kicking and screaming to Norwich Cathedral and then a reception in the county's stuffiest hotel just so she could invite all her ghastly friends. Canapés, a sit-down meal, a reception line, boring speeches and too many tiny, unruly bridesmaids running riot… bleurgh. The thought of it turned my stomach.

Ryan nodded, relieved, and I burst into tears. Oh, thank heavens!

He moved away, rummaging around in the drawers in the desk closest to him trying to find tissues when the door opened and there was an outraged squawk. "What have you done to Gaby, you git?" Katya yelled. Unfortunately, she still had helium in her system. It's difficult, no impossible, to sound serious when you are doing your best Donald Duck impression.

"That does it!" she yelled, as Ryan blustered an explanation, and I said, "No, it's okay, Katya, we're not…" *Not engaged now but okay about it*, I meant to add.

She held her phone up. "Shall I post this?"

I squinted at the screen, cursing the champagne and helium for the lack of focus. She'd taken a photo of Ryan and me, I guessed, and I nodded. So, yes, Ryan and I weren't engaged but wasn't it a nice, positive message to send out to the universe love and friendship was still possible even if you broke off an engagement, and all the cosy, comfortable things that entailed such as liking the same box sets on Netflix, not having to worry about him seeing you in your pyjamas when you decide to wear them at five pm or apologising for being too wimpy to opt for a Brazilian wax…

"You've seen the light, at last, Gaby!" Katya said, the squeakiness still there, "I'm so glad you've had the sense to ditch this loser—"

Oh God, I had to stop her. Ryan growled beside me, and I squeaked back, "No, no, it's not like that."

"What's going on!" Louise joined our happy party seconds later, stomping into the room and glaring at me.

She held her phone to my face. There was the Twitter feed for the garage and in it a picture, the snap Katya had taken earlier of my list of reasons for not wanting to be engaged to Ryan, instead of a picture of the two of us as I'd thought. So far, the picture had fifty likes and thirty-four re-tweets, and it had only gone up a minute ago.

Ryan took the phone from her, his expression pinched and his face flushed. "You fantasise I'm Jamie Fraser?"

"And she doesn't think you're her soul mate, mate!" Blasted Josh, still at the other end of Ryan's mobile, added his tuppence-worth. He must have seen the Twitter feed too.

Behind Louise, Katya held her hands to her face and widened her eyes in mock horror. "I'm so sorry," she mouthed, but she crossed her eyes and, the gesture gave her away. Sorry, not sorry.

Helium, champagne, Louise's outraged face—all of it welled up inside me. The giggles started up, all the more hysterical.

"Sorry Ryan, sorry Louise," I spluttered as her mouth tightened in fury. "I can't m-m-marry you."

"And I never want to see you again. How could you?" He threw back.

The mobile phone cheered. Oh well, at least someone was happy.

Katya began a slow hand clap. "Hooray! Come on, Gaby. Let's get out of here. This party's lame."

CHAPTER SEVEN

"…so we left the party, and the crowd parted like the Red Sea because everyone, and I mean everyone, saw that post on Twitter. I swear I heard boos and hisses when I walked by. I felt like a panto villain."

I finish the story and Mhari nods. The pharmacy assistant and I are now friends. She's not a chemist herself, but thanks to years of detailed questioning of everyone who comes in, there's nothing she doesn't know about every medication known to (wo)man. I'm in for the second batch of super-strong anti-histamines. Dr McLatchie tells me I might find my system has built up an immunity to Mena by now so that I no longer need the anti-histamines, particularly if I take lots of Vitamin C to support my immune function. (Can't wait to tell Katya she's right about the magic powers of Vitamin C).

I'm not chancing it for the moment, and I hand over the script to Mhari who whips out the packet, telling me they ordered some in advance knowing there was a possibility I'd need it.

There are advantages to living in the world's nosiest village. At least you don't have to wait for anything as the residents anticipate your every need.

"Well, it was drastic," Mhari says. "Though, wish I'd been there tae see it."

The thing is, at the time I didn't mind my panto villain status. Whatever I felt about getting married, Ryan hadn't deserved that humiliation. Katya apologised repeatedly, saying she should have double, triple, quadruple checked it with me. But at the same time, the relief was over-whelming.

We left the party, having rescued my mum from the clutches of an air-guitar playing 50-something dressed unwisely in leather jeans, we decided going back to my flat was a no-no, seeing as I'd just finished with the place's other occupant. Katya's flat was too crowded, and Mum's house two miles away. Katya hit on the idea of treating ourselves to some cakes and biscuits from the supermarket and taking them down to the beach. I fired off a text to Ryan, apologising profusely, telling him how much he meant to me and I was sorry it had ended this way. His two-word reply told me forgiveness wasn't coming soon. Not surprising, really.

We found ourselves a peaceful spot away from the late night dog walkers and sat down on our coats. The water lapped the shore, and Katya dished out equal shares of millionaire's shortbread, doughnuts and chocolate truffles.

She picked one up between thumb and forefinger and tapped it gently on the bit of shortbread I was holding. "To you! Sorry again."

"I'm newly single and ready to mingle," I replied, trying the words out for size. They were okay, 'single' wasn't a word I'd used for myself for years and now it emerged from my mouth without too much difficulty.

My mum nudged my shortbread with her doughnut. "Am I allowed to say 'ow relieved I am? Sorry love. I thought you were too young to marry." We'd told her the whole sorry tale as we left the party and she'd gone from concern (*oh dear, love, that was naughty*) to fury (*Kayleigh?! Who's she?*) to giddy delight.

Once Katya stopped apologising for her mistake, she threw in her opinion too. It must have killed her to hold back all those years on what she really thought about Ryan and my relationship with him. She made up for it. After fifteen minutes or so, Mum and I were stiffening up with the cold, and she showed no sign of letting up. (*And then there was the time that douche-bag did…*)

I got to my feet and gave Mum a hand up. "But I do have a lot to deal with. Seeing as my whole life has just fallen apart." Remarkable that even though this was true, all I felt was lightness. Perhaps the helium still floated around my system, making me feel as if I might lift off at any second.

Katya flapped a hand and said she'd think of something and my mum promised I could come back and live with her "if the worst comes to the very, very worst". All right Mum, subtle hint received and understood. As she was still trying to get rid of my older brother who'd decided home-cooked meals, laundered clothes and year-round central heating were worth the lack of privacy, I didn't blame her.

And my mind flickered with all kinds of exciting possibilities—the overwhelming joy of finally doing what I'd wanted to do as a teenager. Get out of Dodge, aka Great Yarmouth.

"And yet you ended up here," Mhari says now, her eyes flicking over the ancient toiletries in the chemist shop. Granted, it doesn't look its best today. But the BBC weather forecaster's promise of sunshine and warmth has come true at last. Unfortunately, the sunlight streaming into the shop, highlights the thick layer of dust over all the products no-one ever buys. The same sunshine, however, turns the waters of the loch closer to blue than grey, and I've even been able to risk coming out sans coat. A first.

"Well, it's a start," I say. "Kirsty promised me she'd give me a top-notch review and my next cat-sitting gig might be somewhere like Las Vegas."

"Oh. Her." There's a top-class sneer if I ever heard one and I lean closer, elbows balanced on the counter in a 'tell me more' posture. So far, I have learned little about the woman whose house I'm living in. I sense one hundred percent quality gossip about to come my way.

"Mmm?" I say. I'm desperate to find out about her and Jack's relationship, but if I ask outright I know it will be all around the village in the next ten minutes. Mhari's part of the Lochalshie WhatsApp group, and blimey they've turned information spreading into an art form. And whoever lets truth get in the way of a good story? I'm glad Kirsty's house is trapped in a signal-free bubble, otherwise, my phone would go mad every night with beeps as the local WhatsApp group updates.

"Weeellll," Mhari begins, leaning in too and lowering her voice even though we are the only ones in the shop. "I shouldnae speak ill o' the departed."

"Whaatt?" I squeal. Is she dead? And does that mean I'm stuck here forever, picking up prescriptions every week and bankrupting myself so I can buy enough smoked salmon stroke organic chicken breast for Little Ms Mean, Mena of course?

"Aye," Mhari says, scowling at me for interrupting. "She doesnae live here any more, does she? As I said, you should be respectful of outsiders. But I think all the website fame went to her heid. Thought she was too fancy/schmancy for this place. She changed a lot after she bought that house. Paid for it all upfront too," she sniffs.

I step back from the counter, my mouth open in surprise. How could someone my age afford to buy a place as palatial as that one without a mortgage? I know house prices in Scotland, and the rural parts especially are much cheaper than they are down south, but still. Plus, everything in that house is top of the range. Kirsty didn't go

81

to Ikea, spend hours wandering around trying to get to the bit of the shop she wanted and then picking the first bit of flat-pack tat she saw. No, no. She's got sleigh beds upstairs, hung her Le Creuset pots and coppers pans all over her kitchen, and draped her cream leather sofas and armchairs with cashmere throws.

I rewind. Website fame? "Is she a YouTube celeb or something?" I ask, imagining her as one of those lifestyle people—the ones who are always promoting freebies they get while pretending to review them. Nine out of ten times, the reviews are positive. Nobody wants companies to be too scared to send you free stuff, do they? Or perhaps she's got a website like Gwyneth Paltrow's ghastly Goop, and she promotes… I close my eyes and shake my head. Gwyneth is famous for telling women they should steam places that are best kept a million miles away from boiling water.

Mhari stirs herself and starts bagging up labelled tablets and medications. When I asked about Kirsty, she gave me one of her incredulous stares—the one all the villages use when I admit to not knowing every single detail about a person because, you know, they haven't told me. Or I'm not a mind reader.

"She's Christina!" Mhari exclaims, and then when I still look blank. "The dating guru!"

Clink, clink—the sound of pennies dropping, like they do when you hit the jackpot on one of those old-fashioned slot machines. A lot of things begin to make sense. A) why Jack McAllan has a portrait of the dating guru in his house. B) why someone my age can afford a house like that. She must rake money in from advertising and affiliate links on her website, YouTube channel, blog and podcast. C) the lovey-dovey way she speaks on the phone. *But, but, but...* my mind protests. Why would Jack still have that picture hanging up, beautiful as it is and a great credit to whoever painted it?

"*That's why, Gaby,*" a little voice in my head pipes up. Katya's this time, I think. "*Because it's such an amazing picture. Not because it has anything to do with residual feelings he might have towards Kirsty.*"

Mhari wears an expression that can only be described as the air of one who has imparted knowledge that has just blown another person's mind.

I go for stating the obvious. "But she can't be much of a dating guru, can she? Her relationship ended, so how can she bill herself as an expert when all that's going on in the background."

Mhari suddenly straightens up, her eyes widening in alarm.

"...and if her subscribers knew she'd split from some-one, they wouldn't take her advice seriously would they?"

I'm about to add 'and follow her online slavishly' when there's the slam of a door behind us, and I whirl around. Oh, this couldn't be worse. Jack McAllan, who today looks even more Jamie Fraser-like than ever. He's in a kilt, for goodness' sake—one of those sexy modern ones, plain black plaid and worn with a black open-necked shirt and black socks that cling to muscular calves, and all of it highlighting a light tan, the freckles on his face and that copper hair I know any woman would kill for. His expression is thunderous. The eyebrows knit together under a screwed up forehead and he purses his lips.

As the ground ignores my second request in only a week for it to swallow me up, I resort to bluster. "Loretta!" I say, turning my gaze from Jack back to Mhari and signalling with my eyes that she go along with this. "That woman who runs the find a husband service. No-one would want to listen to someone whose husband had left her for her best mate, would they?"

Mhari wrinkles up her eyes and then nods. "No, Gaby. You're quite right."

I cringe. If Mhari ever decides to go into acting, I'll be first in line to say, "Don't give up the day job, love."

"Loretta split from her man and ye cannae blame her," Mhari continues, over-emphasising every word and making it worse by looking at me and then Jack after she utters every syllable. I'm not in Jack's direct line of sight, but still I sense disapproval, annoyance and irritation. "I mean, unreasonable of him tae get all het up about a stupid pros and cons list that went viral on Twitter when she said sorry and sent him—"

"Yes, well," I butt in before Mhari recreates all the sorry Ryan/Gaby story and my less than noble part in it. "How are you, Jack?"

He tilts his head towards his shoulder. "All the better for seeing you, Gaby."

I'm reminded of the truth of words. Tone, pitch and eye contact tells you what you want to know far more than the arrangement of letters. I award him ten out of ten for sarcasm and rein in the instinct to blow him a fat raspberry once more.

He turns from the shelf he was inspecting to Mhari. They exchange glances, Mhari to Jack, Jack to Mhari and then both of them to me. Whatever silent communication went on there, minds appear to have been made up.

"The Avon Skin So Soft, Mhari? Have you got any of the stuff in?"

Mhari comes out, 'Mah-rrrie'. I could try saying it a hundred times, and I couldn't roll my 'r's half as beautifully. The woman herself bends down, rummaging around in the boxes underneath the counter and emerging with five bottles of the stuff.

"You're no' to tell anyone I've got stocks of this in," she hisses at me, hastily throwing all the bottles into a plastic bag. "And especially no' Alison. Well, tell folks. But it's special arrangement only. Gaby, I've just let you into a ginormous secret. If you tell folks, I'll have to kill ye."

Gosh. She's serious. Alison is her boss, the pharmacist. I am, as the locals say, flummoxed. What is so special about a cheap spray-on oil from a well-known beauty company?

Jack hands over a stack of tenners that Mhari doesn't bother ringing up through the till. I'd no idea the stuff was so expensive.

"Go," she says, shooing us with her hands. "Both of ye! And mind, this didnae happen. Or if it did, folks have to contact me first, and then I'll arrange the drop."

With that, we are out of the shop—me clutching my anti-histamines and Jack with his plastic bag of black market goodies.

Out on the street, he turns to face me his expression still unfriendly. "I suppose you're headed to my house to do some work?"

"If that's okay!" It comes out as a squeak, and I curse myself. What is it about this man that brings out the idiot in me? Every single time I've met him, I've been at a disadvantage. From turning up late to being caught looking at an embarrassing post on the internet to having him walk in on a conversation about his ex-girlfriend. Not that I rate her advice, but I think Christina the Dating Guru would say, *Whoops girlfriend! A man is supposed to a) fancy you, b) respect you; and c) like you. Ticking none of those boxes? Retreat, retreat.*

I stomp off anyway, fed up of his rudeness. "Yes, I am. If that is okay with your lordship. Do you want money for the electricity or broadband, by the way? I'm more than happy to pay it."

He rushes to catch up with me. "No, his lordship doesnae mind. And apologises for being a rude git."

I slow down. The face now level with me appears to wear a sincere expression. "Apology accepted. The skin-so-soft stuff, Why did you pay so much for it?"

He holds the bag up and, I hear the clatter of plastic bottles knocking together. "It's an anti-midge thing. When I'm taking people out on the Highland Tours, they're not always used to the midges. How are you finding them?"

When I stare blankly, his faces relaxes. "You must be one of the fabled lucky ones. The midges don't bother you. Midges are Scotland's mosquitoes; maybe worse than mosquitoes. And they love fresh blood. I take out tourists, and they're no' going to be happy if they spend the days after their wee tour of the lochs and castles scratching themselves raw. For some reason, the midges don't like the skin-so-soft stuff. I hand it out to the tourists when they get on the mini-bus and tell them to spray it all over. Then their lasting impression of Highland Tours are the lochs and castles instead of the bites and itching. And they give me good reviews on TripAdvisor and the like."

I hear every word, but what strikes me more than anything is that he's stopped frowning by the time he's finished. I think there might be the hint of a smile at the end of his little speech. And we've reached the house too.

"Is this contraband then?" I ask, pointing at the plastic bag. He places a forefinger at his lips and widens his eyes.

"Totally. This stuff's in high demand. If you ever reveal my sources, I'll have to kill you too."

The friendly thing is short-lived. Jack lets us both into his house, makes himself a coffee (without offering me one, I note, marking it as a con in the who Gaby should fancy list) and leaves two minutes later, saying he needs to get the mini-bus valeted. I have a tonne of work to get on with, but I can't resist a phone call to Katya. Apart from anything else, I have the Kirsty/Christina thing to tell her about.

"Woo!" she says. "I was not expecting that. She doesn't sound Scottish."

No, she doesn't. I've now listened to her podcast, *Boyfriend Hunter*, and she's got an American accent. If you pay close attention though, it slips at times, seguing from upper east New York to Scottish.

"Anyway, I've got something to tell you!" Katya's adopted that super-bright voice, and my heart sinks. That almost always means I'm not going to like what she says next. The trouble with—and this sounds rotten ungrateful, I'm aware—with knowing someone so well, is that they signal good news and bad news with hyperclarity.

Here it comes, the bad news.

"Facebook!" she announces cheerily which convinces me what she says next will be dreadful. "You said the signal isn't great where you are?"

I nod, before remembering that we weren't doing FaceTime and she couldn't see what I did. "Nope, not at Kirsty's house anyway," I say, "I haven't been on Facebook for yonks."

And why would I? At 26, I'm only a year or so older than Gen Z. We don't do Facebook. The last time I looked, my mum was too busy posting her hundredth

'Why middle-aged women shouldn't drink' meme—Hashtag Wine O'clock. Hashtag Prosecco—at the same time as uploading endless pics of glasses of wine tagged #WeDontCare. I took a ten-second glance and decided whoever said middle-aged women shouldn't drink was a person of sense, someone my mum and her generation ought to heed. I worked out Facebook wasn't for me and prayed my mother never strayed across Instagram, WhatsApp or anything else she suddenly decided she had to be all over.

Katya ums and aws. "You should check it out. Your Facebook page."

I click on it, and my body zooms in to the screen as if I'm sucked to the monitor. Lordy, lordy.

In the name of flip. What do I do now?

CHAPTER EIGHT

Beneath the last thing I posted is a poster, the words *Gaby! I love you* taking up most of the space.

It's been designed, not a professional job the graphic artist in me notes, but well enough to grab attention. It features a picture of Ryan and me grinning at the camera, and a line underneath—*Help me get my girl-friend back. I dumped her too quickly.* Ryan's poster has been shared on the Ryan Reynolds official account. As a result, it is all over Facebook and Twitter. Some three million (it feels like) people are now screaming at me to get back at Ryan. Someone filmed Louise when she first saw my list of reasons for not getting engaged on the garage Twitter feed, her mouth pursing and her forehead wrinkling in fury, and they've turned it into a meme—the line, 'Louise would be the mother-in-law from hell' popping up endlessly as she reads it again and again.

In the broad light of social media day, none of this reflects well on me. Many people have seen it as their mission to tell me what a cow I am. That's not the word they use. And they add I do not deserve someone as magnificently chivalrous as Ryan. I click out before I read any other nasty comments about me, my appearance and my life choices.

Should I phone Ryan? In a fit of pique—and commanded to do so by Katya—I deleted his number from my phone after he sent me ten texts making his feelings crystal clear. I could email him, I suppose but…

…do I want him back? Um… no?

Back from valeting the mini-bus, Jack sticks his head around the door. "I hear you're off to Glasgow on Monday morning?" he asks, and I nod wondering which villager told him that before narrowing it down to Scottie's owner or Mhari.

"I need to head there on Monday," he says. "Got to pick my next load of tourists up at Glasgow airport." He jangles the keys to the mini-bus in his right hand, and I sense a man wondering whether to take the plunge. He takes a deep breath and appears to decide.

"I can give you a lift…?"

I stare at him, w*hat a lift, what you're offering me is… a lot of hours in your company*. Rude git and all, the idea of it shimmers, a tantalising prospect banishing all thoughts of Ryan and his poster.

"I need to get to Glasgow for nine am as I'm meeting my boss there so we can talk to our client," I say, crossing my fingers underneath the desk the flight he is meeting is an early one.

"No problem. The flight I'm picking up gets in at eight am. I could drop you at the airport, and you can get a bus from there into the city centre. The first day of the trip ends in Glasgow too, so if you don't mind kicking your heels there until five o'clock, I can give you a lift back too."

Melissa had scheduled the meeting with Dexter Carlton of Blissful Beauty for nine till twelve. But I could have lunch with Melissa afterwards and then wander around Glasgow until five looking at all the big shops and getting myself reacquainted with fashion. Besides, nothing will stop me from accompanying Jack on a journey I've worked out takes five hours there and back.

The daft bit of me fast-forwards to fantasy mode. Goodness me, imagine how friendly it might get. Perhaps I can persuade him to call me Sassenach? I fit the criteria for the name, and on a good day with the help of subdued lighting and if I put in a few hours wrapping strands of my hair around curling tongs, I reckon I could pass for Claire, Jamie Fraser's big love…

I spend the weekend working to ensure I can present Dexter with an impressive amount of work, but also to avoid thinking about Ryan and that Facebook post. The heat had died down a little. It wasn't getting the shares and comments it had been receiving; yet another one-second viral wonder. But still my friends and family commented, and most people appeared to take Ryan's side.

Weirdly, he hadn't sent me any direct, private messages either by email or through social media. I composed and discarded endless replies. *Hey Ryan, hope you are okay. The poster was sweet.* But nothing said what I wanted it to, and I couldn't work out what my ideal scenario was. Even if he came up with a reasonable explanation for Kayleigh and he promised me a Louise-interference-free wedding (life), did I want him back? No, yes, no, yes, no. My brain skipped left-side, right-side and back again too many times.

It's a huge relief when Monday arrives, even if the thought of all that time in Jack's company and the prospect of a high-powered meeting ties my stomach up in knots. Breakfast proves too much to ask of it. Mena has decided she likes scrambled eggs. A blessing, seeing as they cost a lot less than smoked salmon, and she ends up the lucky recipient of the meal I can't eat at five o'clock in the morning. Instead, I spend half an hour on the Dating Guru's website where I read up on everything from make-up to sparkling conversation topics on a first date and how to make him want you. Christina the Dating Guru promises me you need a light touch with make-up for a first date. Men, she says, don't like women plastered in make-up. The delicate souls find it intimidating. Although I curl up my lip as I listen to this on YouTube, perhaps she could be on to something. A light pink lip gloss makes your lips seem kiss-able the advice goes, whereas if you opt for red or dark lipstick a guy draws back, frightened he will end up covered in the stuff.

In the end, I settle for an impression I hope screams 'not trying too hard'. I am going to a business meeting, so I choose a pencil skirt with a velour hoodie and slogan tee shirt. As a graphic designer, we're allowed to subvert the suit when it comes to attending meetings. As per Christina's make-up instructions, the foundation I choose promises it is invisible, and I dust on bronzer and apply a slick of the least gloopy lip gloss I own.

When a horn sounds outside at five thirty bang on time, the curling tongs have only made it half-way around my head. I'm only half way through I do the tong thing with my hair. I grab my phone and the old laptop I've loaded with all the Blissful Beauty design work I've done, and head out the door, emerging with a head of hair that is half curly and half poker straight.

Blast it. Jack isn't the mini-bus's only occupant and the excitement I'd allowed to build up trickles away. Next to him in the front seat is Scottie's owner, the man whose name I don't yet know. He waves enthusiastically at me. My return wave isn't quite as energetic.

He throws open the door and budges up so he's in the middle and I'm left with the outside seat. The mini-bus is dark grey on the outside, the decals on the side feature a big sign saying *Highland Tours: Your Authentic Scottish Experience*. Inside, it's luxurious, dark grey seats, little curtains at the windows, and small table trays so people can eat their sandwiches in comfort.

"Aye, aye Gaby! I telt Jack ye were going to Glasgow and suggested he could take the two of us wi' him."

Great. So it wasn't even Jack's idea. I tell myself it doesn't matter. This bloke is tres rude, and it is not healthy to fancy someone so much when you're still recovering from a break-up.

"I'm going on a day course," Scottie's owner adds, "at Glasgow Caledonian. By the way, you havenae finished brushing your hair. It looks funny."

"What is the course?" I ask, fastening my seatbelt and preparing for a long morning. My lift fixer is a nice chap, but if boring people were an Olympic sport, he would qualify for Scotland's national team. During the next two hours, we are going to hear a lot of details about subjects as fascinating as how to make excellent porridge and the number of midges expected to hit the village this year.

Jack puts the mini-bus in reverse, turns it around in Kirsty's driveway—a piece of manoeuvring so precise and professional I would swoon if that kind of thing impressed me—and tilts his face so that only I can see. Was that the ghost of a wink?

At least I get Scottie's owner's name. Jack says it when he reminds him to fasten his seatbelt as we leave the village and Stewart continues his explanation of the course he's off to do. Unlikely as it sounds, he talks about it non stop for an hour. He's off to learn about coding, meaning he will be able to start work developing websites for local businesses. In theory, this might be an exciting subject but by the time Stewart has told us all about the differences between JavaScript, Binary, MySQL and HTML, my head keeps dropping as I struggle to stay awake. Goodness only knows how Jack is staying alert enough to drive.

When I see the sign that says Glasgow is thirty miles away, I butt in.

"Amazing Stewart," I say. "You will learn so much. So, Jack how many people are you picking up today?"

"But I haven't told you yet about CSS and jQuery!" Stewart bursts out, and I mutter 'perhaps later' and that I deal with CSS every day in the desperate hope that between now and five o'clock he loses his voice.

"Ten," Jack says, and I swear there's that ghost of a wink again. "Americans. All of them claim Scottish ancestry that dates back to at least the fifteenth century despite record-keeping not being that great in those days, so I'm taking them to the People's Palace in the morning and Loch Lomond for the afternoon."

I jump in with another question before Stewart can start up again. The scenery's changed. For the first hour, we travelled through stunning countryside. All high hills topped with swirling mists that gradually revealed themselves as the rising sun burnt them off, lochs and fields full of russet-red cows with wide horned-heads. Now though, the traffic has intensified as we head further into the concrete jungle of three-carriage roads, high-rises and large warehouses.

I long to ask Jack personal questions but even if I thought he'd answer them, I can't ask them in front of

Stewart. I settle for the practicalities of ferrying tourists around. What does he do with himself while they explore? Does he know a lot about the places they visit and is he expected to answer all their questions? Jack's answers are short, and he gives me no openings to ask for more details. It's all 'yes' 'no' and the occasional, 'I'm not sure'. So much for my Sassenach fantasies.

You are such a wa—my inner censor draws the line. 'Terrible person', it adds instead. *Why do I bother liking/ lusting after you?*

We get to the airport five minutes ahead of time, and Jack jumps out to show us where we need to go to get the bus. He's wearing that kilt again, as you might expect a Scottish tour guide to do. It falls just above his knees, and what fantastic knees they are too. Bear with me on this one. Some knees are knobbly and almost repellent; Jack's are smooth and big, hinting at an impressive set of quads above them. My mind does that half-naked towel imagery again, and I have to shake my head so I can focus on what he's saying. He says goodbye and repeats the directions I'll need to get to where he is to pick me up later.

Stewart starts up the coding conversation once more when we get on the bus that will take us to Glasgow city centre. Thankfully, the trip only takes twenty minutes. Stewart's coding chat is still ongoing when I get off outside the main train station, the one Jack promised was nearest to West Nile Street where Blissful Beauty has its office.

The streets are busy with people making their way to nine-to-five jobs. I'd forgotten what 'busy' streets are like, the sea of people you get waiting at traffic lights, the honk of horns when cars and people dodge red lights and the courier and Deliveroo bikes that weave in and out of the crowds. Glaswegians sound different too. I've grown used to the Lochalshie accent. It's still indecipherable at times, but the snatches of conversation I hear now are voices that are harder and edgier.

West Nile Street is off Buchanan Street, and Blissful Beauty has taken over all three storeys of the part of the street where the road curves around a large church, the company's logo and branding plastered on the front. I stare up at the building and the logo, the Bs a swirly mass of silver stars. Melissa is there already, left wrist held up so she can glare at her watch even though I am bang on time. Suddenly, the nerves ramp up. Most clients I meet with do not understand design. Farmers are grateful for anything you do, but Blissful Beauty is a well-established brand. I won't be able to palm off half-baked ideas on these people. I wish I'd put more thought into this.

"Gaby!" Melissa nods, as I juggle the laptop so I can give her a clumsy hug.

She steps back quickly. "Country life appears to suit you. Leave the talking to me, okay? You just show him the stuff and promise him you've followed every directive in the Blissful Beauty brand bible, okay?"

Phew. My role is to appear hard-working and serious. *Say nothing, Gaby,* I repeat to myself.

"Hi!" a voice behind me makes me jump and then start once more. Am I fated to meet only men who remind me of my favourite TV programmes? The guy behind me is the spitting image of Tobias Menzies, aka 'Black Jack' Randall in Outlander. A younger version of him, I decide as I inspect him as discreetly as I can. He's all dark hair, pointy chin and serious eyes that fix on a person. 'Black Jack' Randall was not a nice chap, but Katya and I often had the snog-marry-avoid conversation about all the male characters in Outlander, and he always turned up on the snog list, despite being one hundred percent bad.

"We're meeting someone," I say, and curse as my voice comes out helium style. Already I've broken the say nothing edict, and Melissa sighs, introducing herself and me.

"I'm Dexter Carlton, Blissful Beauty's UK marketing manager? We're meeting to discuss the website and what we need for the launch, right?" he asks, the accent taking me by surprise as it isn't English, a lilting American one I pin down to the south of the US. It's another reminder that the guy in front of me is not Jack Randall and I'm not in an episode of Outlander. He shakes hands with Melissa then sticks his hand out for me.

I stick my hand and drop my laptop. "Nooooooo," I scream. The next bit takes place in slow motion, the three of us watching in powerless horror as it bounces on the kerb, flies into the air, lands on the road and is driven over by a double-decker bus and the two black cabs following it.

Melissa has closed her eyes, mouth blowing out deep breaths while Dexter tips his head and looks at the remains of the laptop the manufacturers had advertised as the lightest, flattest one money could buy. Not as flat as this, though.

"Wow, that's…" Dexter starts, then shakes his head.

Gabrielle Richardson, professionalism personified. If blushing turns you red, I match the nearby traffic lights for shiny brightness.

Melissa opens her eyes. "Gaby here," she says through gritted teeth, "is much better at design than she is at life. Luckily, I've always taken out the best public liability insurance I can afford, which includes damage to leased equipment."

As the traffic has halted, I pick up the laptop. I don't want to be landed with a littering charge too. It's paper thin, thanks to seven and a half tonnes of double-decker rolling over it. I thank the universe and all the stars that I'd backed up everything on that laptop on the iMac back at Jack's. Melissa tells me I can find some way of disposing of it. I put it in my bag and try to rearrange my features, so I look professional and capable of mind-blowing design work once more.

"Um, shall we?" he points at the door, and I offer prayers begging any deity who will listen that it is true everyone exaggerates when they talk about the importance of first impressions.

Tobias stroke Dexter grins broadly, the upturned mouth spreading so wide it threatens to split his face in two. It's nice, I decide, a man smiling at me so much when I've grown used to Jack and his taciturn ways.

"Come in," he says, sweeping an arm before him. "Do you think you'll manage the journey to the office with no more accidents?"

Melissa smiles. "Just keep her miles away from any electronic equipment in your office, and we'll be fine," and he grins at me once more. I return the gesture sheepishly. At least I'll be able to entertain Katya later when I tell her what happened.

Dexter doesn't seem to have taken against me for being an idiot. I like his accent, I decide. Scottish accents have hard consonants in the main, and his are silky smooth. The best way to describe it is, speech like melted dark chocolate.

Inside, the Blissful Beauty branding is everywhere—silver stars and blown-up pictures of the reality TV star who founded the company wearing what looks like every one of their products at once. The reception features an enormous cut out of her doing her best duck pout and blowing a kiss to the camera. The tag line underneath reads, *Make-Up and Skincare so Good You Won't Need to Cover Up*. Dexter sees me gawping at her, and he nudges me. "Maybe you'll get to meet Caitlin at some point. She's awesome. It's hard to believe she's created this multi-billion-dollar company, and she's only twenty-one years old."

"Mmm," I mutter, while the voice in my head argues that it doesn't hurt when your family are already millionaires anyway, and you can employ all the experts you need to launch a successful business and brand. She spends all her time on Instagram promoting her products. "You guys!!!!!!!! I'm super-excited for this new eyeshadow you're gonna LOVE!!!!!" Does that leave much time for doing business type stuff?

Dexter's office is at the top of the building, and the bay window looks out over rooftops. To my right, I see the big shopping mall I plan to spend too much time in later and to the left are spires, the golden dome of a Mosque and high-rise offices. He invites us to sit down at a table in front of the window and asks if we want coffees. After this morning's little incident, I'm too nervous to add caffeine to the mix, and Melissa's nod tells me I've made the right decision in her eyes. Dexter pushes a button on his phone and orders two espressos. Coffees delivered, Melissa takes out her laptop, finds the pages I've created and turns it so Dexter can see them.

"I used—"

"As you can see, Gaby followed the brand bible religiously," Melissa cuts in.

"I'll print them out," he says, pointing at the top of the range laser-jet printer in the corner of his office. He studies every idea I've come up with, rotating the papers and bending his head to look at them closely. I'm just running through my speech for Melissa, "*Sorry. I tried so hard, and I'm sorry he hates everything, and I accidentally ruined more than £1,000 worth of kit,*" when he sits up straight once more and pushes the papers away.

"These are amazing. You've done just what we wanted."

The glow starts in my belly and spreads its warmth through my body…

"Seriously. These are amazing. Blissful Beauty will take the UK by storm, and you will be part of our exciting journey… That's fantastic, isn't it? Like a dream come true."

I'm still nodding along, enjoying the glow. I might qualify the dream come true bit. I don't enjoy working as a designer that much. But at least I've got one satisfied customer. Again, I take a few seconds to realise he's still talking.

"What you want to do now," he says, pointing at the print-outs one by one, "is go back to our brand bible and then you'll be able to adjust the colour palette on this one, this one and this one to ensure it meets our standards. Then, if you take the website template, move the menus here and arrange for the pictures to appear in this sidebar. Here, I'll show you."

He takes a pen out and scribbles all over my designs. When he hands them back, they are unrecognisable. 'You did just what we wanted' and 'these are amazing' must mean different things in US English. My designs lie buried under a mass of red ink, and yet that super-watt smile is still in place and the words coming out of his mouth continue to wax lyrical about my design genius.

The main point is, however, that Blissful Beauty still wants Bespoke Design to carry out the work for them. Melissa's expression is no longer tense. My odds of hanging onto my job are once more fifty-fifty.

I leave the office in a daze, Dexter calling out after me he'd like to see more of the Scottish countryside, and why not arrange our follow-up meeting nearer to where I live? It's hard to imagine the ultra-urban Dexter in an ultra-rural setting, but I plaster my best 'great idea' look in place and wander out.

Out on the street, I turn to Melissa.

"I'm so sorry," I squawk. "I'll pay for the laptop if the insurance doesn't cover it." No idea how. "And I followed the brand bible instructions exactly."

"Yes, the insurance will cover it, though please never, ever do that again. And as for the designs, welcome to the corporate world, Gaby. Go off and re-do everything as he specified. Then, he'll ask you to re-do it again right back to what you presented him with originally. After that, we'll change it back to his first request. Other people will see your designs. They prefer you to give them your first ideas. You change it and after that, we go back to Dexter's requests. Multiply this by ten, and eventually, we get to the end."

"What is the end?" I ask.

"Your original designs," she says. "Let's talk tomorrow when you've re-done them the first time. Send me the originals just in case and I'll make sure they're backed up in our office too."

My stomach, unfilled since last night's dinner, rumbles so loudly it is audible above the traffic. Melissa raises her eyebrows. This is my day for mortification.

"Um, do you want to go for lunch?" I say. "My treat." It's the least I can do.

Melissa shakes her head. "No, if I go now I can get the earlier flight to Stansted."

She sticks her hand out, stopping one of the black cabs passing us. "Goodbye, Gaby. Treat the rest of the equipment I've sent up to Scotland with you as if it is your newborn child."

I've five hours 'til the pickup point. Time for some food and a little retail therapy.

CHAPTER NINE

Jack raises an eyebrow when he picks me up at the front of Glasgow Central Station loaded down with bags. "Retail therapy," I say. Fortune had smiled on me, and it was the start of summer sales. I picked up some serious bargains. The shops were selling off their winter stuff, and as the Lochalshie summer is yet to prove warm enough for tee shirts and short skirts, I loaded up on sweaters, scarves and gloves.

"Where's Stewart?" I ask, fingers crossed behind my back.

"He decided to stay in Glasgow. He met someone on the course who's just as... keen on coding, and the guy offered him a bed for the night so they could continue their chat."

Oh, one hundred thank you's, the Gods of Entertainment for stepping in to save me from death by boredom.

The mini-bus's inhabitants, those Jack picked up from the airport earlier in the day, stare at me from the windows of the mini-bus, and I wave. It's not ideal—having Jack to myself would have been the perfect situation—but chatting to a group of Americans will be fun.

"Hey everyone!" I say as I get in.

"Gaby! Darcy here! I thought I recognised you. How awesome to see you again."

The woman at the front of the bus leans forward so she can grasp my hand. I bumped into her when I stopped at Glencoe on my way up to Lochalshie all those weeks ago. Hadn't she been doing a Scottish tour at the time and didn't she see everything she wanted to then?

Something must show in my face as she grins at me. "I love Scotland," she says. "And now I'm retired me, and John Junior here can spend our time just as we like. This is our third tour this year." She lowers her voice. "And what do you think of our tour guide? Ain't he the spit of Jamie Fraser? When he picked us up, I couldn't believe it. I said to John Junior, will you lookie here! We've got our own private Outlander experience. You must have been over the moon when you met him, what with you being such a super fan too."

Darcy's idea of lowering her voice means that only everyone in the mini-bus and surrounding 100 metres can hear her, instead of just people within the entire city of Glasgow. Perhaps this is what comes of living in a huge country where you have far more space around you.

The smile I wear is decidedly fixed as I turn from her and take my place beside a smirking Jack. "Super-fan, eh," he says out of the corner of his mouth. "Not that much," I say, breezily, hoping Darcy can't hear. When we last met, she and I quoted bits of the book to each other and confessed to having read most of the books three times each.

We drop the mini-bus tourers at a hotel half an hour from Lochalshie. It is fairytale-like, and all the guests sigh and coo behind me as we drive up. It sits on the edge of a loch and had been built centuries ago, according to Jack who delivers a thrillingly knowledgeable running commentary as we head back, the ancient seat of the Mc-Gilmours of Lochalshie. When they went out of favour for picking the wrong side in the Jacobite uprising, the castle fell into disrepair but was bought many years later by a wealthy banker who eventually sold it to a property trust that turned it into a luxury hotel.

The sight of the turreted towers, the sweeping drive-way and the stairs to the main entrance hushes even Darcy who'd kept us all up to date on her tours of Scotland and thorough knowledge of everything Outlander. By the time we drop her off, I am back to bargaining with the Gods of Entertainment. Come back Stewart. All is forgiven.

She winks at me as she leaves the mini-bus. "Now, you kids have fun this evening! Someone told me what proper Scotsmen wear under their kilts, and I'll want to know if it's true when I see you tomorrow."

John Junior, a hefty, silent bear of a man rolls his eyes at us as he lumbers behind her out of the bus. It must be my day for blushing, I decide. What with the laptop accident and encounters with women who don't know the word shame, my skin has taken on every shade of pink, from a delicate flush to the full-blown scarlet face. Thankfully, the sun is setting, lending the cover of subdued lighting to the mini-bus's interior. I get back into my seat and pull on my seatbelt. My heart races as the door opens beside me and Jack gets back in. He grips the steering wheel in both hands and tips his head forward so it rests there. The seconds tick by, and I am just about to prod him when he pushes himself back again. To my astonishment, the dimples have returned to Jack's face. I suspected he is trying not to burst into hysterical laughter.

"What a day," he says, and I nod fervently. If only he knew the extent of mine.

He puts the bus into reverse, performs yet another textbook manoeuvre and drives away, adding a jaunty honk of the horn aimed at the American visitors who still stand outside admiring the loch.

As my heart continues its yammering, I decide silence is the best policy. Katya, a fan of police dramas, once told me the best way to get people to talk was to say nothing and wait for them to become uncomfortable enough to want to fill the silence. Excellent mode of attack is silence. You just sit there and wait and…

"I'm really not that big a fan of Outlander," I burst out. It turns out only being able to hear engine noise was more than I could bear. "And you don't look that much like Jamie Fras—I mean, the actor Sam Heughan."

"Don't I?" he says. "I am his cousin."

"Gosh, are you? That explains it then. You're the spitting image of the—"

I stop, aware that I've contradicted myself in three sentences. "Well, your skin's different, and your knees don't look the same, and your hair isn't the exact shade—"

Katya's face swims in front of me, appearing on the windscreen, her head in her hands. "*Shut up, Gaby! Stop now before he decides you are a total fool.*" And works out that I've paid a lot of attention to what he looks like.

"I'm not," Jack says. "But ever since that programme came out, I keep getting mistaken for him. Or his far better looking younger brother, anyway."

And at that, he winks at me. Earlier that day, I've seen ghosts of winks but nothing I could claim as definite. This is a bold sweep of an eyelid and lashes that makes his nose and mouth move at the same time. It is so heady I gulp and then have to hide it with a bout of fake coughing.

"You could capitalise on it," I volunteer, determined to seem semi-intelligent in front of him for once. "Um, run Outlander tours dressed as Jamie Fraser and take people to the places in the books and on the TV."

"There are a few of them already," he says, his tone regretful. "Don't want to over-crowd the market. And if people like Darcy turn up to a tour like mine and discover the guide looks a tiny bit like Jamie Fraser and she does her word-of-mouth thing that might make me popular, anyway."

He flicks his gaze to the mirror, and I catch his eye. He is back to being nice again. Heck.

"I'm sure Darcy's mouth can do all sorts of things," I add and cringe as soon as I've finished the sentence. What is it about me that I can't help saying stupid things in front of this man? I'd been tempted to share my laptop story, but silence on that subject seems wise else he thinks I'm a total klutz. "Er, you're right. Word of mouth. Best way. Darcy. Lots of friends." Short sentences, I decide, are the way forward. They allow less room for mistakes and stupidity.

The sign for Lochalshie appears all too quickly. I have three minutes left to say something so mind-bogglingly brilliant, it blasts away all previous impressions Jack might have had of me.

"Kirsty's house is so pretty, isn't it?"

"*Genius, Gaby.*" Katya is back and unimpressed.

The mini-bus has come to a halt, and Jack stares at the place. "If you say so. I prefer places that don't look as if they've been decorated by interior designers. Goodnight, Gaby."

He drives off so quickly my thanks for the lift are shouted at the wind.

Back in the house, I update Katya, which means a phone call outside in the right-hand corner of the front garden—the only place I can get a signal.

"You were with me today," I tell Katya, and explain the whole windscreen appearance thing when she prevented me making too much of an idiot of myself. "I let you down, Gaby," she says solemnly. "If I was supposed to stop you making an idiot of yourself I failed spectacularly."

Oof. "So!" I say brightly. "You coming up to visit me? Commit."

There's an awkward silence the other end.

"You know I love you, right?"

"Katya!"

"It's just this ruddy book I'm writing, the self-help one. The publishers have moved the release date forward. They're aiming for the Christmas market. And I'm doing work for Blissful Beauty too, remember?"

True. At Bespoke Design, it's all hands on deck, and Katya writes for us from time to time so we can offer clients everything they need for a website.

"I sent Dexter all the stuff I'd written so far the other week. He phoned me up, told me it was beyond awesome and then sent it back with tracked changes all over it. He'd rewritten every second word."

She asks me if I'd done anything about the post Ryan had put on Facebook where he declared his undying love and begged for my forgiveness. Oh, that. I realise I have thought little about it or done anything. How strange that Ryan, the guy I was with for ten years, should feature so seldom in my thoughts now. I guess that answers the 'do I want him back' question.

"I almost feel sorry for him," Katya muses, which makes me squawk in surprise. Katya was never Ryan's number one fan. After the engagement party, she didn't miss a chance to tell me how right I was, and that my life was about to become a million times better. "I saw him the other day," she adds, "and he asked after you. I thought he'd lost weight. Not enough to look like he'd got a fatal illness. Shame. But when I told him how far away Lochalshie is, he slumped."

Guilt threatens, but I think of Kayleigh and what Ryan said to Josh, "You've heard from her?", in tones of awe and wonder. If I'm honest, Kayleigh did me a massive favour. I'm the woman who said 'yes' to a proposal because my intended asked in front of an audience and I couldn't bear to let them down. That's not a solid reason for deciding to stay with someone the rest of your life, is it? It's up there with getting married because your surname is Pratt and you're sick and tired of hearing people in customer services snigger when they ask you to repeat your name, so tying yourself to someone with any other surname (bar Ramsbottom) makes sense.

"You will visit me as soon as you can?" I ask, hating how needy I sound. I settle for an 'I'll do my best!' and hang up.

The rest of the week flies by. As Melissa predicted, Dexter and I exchange a lot of emails. His ones start the same way every time. "Gaby, you are A WONDER. The page you have designed where people can upload pictures of themselves and try out the different make-up shades is beyond awesome. Seriously, I looked at it and knew Caitlin will jump up and down in excitement when she sees it. If you could just change the colour, shift the text box to the right, use this font instead, swap the stars for glitter dust… Etcetera, etcetera."

By day three, I'm beginning to wish he'd start his emails saying, *no this isn't good enough. Do something else.* Or sack me as the head designer. He's terrible to work for. Katya sends me the odd message and her experience of writing for him is the same. Melissa tells me to be patient. At the end of the day, he'll go back to the original designs and words. Our job for the moment is to make him feel he earns his fat marketing manager salary.

I've seen little of Jack, apart from the bus passing Kirsty's house early in the morning and late at night. He'd said the average tour is five days/four nights and the bus that passes me on the high street on Friday evening as I head off for the general store is empty of tourists. He gives me a cheery wave. I can't see clearly enough, but I think he smiled too. My heart dances. Small victories, eh?

In the shop, Jamal un-props himself from the counter when I come in and ambles to the fridge. "Chicken or smoked salmon? We've got some venison in too if you're interested. Very lean meat is venison, so better for the cat's heart."

"Is it cheaper than the chicken?" I ask, taking the packet from him. The label promises me that venison is the best health and ethical choice for the modern-minded shopper. It features a picture of a stag with enormous antlers glaring at presumably whoever is about to shoot him.

"No," Jamal shakes his head. "A wee bit more expensive, but you cannae put a price on Mena's well-being can you?"

I leave the shop wondering why I fell for that line. Now that Ms Mena doesn't make me sneeze, I've developed a wee (as the locals would say) fondness for her. This morning I woke up and found her curled at the bottom of the bed in between my legs. And when I return from Jack's and open the door at night, she runs towards me tail up. Mostly to do with me bearing packets of smoked salmon, I suspect, but it makes me glow with pride. Gabrielle Richardson, by day graphic designer; by night, cat whisperer. I've also got in the habit of posting pictures of her on Instagram, and she gets a tonne of likes. Still, does my new-found love of her justify spending £8.50 on a packet of venison? The jury's out.

My neighbour is coming out of his house as I open the gate to Kirsty's house. He raises a hand.

"How're ye? How're ye?" he says, his usual form of greeting. I don't know if it's because he's so ancient or if his accent is much stronger than everyone else's in the village, but everything he says blends into a thick gloop of words. I only understand one in twenty of them, and I go by body language most of the time. 'How're ye' is a general inquiry after my health and/or happiness and only needs a nod. I say it back to him, hoping that what-ever he answers, it is not 'I've only got six months to live, bummer eh?' seeing as I only reply 'Good, good!' every time we have a conversation.

He moves to his side of the hedge that divides his and Kirsty's property.

"Tonicht," he adds, and I smile along nodding my head like a marionette wishing we could use sign lan-guage to make this easier.

"Perty tonicht. An' McCollin's telt me tae ask't ye. Big perty."

I nod some more. I have no idea what he means. He smiles and waves his phone.

"Aye, got wan' of they speshull Tinda ladies cummin' tae!" and at that he winks at me, his wrinkled pixie-like face creasing up with mischief. Again, I'm none the wis-er but take it to mean he is going out, and he's over the moon about it.

I gesture towards the front door where Mena sits on the step howling furiously. "Well, I'd better get in and feed the cat. See you later."

My neighbour smiles. "Aye, aye! Shud be a great perty."

At that, he's gone hobbling up the street much faster than I would have expected a man of his age to move. As I search for the keys in my handbag, I note he's stopped to talk to Mhari who asks him something and looks in my direction. She shouts something at the same time as Mena lets out another ear-splitting yowl. I'm taking far too long to get in the house and sort out her dinner. I wave a vague reply, and she nods, heading off in the same direction as my neighbour.

I let myself in the house and apologise to Mena for keeping her waiting. If she can just hang on a minute, I promise her, waggling the packet of venison in the air, it will be worth her while. And then the two of us can curl up on the sofa and catch up on episodes of Outlander series one on the TV. Again. Her tail waggles in the air furiously. Approval, I guess. Who knew cats loved Outlander too? Both of us fed and watered, we settle down for an evening of heavy-duty binge-watching. One hour later, the Lochalshie fresh air defeats me once more (not my fault I'm battling fatigue this early of an evening), I say 'bed' to Mena and she bolts up the stairs ahead of me.

Lochalshie seems too quiet the following morning. Usually, I spot at least two or three dog walkers taking their pets on a stroll along the water's edge and the odd car or van making its way along the high street. Every house facing me has its curtains shut too. Odd. Mena adored the venison. I'm now on a cat owners' forum, and several of them suggested I feed Mena raw meat from time to time as cats love it and it does wonders for their teeth and bones, so £8.50 a packet or not I'm off to buy yet more of the stuff.

To my astonishment, the general store is closed when I get there. On a Saturday, it opens at six am to take delivery of rolls and loaves from the local bakery. The closure added to the street's desertion makes me uneasy. Where is everyone? My mind leaps to horrible theories.

Eeks, eeks, eeks, is the zombie apocalypse upon us? And should I have taken up jogging when I moved here so I can flee from them when they appear on the streets, craving fresh brains?

I'm on the point of dashing back to the house when Jamal's van pulls up. The door opens, and he stumbles out, his face pasty and his eyes bloodshot. He takes a bottle of water from the seat next to him and drinks the whole thing in one go, leaning back against the van to do so.

"Are you okay?" I ask. And, er, don't zombies have bloodshot eyes? I take a few precautionary steps back from him and grip my bag so I can bolt if necessary.

"Hangover," he mumbles. "That last whisky was a mistake."

"Dear oh dear," I say. "Um…"

Jamal's a Muslim. I'm not one hundred percent up on Islam and the do's and don'ts, but I'm 90 percent sure they're not supposed to drink.

He shakes his head sorrowfully. "Allah is not pleased with me today. And he makes his displeasure known."

Water drunk and van locked up, he opens the shop and invites me to enter. I pick up another packet of venison, wincing when I notice it's a pound more expensive than the last one, and hand it over.

"Special occasion, was it?"

"The annual party," he says, eyes squinting against the overhead lights. "It started out a few years ago. Just a few people and now it's the village's biggest event." At that, he opens one eye.

119

"I didnae see you there. Mind, there was an awfy lot of people there so I might have missed you."

"A party," I say stiffly. "I didn't know."

Jamal's face changes from tiredness to dismay. "Oh? Eh. I suppose it's not really the biggest event. That would be the Highland Games in August. No, not that much of party. You didn't miss anything."

The bell above the front door jangles and Mhari walks in and heads straight for the fridge, helping herself to a bottle of Lucozade, not bothering to wait until she's paid for it before gulping the lot down.

"That last Aperol spritzer was a mistake!"

She spots me. "Gaby! Didnae see you last night at Jack's party. You missed yourself. More folk than ever before, don't you reckon Jamal? And when Jack did that thing with his kilt to that Purple Disco Machine song, I swear I died and went to heaven."

"NFI," I mutter and leave them to work it out for themselves as I walk out without bothering to pay for the venison. I'm half-way down the street when I realise and have to shame-facedly walk back into the shop, inter-rupting Jamal and Mhari's conversation which no doubt was about me.

As I let myself back into the house, I feel tears starting, and I brush them away angry with myself for caring that much. But if ever there was a reminder of how much of an outsider I am, it is this. The village's biggest event and I don't even get an invitation. Thank you, Lochalshie. And Jack. Message received loud and clear.

CHAPTER TEN

I stay in Kirsty's house the rest of the day, too scared to go out in case I meet yet another villager who asks me why I wasn't at Jack's party and what an amazing night it was. I can't face telling them I wasn't invited, and I appear to be at the bottom of the Lochalshie popular persons list.

Mena seems to sense something and decides I am now her best friend. She insists on sitting on my lap most of the day, happy to re-watch Outlander series 2 with me as I mutter that Sam Heughan is one hundred times better looking than Jack McAllan and surmising that he, Jamie Fraser stroke Sam Heughan, would never think of holding a party in his home town and not inviting the village new-comer.

When I risk creeping outside to phone Katya, picking my moment to minimise the risk of people passing by who might hear my moans, she suggests my invite might have got lost in the post.

"Katya," I say, "we're not living in the eighteen hundreds. People don't send invites out. They ask you themselves. I sat in a mini-bus with him for six hours. Don't you think he might have mentioned it then? 'Hey, Gaby! I'm having a little party this weekend. It's the annual do I have to celebrate the tourist season and the first few successful tours. Nothing formal. It would be great if you could come.' But he didn't. Or there's the Lochalshie WhatsApp group. He could have asked me through that."

"Is he on that group?"

"No. But he could have gone on it. Joined it for a minute or so, asked me and then left."

The Lochalshie WhatsApp group is so active, any sane person doesn't stay in it for long. Whenever I'm in Mhari's company, her phone beeps with updates every second. How she keeps on top of it is beyond me.

When I moan again about my Norma No Mates status, Katya loses patience. "Gaby, you're already at a party—a pity party for one. Let's talk about Dexter, stupid accidents aside." When I told her about the laptop incident, she spluttered with laughter so much she had to hold the phone away. Close-to snorting isn't something you want to hear from anyone, even your nearest and dearest.

"You said he reminded you of Tobias Menzies.," Katya goes on, still on the Dexter subject. "Did you notice if he was wearing a wedding ring or not?"

He wasn't, but that doesn't tell you if he is with someone or not. I'm sure that the Dating Guru would say dating someone I work for is a no-no. Or at least until after Bespoke Design has finished the contract we have with his company. Anyway, he's used to glamorous people like Caitlin. In any picture I have ever seen of her, she is immaculate. Smooth, shiny hair, skin glossy her make-up immaculate and head to toe in designer gear. When I caught a glance of myself in the mirror this morning, I was red-cheeked, my hair was doing its best impression of part finger in an electric socket, part hasn't seen a brush in months. And my coat had a hole in it torn out by the wind here. (Feels like.) Dexter has those American teeth too—you know the kind I mean, big, straighter than the line you draw with a ruler and so white they dazzle in the dark. When I was with him, I didn't smile and kept my lips over my mouth when I was speaking as I didn't want him to draw unfavourable comparisons with my unstraightened, undazzle in the dark teeth.

And what if Dexter's personal self is like his work self? "Gaby! You are beyond awesome. I've never had such an amazing girlfriend. If you could just change the way you say 'I love you', and when we go out hold my hand and not my arm, and make sure you brush your hair at all times…" And so on, a never-ending list of everything I need to do to improve myself before he decides I was okay all along.

I force myself out of the house on Sunday, having rehearsed beforehand what I'll say if anyone asks me why

I wasn't at Jack's party. "Oh? That. I was too busy working." Hopefully, no-one will suss that makes little sense seeing as my 'work' place is Jack's house. Luckily, it's a beautiful day. The higher temperatures the BBC weather forecaster promised mean it is warm enough to go coat-less, but I wear a long-sleeved top anyway. The wind that blows off the loch here is always present and most of the blame for my permanently messy hair. Plenty of people mill about, but I walk the loch edge and avoid getting close enough to anyone for them to speak to me. The sharp chime of an ice-cream van pierces the peace and quiet, and I decide to cheer myself up with a gigantic cone. The rainbow-wrapped van is parked at the far side of the loch. With any luck most of the surrounding crowd will have gone by the time I get there.

"How're, Gaby!"

Dang. That was badly timed. The kids have vanished, but Stewart and Scottie appear from behind the van just as I approach.

"I was working," I say, determined to nip the 'you missed yourself at the party conversation' in the bud. Scottie does his usual wild circling around my legs and hobbling me with his lead. I don't bother waiting for Stewart to take the initiative and I undo the lead from his collar myself. This pleases Scottie a great deal as he barks enthusiastically and races off towards the water chasing after the ducks, who rise from the water in perfect V formation.

"Aye? But you're no' at your computer?" Stewart's face wrinkles up in puzzlement. "By the way, I looked after your iMac for ye at the party. Mhari spilt her last Aperol spritzer all over it—and I dinnae think she was the first to do so either—but I gave it a wee wipe and it was as good as new. I switched it on and off to make sure too."

Dear heaven. That iMac, equipment borrowed from my work, is worth upwards of two thousand pounds. Explain that one to Melissa. I'm already living on borrowed time when it comes to care of computers and laptops.

"You're not suffering a hangover yourself?" I say through gritted teeth. Jamal still hasn't recovered. The man who greeted me this morning in the shop was bleary-eyed and vowing never to touch alcohol or attend a party again.

"No, no!" Stewart says cheerily, breaking off to yell at Scottie to come back. "A lot of the folks who go to Jack's party are amateurs. They dinnae ken how to drink properly. Or how to prepare. You see what you must do is start the day before and…"

Enough of this. I can't face what will be a long and detailed explanation of party prep which will undoubtedly involve porridge.

"Ice-cream, Stewart?" I bleat as the van's owner leans out of the window.

"Aye, don't mind if I do," he says and presses against the van's side to read the menu at the back. The van offers everything—from soft-whipped 99s to Magnum bars and cones with sauce, nuts, sprinkles and bits of shortbread. Stewart opts for one of them (the most expensive option), and I choose the Mr Whippy cone with a chocolate flake. As I lick it, I close my eyes and zone out Stewart who keeps talking through every mouthful of his Millionaire's Shortbread cone.

"...aye, so as I was sayin', ye need a big bowl of porridge just..."

The words come to an abrupt halt as Stewart's cheeks inflate and he makes odd gulping noises as if he's about to vomit. He must have taken too big a mouthful of ice-cream, shortbread bits and the toffees pieces sprinkled throughout.

"Are you okay?" I say. Scottie, having returned from his duck chasing, plants himself in front of his owner and barks furiously. The canine equivalent of the same question, I guess.

Stewart, a maroon-faced man at the best of times, is now scarlet. But there's a blue tinge to him too, and I scan our surroundings trying to find help—a handy ambulance or Dr McLatchie ready to step in and save the day.

The ice-cream van owner leans out of his serving hatch. "No' my fault!" he says, "He ate that thing too quickly!"

He pulls up the hatch indecently quickly, and the van drives out of the car park seconds later.

"Stewart!" I put a hand on him, thoroughly alarmed. I've reached the grand old age of 26 without ever seeing someone die in front of me. Please do not let this be the first time.

The loch side is deserted—the kids vanished, the dog walkers tucked up back in their own homes and no handy ambulance or GP nearby. Pity as this seems like a situation the good Doctor McLatchie would relish. The man beside me flays around, arms out and face turning bluer by the second. His dog mirrors every movement as if somehow that will help.

Last year, Melissa rail-roaded me into the role of appointed first aid person. I went on a training course and returned to the office promising everyone I'd kill them if they dared so much as get a paper cut.

First aid training included the Heimlich manoeuvre. I take a deep breath and get in close and personal with Stewart, wrapping my arms as well as I can around his substantial girth and forming a fist below his sternum.

I thrust my fists up as hard as I can, trying not to mind too much as Stewart's bottom and my crotch make closer contact than I've had with anyone in months.

He's still choking, and Scottie circles the two of us, pausing every now and again as if to tell me off for being a rubbish first aider.

The first aid folks told us not to worry about cracking ribs. They're far easier to repair than an oxygen-starved brain. I visualise Louise and her snarly face and my arms tighten in a choke hold. My right first thrusts up in an upper cut move Joe Calzaghe would be proud of, and a tiny object flies out of Stewart's mouth. Shortbread, toffee— who knows? Blockage ejected, he drops to the ground, panting hard. Scottie rushes over and licks his face.

"Are you okay?" I ask, hands on thighs and breathing heavily myself. Is this what marathon runners feel like at the end of their 26 miles?

Stewart staggers to his feet, wrapping his arms around his torso and wincing. "Aye. Much obliged to ye, Gaby. I need a pint. It's an awfy shock, ye know. Seeing your whole life flash in front of ye!"

With that, he's off—another 'thank-you' thrown hastily over his shoulder as he leaves, heading toward the Lochside Welcome. Scottie, still off the lead, runs alongside. When the dog stops for a second and looks back at me, I tell myself his expression is apologetic. *Sorry about my crap owner who should have thrown himself at your feet in thankfulness.*

"Well!" I stamp my feet, a pointless gesture seeing as no-one's around. "You might have offered to buy me a pint."

The remains of both our cones lie pointing upwards in the sand. Nine pounds fifty those cones cost. I curse Stewart, Jack McAllan, Scotland and rip-off ice-cream merchants who vanish at the first sign of trouble.

All in all, a dreadful weekend.

CHAPTER 11

"How's the book going?" I ask Katya. I've finally got hold of her one week after the Stewart incident. Our conversation had been uneven. My side of it far too long because so much had happened since I'd talked to her last. It has taken me two hours to fill in, not helped because Katya likes to interrupt and make sure she understands everything, but after a while, I had to steer the conversation back to her if I didn't want to come across as a total narcissist. Even if I needed her interpretation of all my events—Monday evening, for instance.

I'd been about to settle down on the sofa to a re-read of *An Echo in the Blood* when there was a knock on my door. I opened it to a sheepish-looking Stewart and a stunning woman I didn't recognise.

Stewart thrust a bunch of flowers into my hands. It looked like he'd picked them from the displays that surrounded the car park, but I supposed it was the thought that counted.

"Eh, aye Gaby. I didnae thank you enough for saving ma life. I'm awfy grateful. Jolene telt me I should come and say thank you properly." He nodded at the woman by his side who extended her hand and gripped mine so tightly I winced.

"Pleased to meet you, eh?" she said. Not Scottish then, the antipodean accent turning every sentence into a question. Katya once told me that just as you should always guess someone as a Canadian when you're not sure if they are Canadian or American, the same applied to Australians and New Zealanders.

"Auckland?" I asked, and a broad smile split her face in two.

"Manukau, South Auckland. Can we come in? I want to chat to you about something, and my boyfriend here still needs to thank you a thousand times over for pulling him from the clutches of death."

Boyfriend? I had to rescue my jaw before it dropped to the floor. Seriously? As my nanna used to say, there's a lid for every pot, but Stewart is—to use another Nanna-style saying—punching way out of his league. I guessed Jolene to be Maori, long dark hair, light brown skin, dark-eyed and muscular if that handshake was anything to go by. Stewart must have hidden—I shook my head, unwilling to guess what talents for attracting beautiful women he might possess.

"Of course," I said, doing a quick mental run-over the house wondering if I'd left out anything embarrassing such as that book I'd ordered from Amazon the other day, *How to Find Lasting Love with the Right Man*. Nope, it was hidden away upstairs next to my bed.

Stewart and Jolene stared around them. "We've never been in this house," Stewart said, moving to the windows at the front and running his fingers down the neat join in the panes that let no draughts in at all.

"Yeah, that stuck-up cow never let anyone in here, eh?" Jolene said, making me like her one hundred times more than I had five seconds ago. She stared up at the atrium.

"Isn't that annoying in the morning when it gets light at four thirty?"

Not really, I told her. I liked the light waking me up in the morning, and I always managed to fall back asleep again. "Have a seat," I said, and Jolene eyed the sofa and chairs warily.

"This is the kind of house you're too frightened to sit down in," she said, "in case you make a mess."

Funny that. Jack had said something similar when he told me he preferred houses that didn't look as if an interior designer had done them. Maybe I was wrong to think Kirsty's house was so amazing.

"Don't worry," I said, "the cat sitting service website includes full house cleaning afterwards. And I'd rather have people in here. What did you want to talk about?"

Jolene sat down opposite me. "I do the Lochalshie website. And you're a graphic designer, eh?"

The New Zealand question thing—it's hard to tell when someone is asking you something or it's a statement. This one's a statement and I am proved right when Jolene doesn't bother waiting for a reply.

"Anyway," Jolene said, the death stare departed and a smile lighting up her features. "Stewart built the site, so it's brilliant," she flashed me a smile that suggests otherwise, "but it needs a tiny bit of updating."

Ah. I'm pretty sure I can guess where this is going.

"We've got the Highland Games coming up in August and we want to attract as many people as possible this year. It's a big money-maker for the village. Or it used to be."

The games, she told me, brought in lots of visitors in the old days. People loved watching strong men wrestle with cabers, whatever that is, or tosses and throws where you fling hammers over bars. The dancing displays went down a treat. And the sight and sound of pipers marching down the High Street playing Flower of Scotland were enough to melt a stone heart. Visitors flooded the place, staying overnight in the two hotels and the B&Bs, spending their money in the general store and the pub, and many of them made it a proper holiday staying a few nights or even the whole week.

I stirred in my seat. Something must have shown on my face because Jolene anticipated what I was about to say.

"I know it doesn't sound exciting. Especially these days. The committee is working on new ideas for the games this year. We've got a travelling fair coming along so we can offer rides and we've lined up Psychic Josie, that woman who speaks with the dead to help you work out who you're going to marry."

I kept my expression neutral. Neither idea sounded promising.

"...so we wondered if you could update our website for us—make it look modern and exciting? And then more people will decide to come to our games and perhaps think staying in the village for a few days is a good idea."

I could hardly say no, could I? Over the years, I've found that when you tell people you're a graphic designer, they think it's easy for you to create images or websites. Or that it doesn't take long. And I didn't need to ask if the Lochalshie's village committee had money in their budget for professional photos. The answer would be no.

Mena chose that moment to appear, strolling down the stairs and yowling. Stewart leapt to his feet, whirling round to face her and yelling 'go away!' at the top of his voice. Mena stopped, looked him up and down disdainfully and walked past him to the kitchen. At that, Stewart had a sneezing fit, droplets of liquid flying from his nose so fast they hit me full on the face. I gulped hard, swallowing back nausea. Other people's bodily fluids should stay in their own bodies unless...well, we all know the exception to that rule.

Jolene leapt up too, pulling tissues out of her handbag. "Stewart, you muppet! Gaby, I promise you he is house-trained even if it took me three years to get him to put the toilet seat down after using it."

Stewart wiped a hand across his nose and then over his trousers. Jolene's definition of house-training must have differed from mine.

Time then to end my first Lochalshie visitors' event. Nice as it had been to welcome people in, what might Stewart do next? In my rush to get rid of them, I ended up not only agreeing to a full update of the village website but also to design all the posters and signage for the Highland Games. Oh well. Perhaps it meant that if the villagers held a party afterward, this time I'd get an invitation.

Unlike Jack's event.

"The book," Katya says now as we catch up, "is a total nightmare. Remind me never, ever to ghostwrite for anyone ever again. And there's a meeting in London I have to go to next week to discuss a 'change in direction', so it looks as if everything I've written so far is about to be trashed and I'll need to start all over again."

I try my best to sound soothing. There's a loud trill in the background—the landline.

"What's that?" Katya asks and exclaims too when I tell her. Like me, she's never used one before. I beg her to carve out some time to visit me and hang up, picking up the other phone just as the answer machine kicks in.

"Gaby!"

Aha. Mena's owner, no doubt checking up on my care of her cat. And yet again, sounding breathy almost as if she is jogging at the same time.

"Mmm?" I say and mouth 'Miaow, Mena' to the cat who ignores me, busy as she is with her advanced cleaning ritual. As Kirsty talks, she begins on her bottom. I tell myself this means nothing.

"I thought I'd update you on my plans! I knew you'd be desperate to know what I'm doing!"

I make agreement-type noises. Kirsty's original reason for needing to employ a cat sitter was that she had to escape after a relationship ended. At that stage, I wasn't aware she was an internet star and a YouTube celebrity. Maybe she's in London meeting with sponsors or something.

"I've come up with this A-MAY-ZING idea! I'm going to personalise my blogs and podcasts, you know? I've always concentrated on giving people advice, but it's my story they want to hear, isn't it? I need to take my own advice, Gaby, and I'll document every stage of the journey. Guess what my destination is?"

"Um," I say, but she doesn't bother waiting for the answer.

"Jack, of course! I mean, I've got millions of followers, and they all use my advice to find a man. It makes perfect sense for me to do so. *Boyfriend Hunter* takes a new direction. I've already hinted at it in blog posts and updates, and people tell me they can't wait to see what I do. I'm going to call the blog *Christina's Tips for Moving Date to Life Mate*. Isn't that brilliant?"

Lame, Katya says in my head. I nod agreement. If you need someone to think up a red-hot title for you, don't do it yourself, ask my mate. She's the words woman.

"Why did he break up with you?" Kirsty is more likely to tell me what I've been dying to find out ever since I moved here. Mena stops licking her bottom and looks at me. I have tried asking her, but so far the answer has only been a yowl.

There's a pause, then the words come out in a rush. "He said we didn't want the same things. He's wrong, though. Jack doesn't know what he wants, but by the time I've finished with him, he'll want me more than he's ever wanted anything in his life. I'm going to implement a ten-step process and when people see how successful my methods are, imagine how many followers and fans I'm going to get."

As well as Jack. I keep the thought quiet though. I don't want Jack to go back to Kirsty for obvious reasons. I'm under no illusions I stand any chance with him, but at least if he's on his own, I have a five percent chance instead of a big fat zero. Besides, Kirsty is the Dating Guru. She'll have lots of information to hand to help her. And she strikes me as one very determined lady. This. Is. Not. Good. News.

"Will you help me, Gaby?"

Argh. "Um, I don't know what—"

"I can tell you're on my side. Jack is the love of my life. He just doesn't know it yet. But I know it. The first time I met him, my heart fluttered to new life and flooded with joy."

I must repeat that one to Katya. She'll howl with laughter.

"Tell me," she says, the voice dropping to a purr that would do Mena proud, "Does he still have that painting of me hanging in his upstairs hallway?"

"Yes," I say, the word coming out through gritted teeth.

"All I need you to do is talk about me from time to time when you see him. Mention how heart-broken I am, that I spend my evenings crying and confused, trying to work out what I did wrong. Oh, and also say that there's a bad boy billionaire who is very interested in me."

"A bad boy billionaire?" I repeat. "Like Christian Grey?"

"Yes. Jack's beautiful looking, but he's not a billionaire. I need him to feel guilt and pain that he's hurt me, but also threatened. These are the emotions that will bring him back to me. My agent says if I can get him to propose in two months, we'll be able to generate amazing publicity for the… oh, nothing."

She pauses and then goes back to telling me how dreadful the split was for her and how unexpected. There she was, drifting along totally in love and making plenty of money from her website when BAM, out of the blue it came. The text Jack sent her telling her he needed to talk. She thought he was going to propose and spent ages making sure she looked her best so that when she uploaded the pictures on Instagram no-one would be surprised her boyfriend felt the need to ask her to marry him after only three months. But no! He'd told her instead that he didn't feel they wanted the same thing, and he wasn't comfortable continuing their relationship. Jack, she mutters darkly, has a history of never lasting longer than three months in a relationship. She'd thought she would be the woman to change him.

Kirsty even cries and, I wonder uncharitably if this is just to convince me of her heartbreak. I mean, when she talked about the living proof her solutions worked, I wondered if she only wants him back so that her website will do better if she has Jack in tow.

"So, you will help me won't you, Gaby? Imagine how amazing your review on the cat sitter site will be if you help me with this too!"

That almost sounds like a threat. And imagine how terrible it will be if you don't. But then she adds one more thing, and the tearfulness sounds genuine. "When I lost my dad seven years ago, I vowed I'd only ever date or marry a man who was every bit as good as my father. Jack is such a man, Gaby. I must get him back."

My mum and dad split twenty years ago, but I saw a lot of him as I was growing up. The thought of either of my parents dying sends shivers down my spine. Kirsty lost her dad at a young age.

Yet again, I could hardly say no.

CHAPTER 12

"Mena, have you ever heard of FOMO?" I ask solemnly, and she shakes her head. I'm kidding. She's a cat and does not understand anything I say, but I've succumbed all too quickly to crazy cat lady behaviour and now carry out serious conversations with her. This works best if you make up the answers yourself.

"Fear of missing out," I say, pulling open my bag to check I have my notepad, pens and phone. "Rhetorical question, Mena. No-one could argue that going to the village library for a meeting of the Lochalshie Highland Games committee comes anywhere near the top ten things to do."

Yes, Jolene might not be Dexter-like in her assessments of my work, but things I thought were requests turn out to be orders. Attending the next meeting of the games committee is one of them. It's a Friday night—yup, Friday, not a Tuesday or anything—and I'm heading to the library to discuss the plans for this summer's Highland Games. How did this happen? And yes, if I were to post my plans for this evening on any social media site, I doubt my followers would call it a FOMO moment.

Still, a library outing hardly rates appearance preparation, which fits in with how lazy I feel. My 'work' uniform of leggings, a slogan tee and a hoodie will do. I've got into the habit of not showering in the morning. When you work in an office with zero colleagues, why bother? Strictly speaking, I should have done so before heading off to a meeting with other people. But when I ask Mena if it's worth the effort, she shakes her little furry head. That's how I interpret it. The thing with conversations with cats is that they almost always work out in your favour.

The library is yet another of the Lochalshie buildings that disguise themselves as a home from the outside. Only the council logo on the front door shows it might not be what it seems. Inside, a huge display of new books on offer catches my attention. As I inspect them, Dr McLatchie slides up to me and points at every one. "Pish. Pish. Pish." If you have ever wondered what might appear on a doctor's recommended reading list, now appears to be the best time to find out what shouldn't.

"What about this one," I pluck a random book from the display, *You Lost Him at Hello* by Jess McCann. "It's the secrets of one of America's top dating coaches," I say, reading from the back cover and wondering if Kirsty knows her local library stocks one of her rival's books. Dr McLatchie takes it from me, bends it open in a way that makes librarians up and down the land shudder, and reads the page in front of her.

"What total tosh! Daters have to apply successful sales techniques and know and love the—"

Whatever she is about to say is cut short. Jolene appears from behind a bookshelf armed with a bell and telling us the meeting is to begin. She nods a greeting to me and sits at the top of the table in the centre of the library. Others fill the surrounding eight chairs. I slide into the seat next to Dr McLatchie and nod a greeting to every other committee member.

I get to my feet. "Hello! Lovely to join—"

FOMO comes back and bites me. Here I am, stuck in a small room on a Friday night with…

… a guy who makes every bit of me heat up, even though he is a non-party inviting, rude, sarcastic, horrible… Oh, woe.

I'd been in the middle of that 'authenticity' thing, where you look around the table at everyone, trying to make your intro sound sincere, couldn't be happier to be here, etc. Then, my eyes landed on Jack McAllan, Lochalshie Highland Games committee member so far unknown. He nods, and as per usual it's a gesture that gives nothing away.

Jolene stands and waves at me to sit down. "Thanks, Gaby! We'll be coming back to you later. Now, back to the important stuff—the games and Psychic Josie!"

Jack pulls out his phone and checks something out. "So far, we've got ten entries to the Highland Games."

Even as an outsider, I know this isn't good.

"What's the prize?" I say, and I'm met with blank stares (most of the committee) and glares (Jack).

Jolene rustles the papers in her hands, flipping a page over so she can read the relevant bit. "First prize in the Highland Games is a 'wee dod o' shortbread'".

"Shortbread?" I say, "Big wow. Jack makes the best shortbread I've ever eaten." I nod at him. His face doesn't flicker. "But is it enough of an incentive?"

There must be better possibilities. People come to the games for… Big Men. Big Muscles. Strength. Whisked away on a Highland Tour… now, my brain does cart-wheels, flourishing pictures and images online of all of the above. Present the ideas neatly on a website so that FOMO is obligatory. Come to the Lochalshie Highland Games or forever miss out.

"Why not install a plug-in on the website where people can view themselves in their family tartan kilt? And then you could print out the results and have them on a stall at the games? Or what about a recreation of the Battle of Stirling Bridge, a glorious Scots victory?"

I'm about to add, "the only one, eh?", when common sense stops me at the last minute. *Invitations to parties, Gaby,* no need for further reinforcement of your outsider status, hmm? And possibly the Scots don't take too well to reminders of Scots-English battles.

Nods start around the table. Phones or tablets emerge—the library must be one of the fabled hot spots—and other people pitch in with ideas. The pipe band major clears his throat. "We could ask Big Donnie for a money prize for the games. That would attract competitors. He can spare a hundred pounds."

Jolene agrees. "Can you ask him, Jack?"

From where I'm sitting, I can see Jack roll his eyes and a tiny frown crease his brow. My heart flutters, as the memory of that first meeting I had with Jack resurfaces. Turning up two-and-a-half hours late ensured I lost him at hello, as Jess McCann might say. And why didn't I make an effort for this evening, or at least shower? It's a good job I'm not sitting next to him. The Dating Guru advises her clients to smell 'flowery and fragrant' at all times when trying to attract a man, and I haven't showered since yesterday morning.

"No," Jack shakes his head. "I don't think a money prize will make any difference. The guys who compete in the games aren't motivated by filthy lucre."

Oof. That seems aimed at me, and I flare up forgetting for the time being that the Dating Guru advocates agreeing with a guy all the time to make him like you. (Honestly.) "You think?" I say. "Shall we vote on it? I'm willing to bet a big sign on the website saying first prize £1,000"—Big Donnie sounds just like a guy who'd have a spare grand lying around—"the entries would fly in."

Six of the eight people around the table raise their hand in agreement. Even Dr McLatchie sticks her hand

143

in the air, though her son sends her a filthy look. "Sorry, Jack son," she says. "But the lassie's right. And she's fae the big city too, so she knows how these things work."

Oof, really? Great Yarmouth is nowhere near city size, and I'm not sure me being from a city, accurate or not, gives me added insight into how competitions work. It's common sense, isn't it? Jolene agrees she'll approach Big Donnie, who is a lady's man and more likely to agree to the request if it comes from a woman.

Jolene shuffles her papers. "Now, Psychic Josie! Scotland's number one psychic. You're our contact, Doctor. Has she said yes?"

The doctor nods. "Aye, she can make it. Here's her contract." She takes a folded sheet of paper out of her bag and slides it across the table. Jolene studies it, her expression changing to disbelief. "That's her fee?" she asks. "It's more than the proposed Highland Games prize. And she'll be charging people on the day. She'll make a killing."

The doctor shrugs. "Have ye seen how popular she is? Every time she does an event in Glasgow or Edinburgh, it's sold out months in advance. Ye'll make your money in the numbers who come through the park. The games are not free are they?"

Jack whisks the paper from Jolene's hands and studies it too. "No fee," he says firmly. "Tell your contact, Mum, that Psychic Josie can keep all her takings from the customers she gets and we'll only charge her a stall fee the way we're doing with everyone else."

"But—"

"Mum!"

"Oh all right then," the doctor says, taking back the contract. "Mebbe she might no' be as keen."

Blast it. That little show of authority sent my treacherous, ever-moving emotions back toward passion and want. Who doesn't love firmness?

The rest of the meeting is taken up by a discussion of the various stalls and speculation if the Lochalshie Highland Games budget stretches to weather modification so that the sun shines on the day or that at least it doesn't rain. When someone mentions how much the Soviets were once rumoured to have spent on making the sun shine on a military parade, they quickly drop the idea. The budget couldn't cover a minute of modified sunshine, never mind four hours.

Jolene declares the meeting over at nine pm, and most people drift off. I'm about to sneak over to the new book stall and pick up that copy of *You Lost Him at Hello*, which sounds more promising than the Amazon one I ordered *How to Find Lasting Love with the Right Man*, when Jack makes his way over, and I have to grip the table top to stop my trembling legs giving way underneath me. Pathetic that such things excite me so much.

"How are you?" he asks. Oh, that smile—when it's given without the qualification of sarcasm, cockiness, and appears one hundred percent genuine I defy any woman not to melt.

"Fine, fine," I say, managing not to squeak, "*why didn't you invite me to your blasted party?*"

"You're probably right about the prize for the Highland Games. Shortbread isn't much of a reward for spending your afternoon flexing your muscles and panting hard."

STOP IT, Gaby! When he said 'panting' my imagination ran away with itself. Dear oh dear oh dear—it planted the lovely idea of Jack McAllan, pupils dilated, mouth open and his breaths coming in ragged gasps. I was in the room too, if you get my meaning.

"I've never met anyone who's done the Heimlich manoeuvre before," he continues, and the doctor materialises beside him. She must have been in the loos.

"Aye, aye, Gaby," she says. "Awfy good job for an amateur. I checked him out on Tuesday morning and he's got two cracked ribs. I wouldnae have thought a wee lassie like you had the strength. You should enter the Highland Games. What d'ye say, Jack? Gaby here might walk away wi' that £1,000."

"Maybe she might," Jack says, "though I don't know if future Lochalshie villagers will thank her for making sure Stewart's gene pool continues." With that, he cracks a smile that totally changes his expression, the sight of it joyful. My mission in life might be making Jack McAllan face light up as often as I can.

"See you next week then," he says, a question I take to heart. That signals he's looking forward to it, doesn't it? I nod agreement, and we let ourselves out of the library, Jack and his mum heading in one direction and me in the opposite.

The darkness is like a velvet cloak, soft, comfortable and nothing to fear. I skip back to Kirsty's house. When I open the door, Mena comes running. "You'll never guess what, Mena!" I say as she yowls encouragement. "Jack said I was right about something. And he smiled at me. That's got to count as a positive, don't you think? And also, unlike earlier when I said going to a village meeting in the library was no-one's idea of FOMO, my evening turned out very well indeed!"

She sashays her way through to the kitchen, pausing pointedly in front of the fridge. I open it as she miaows with approval. "Organic chicken for you," I say, "and a lot of water for me. Wake me up when it's time for work."

CHAPTER 13

"You're working late. I don't usually see you at this time." Jack says.

It's nine pm, and I'm still at Jack's. Once I'd finished dealing with Dexter's demands—I'm on the fifth lot of templates for the product pages, a batch that looks remarkably like the second set of designs I presented him with and he rejected—I made a start on the Lochalshie website. It is charming, but the design is a mish-mash, and there's no consistent use of font, styles or pictures.

"Bitten off. Chew. More than you can," I told myself. "Rearrange these words, Gaby, so they form a popular saying. And then promise yourself you will never do it again."

Luckily for me, Jolene is nothing like Dexter. When I emailed her my first suggestions, she rang me back

149

straight away. "Gaby, these are so fantastic." I sucked my cheeks in waiting for her to tell me to make them stand-out awesome by changing them in ten different ways, but no. Her 'fantastic' means just that. "I can't wait to run a social media campaign when the new website is up and running. It'll make everyone come here!" Nothing like a bit of pressure, eh? I hope the villagers don't blame me when visitors don't flock to the games because a few carnival rides and Psychic Josie don't do it for them. Even if she isn't a demanding client, it doesn't change the fact the website needs a complete overhaul. It's got so many pages too. Who knew that one tiny little village had so much to tell the world?

When I heard the door open, and Jack come in, my heart did its usual treacherous soar to the ceiling, despite me telling it to stay right where it was. Off-limits, remember? Belongs to Kirsty or about to do so again.

I swing around in my seat. "So are you. Working late, that is." He looks tired, I decide. Not that it does anything to distract from his appearance. Jack's got the looks that can carry off tiredness—light shadows under his eyes that only emphasise their size and a droop to his shoulders that begs a girl to throw her arms around him. I'm almost out of my seat involuntarily, ready to do so.

"It's always like this in the summer. But I don't work October through to April, so it's bearable."

Aprrrill. Bearrrable. Jack's voice suits his cosy home. The words swirl comfortably in the air.

"Where were you today?" I ask as he dumps a rucksack full of water bottles and Avon Skin So Soft on the sofa.

"Clava Cairns—the standing stones just north of Inverness. Everyone wanted to touch them to see if they vibrated. I've no idea why."

I'm about to jump in and tell him when I realise he's being ironic. Clava Cairns is meant to be the place where Claire Randall travels through time from the 1900s to the 1700s in the first Outlander book. If you can feel the thrumming of stones, it means you're a time traveller like her. Imagine the explaining he would need to do for that when he took his tour party back to their hotel minus two people who'd inadvertently ended up in the 18th century.

"I bet they all asked to get their picture taken with you standing next to the stones," I say and am rewarded when he smiles at me, the upturn of his mouth banishing the shadows and lighting up his eyes.

"Want to take a guess how many photos they took?"

I'll bet. He's dressed in the black kilt and tee shirt that seems to be the standard tour guide uniform. He's paired the kilt with long socks and a pair of Doc Martens to make it more modern and less tartan shortbread tin. I sneak another look at his knees. I'm not sure why I'm so fascinated by them. Few other women would say, "It was his knees, m'lud!" when they stood in front of a judge, accused of a ferocious crush on a man. There's a tiny smudge of dirt on one and I long to lean over and wipe it off. I resist. Doing that to a stranger might count as assault.

Jack stretches an arm out so he can look at his watch. The move makes the tee shirt rise a little, offering a quick glimpse of a flat, muscular stomach. I knew it! My imagination, when it conjured up that half-naked dressed in only a white towel picture, wasn't far wrong. And now I've got actual, real flesh to pad my fantasy out. The sun catches a dusting of coppery hair there too. I blink a few times and turn back to my computer system before he sees the expression on my face. Wanton desire is signalled there almost as much as it would if my tongue was hanging out.

"Do you still need to finish stuff off?" Jack asks. "I was going to grab some food at the Lochside Welcome. Do you want to come, the hotel being next door to it means you won't have far to stumble home."

OOOHHHH. A date, a date, a date. Kirsty's plans wrestle with my conscience. She wants him back so badly. And that stuff about her dad dying and wanting a man who was as good as him struck home. I'd worked out how young she'd been when her father died. She was still a teenager. Tough. It would take a heartless and horrible person not to be on her side.

"I'll see if Jolene and Stewart are around too," Jack adds, and my helium-balloon-floating-on-the-ceiling status deflates. Not a date after all. Just as well perhaps.

"Do you want to get changed or anything?" he asks. I shake my head, then wonder if I should have said 'yes'.

Kirsty is very glamorous, and that's what he is used to. In all her YouTube videos her make-up is trowelled on and she dresses in glittery things most of the time, whereas I'm a jeans and hoodie person. At least today's version isn't too faded. And, bonus, my top is hole and (almost) cat hair free.

Jack tells me he needs to get out of his kilt—shame—and heads upstairs. Sartorial slobbiness aside, I whip my make-up kit out of my bag for a subtle touch-up, rubbing highlighter on to my cheekbones to add emphasis, top up my mascara and apply more lipstick, shoving it all back in my bag quickly when I hear him coming back down the stairs.

He's changed into a pair of faded jeans and a woollen tank top over a black tee shirt which sounds as if it shouldn't work but does.

"Stewart's in the pub already," he says. "Though that's his second home so no surprises there. Jolene says she'll be there in five minutes. You coming?"

"Five hundred," I say when we're out on the street, heading towards the Lochside Welcome. "That's how many photos the tourists tried to take of you."

He shakes his head. "Not quite. But four hundred wouldn't be far off. It's a good job I have the patience of a saint."

"You have?" I ask, and the astonishment makes him laugh.

"Fair enough. Some people might disagree and add other accusations too."

Quite the admittance. Still, in hotel rooms not that far from here, I bet visitors to Scotland scroll through the pictures they've taken today flicking back heather-topped mountains and shaggy-haired cattle with impressive horns and lingering far too long on the photos of a red-haired man in a kilt. Should I get in touch with them myself and ask if they could send one on?

It isn't warm, but at least it's not raining this evening. Clouds roll in from the top of the hills above the loch dark and velvety now that the sun is setting. We pass the odd dog walker and exchange hellos. I see at least one raise of eyebrows. How long will it take for the news that Jack and I have been seen together in public to reach Mhari and from there all around the village via WhatsApp?

This is the first time I've been in the pub, and the interior is both expected and unexpected. The surroundings are dark wooden panels' and a stag's head has pride of place above the bar. There's even an open fire too, but the musician in the corner isn't singing in Gaelic, instead mumbling his way through Emo's greatest hits. The corner bar isn't horse brasses and old optics either, sleek polished chrome instead, draft craft beers and the biggest selection of gins I've ever seen.

Stewart is at the bar, on a seat that has his name on the back of it. Second home indeed. In front of him sit two empty glasses, and the third one he holds is about to become empty too.

"Jack, Gaby!" he throws his arms wide and the seat wobbles. The barmaid sticks out her hand and yanks him by his shirt, pulling him straight again. I can tell it is a well-practised move.

Jack doesn't bother with a menu, but he hands me one. My mouth waters. It's a long time since lunch, and this place does brick oven fired pizzas. They don't bother with all the stuff you often get down south, all rocket this and smashed avocado that. Here, I have three choices— Marguerita, pepperoni or three cheese. When I say 'three cheese', Jack nods and says he'll share it with me.

"You're a lucky lass!" Stewart says, pint number three finished. "He doesnae share a 12-inch with just anyone."

"Stewart!" I hiss, as heat starts in my chest and spreads to my cheeks, while Jack merely raises an eyebrow. Blame it on having an older brother. As a teenager, Jason found innuendo in just about everything I said. Other people obviously aren't as dirty-minded.

"Make that two three cheese pizzas!" Jolene says, appearing behind us and flashing me her big smile. "Stewart and I can share one too."

A muffled bark sounds, and Scottie comes out from where he was hiding underneath Stewart's chair.

"Scottie gets none of it, Stewart," Jolene adds. "The vet said he's obese." The dog wags his tail delightedly. References to fatness don't seem to bother dogs in the same way they do we humans.

Drinks and food ordered we settle on a table as far from the Emo singer as possible, seeing as he is determined to put a downer on everyone's mood. Jolene sings my praises as she talks about the website. I try not to watch Jack too obviously, wondering how he is responding to someone else's endorsement of me. When the pizza arrives, I'm not sure of the etiquette. Should I eat it with my a knife and fork, or do we just dig in and rip it apart with our fingers? Ryan was funny about sharing food. He hated me taking chips from his plate, and if I ever asked for a taste of anything he was eating, he would sigh, spear up a tiny bit with his fork and dump it on my plate. The pizza comes with chips wrapped in fake newspaper and a garlic dip, that the waiter places between us.

"You go first, Gaby," Jack says, and I pretend lady-like-ness. My mum once told me that when she was a teenager, girls weren't meant to eat very much and especially not in front of men. Jack watches me spear a chip with my fork. He shakes his head and tips half onto my plate, dolloping spoonfuls of garlic dip on top and handing me the slice of pizza that is most generously covered in melted cheese. Oh heck. This is doing nothing for the campaign I wage where I persuade him Kirsty is his one true love. I count up the chips he tipped on my plate and realise it's not half the portion, more like two thirds.

He gave me two-thirds of his chips, Katya. My best friend gets it straight away. *Jeez, Gaby. He's a keeper.*

Stewart and Jolene finish their pizza in double-quick time, all to the backdrop of further tales of coding from Stewart. Thankfully, Jolene chips in so it's not the kind of chat you zone out of after two words. She stands up as soon as they have eaten their pizza and holds out a hand.

"Stewart, we need to go. Before you lose two more friends by boring them to death."

"Now!" she snaps when he looks as if he's about to object.

Goodbyes exchanged, I find my blood fizzing once more with excitement. I'm on my own with Jack, if you don't count twenty or so other folks in little groups around us. The Emo singer is having a break—thank heavens—and cheery chat fills the air instead. There's one slice of pizza, three chips and a ramekin dish full of garlic dip left. I sneak two fingers forward, destination final pizza slice, and Jack's hand clamps on top of them.

"Oh no, you don't."

Funny how a vice-like grip doesn't bother me. He holds my hand above the plate and grins at me. Out of the corner of my eye, I spot the barmaid alternating between gawping at us and shifting her focus so she can move her thumb lightning speed over a phone. Looks like I've clocked yet another member of the Lochalshie WhatsApp group. When Jack uses his other hand to pull the last bit of pizza towards him, I marvel at myself. Once upon a time, Gaby of Great Yarmouth would have told you no-one kept this girl from her last slice of three-cheese pizza. Or they did so on peril of death. Now, it looks as if I might relinquish without a squeak that perfectly cooked, thinly sliced bit of dough topped with herb-rich tomato sauce, Parmesan, Gorgonzola and Mozzarella that melts together into a puddle of cheesy perfection.

He takes the pizza slice, opens his mouth wide, and bites off a third. My hand still hovers in the air above us and I feel the vibration of every chew. He waves the remains in front of my mouth.

"Want some?"

Oh goodness, gracious yes. I was wise enough not to make the mistake of ordering anything alcoholic when we came in here. I stuck to diet coke. But the pizza waving, hand in the air stuff has gone to my head. Alcohol lowers your inhibitions, my mum always warned. I'm drunk on whatever knows else and just about to do something I might regret in the morning, like bite the blasted pizza slice suggestively and forget everything I'm supposed to do to make Jack weigh up his options and decide Kirsty is his best bet.

I jerk back my hand. Jack stares at me, as does the barmaid. No doubt this is update number two to the WhatsApp group.

"You eat it," I say, and his eyes narrow and widen again. He does that taking you literally thing men love to do—why? why?—and wolfs the slice in three bites. As he reaches for the chips, I stir myself, grabbing the plate and moving it to one side. It's not my prettiest move, but I grasp the three of them, use them to scoop up a ginormous blob of garlic dip, open my mouth as wide as I can and cram the lot in. I think this counts as a nil-nil draw. Jack shakes his head, but he smirks.

"Jack!" The man who stands in front of our table slaps him on the back so hard, he flies forward, the plate in front of him shooting straight across to me. Jack straightens and regards the back slapper warily.

"Donnie. What can I do for you?"

Donnie fits the width and breadth of the table we're at. He wears a leather trench coat—and even I'm not that cold in Scotland—along with a waxed hat pulled low over his forehead. He plants fat fingers on the table. My razor-sharp detection skills tell me this is the infamous Big Donnie, he of the money to throw around fame.

"I want that picture. Five thousand pounds."

Unlike me, Jack has been drinking. He lifts the bottle of beer to his mouth and takes a hefty swig before answering the man.

"It's no' for sale."

My mind goes haywire, thoughts firing off left, right and centre. I've walked my imaginary self back to Jack's house, and in there, I've looked around the living room, taken myself into the hallway and perused the upstairs. What picture do I think he means? And ninety percent of me is sure I know the painting he has in mind. The other ten percent crosses its fingers, toes and offers all kinds of promises to deities etcetera that Mr Serious by the Look of it Doesn't Want Golden-Haired, Beautiful-Skinned Woman.

"You're a hard man, Jack. Five and a half and that's my final offer. You could do a lot with that money. Plus, I'll double the prize money for the Highland Games."

Silence. I've got hand it to Jack. He does mean and moody magnificently. I'd have cracked by now.

Jack gets to his feet. "Sorry, Donnie. Thanks for the offer, but as I said it's no' for sale. C'mon Gaby. I'll walk you home."

Outside, the streets are silent. All the dog walkers have retired for the night, and the clear skies mean it's colder than it was earlier today. I've only got ten metres or so and I'll be outside my front door. At certain stages, the evening looked so promising. When he asked me out and when we competed to see who could finish the pizza in the greediest way, and now that air of fun and expectation has slipped away. *You're still meant to be persuading him Kirsty is the love of his life.* Even if I'm not one hundred percent convinced that is wise. If I make the voice stern in my head, perhaps my disobedient and unruly imagination will come round.

"What painting was he after?" I ask, hoping I sound mildly curious and not desperate to know.

"The one of Kirsty," he replies, pushing my gate open for me. "Night, Gaby. Sleep well."

I treat myself to the luxury of watching him retreat, noting the hands thrust deep into pockets and how his head dips downwards.

What's the point of continuing this unrequited crush? If someone is offered five and a half thousands pounds for a painting of their old girlfriend and says no, he's not over her at all. I don't need to do any convincing on Kirsty's behalf. When I tell her this, she'll be over the moon.

CHAPTER 14

Today's 'to-do' list included 1) Stop Fancying Unavailable Men and 2) Throw Yourself into Your New Job.

If only Jack hadn't sent me a text the morning after our night out. "Enjoyed sharing my twelve-inch with you. Gotta love a greedy girl. Have a nice weekend." He'd added emojis after the greedy girl bit in case I took offence, and I decided not to. I wished he hadn't put the 'love' in there. The logical bit of me tells me that taken in context, the word means nothing. The illogical bit, and often I wonder if I'm far less governed by common sense than most, screams *he loves me, loves me!*

Kirsty phoned on Sunday and asked if I'd spoken with Jack. She sounded tearful, and the sound of her choking back tears as she reiterated how dreadful the split with Jack had been guilt-tripped me into telling her about Big Donnie's offer for the painting.

"And he said no!" she says, the cheerfulness level cranked up one hundred percent on one side of the conversation and plummeted by the same on the other. "Goodness me! He was always telling me that five grand would help him enormously with the marketing of the tours."

I concentrate on throwing myself into the new job. On Saturday, Dexter sent me an email asking if he could meet me in Ardlui on Monday morning. He was there doing a two-day mindfulness and yoga retreat, so if I could drive there, we could discuss the design work I'm doing for Blissful Beauty. Not much of a retreat, I thought, if you're sneaking out to send work emails. But Ardlui is only a fifty-minute drive from Lochalshie, so much easier to get to than Glasgow. And meet-ups with our biggest client were Melissa's number one reason for letting me work away from the office.

Relaxed Dexter, I decide when I meet him later, has a hypnotic trance-like state to him I find unnerving. Ardlui sits at the top of Loch Lomond, and it makes Lochalshie look like a metropolis. All I can see as I drive up is a few houses and a lot of wooden lodges that nestle behind lush green trees. I dump my car in the park outside the reception. The woman at the desk directs me to chalet number four, which is the biggest one in the place—three floors, a porch big enough to hold a table for ten and chairs, and a garage. It's here that Zen-like Dexter greets me.

"Gaby!" he says, the exuberance dialled down three or four twists. He plants his hands in prayer position and bows. I do the same back and then hate myself. I am an idiot.

"Come in, come in!" he waves me through the door. "We have so much to discuss."

"How was your retreat?" I ask. He looks the part—dressed in baggy linen trousers and a loose white tee shirt, no shoes and his hair tied back in a ponytail at the crown of his head. His bare feet hold no horrors such as dirty toenails, freakishly long toes or hobbit hairiness. When I choose the armchair in the chalet's living room, he drops to the floor and crosses his legs into the lotus position. Show-off.

"The retreat was beyond awesome, Gaby. And what I needed. Modern life is stressful. You need to come on these weekends so you can appreciate life at a much slower pace, do you know what I mean?"

I nod, and he pulls his laptop across the floor towards him, fires it up and glares at it, his expression performing an 180-degree turn from placid to furious in a second. The next few words are not Zen. Quite the opposite in fact and not repeatable. The gist of it is he is sick and tired of the backwardness of Scotland and the inability to get decent Wi-Fi anywhere outside the central belt. I pull out the print-outs of my designs I had the foresight to bring with me; pass them to him, and talk through the changes I've made in what I hope are soothing tones.

The changes, just as has been the case with all the changes I've made so far, involve one tiny tweak here, one miniscule tweak there, and make the pages closer than ever to the original designs I presented Dexter with way back when we met in Glasgow. It's a mark of his distraction that he only glances at them and when he does, says "Fine, fine." I heave a sigh of relief. If I'd had to change them yet again, I might have added to the blue turn to the air myself, and that wouldn't have been professional.

Dexter thumps his keyboard in a move a yoga teacher would disapprove of, and it beeps at him in response.

"At last. My emails have come through. I don't think they understand here how crucial it is for me to be contactable at all times."

I watch his face change as he reads the screen in front of him. It turns white. People always use that to describe someone as they receive bad news, but I've never seen it in real life before. The colour drains from his face, making his eyes stand out as tiny muscles twitch at his jaw. I scan the room, searching for a bottle of brandy convinced I'll need to pour it down his throat.

"This can't be happening, this can't be happening…" Dexter reaches for his phone, then flings it across the room when he realises he can't get a signal. He starts to rock back and forth, a lotus position variant no yoga teacher would sanction. "No, no, noooooo."

I stand up and get down on the floor myself, scooting across to join him. Working with clients has given me some background in dealing with melt-downs, though none as full-scale as this. I go with back-patting and saying 'there, there', 'everything will be fine'. When he turns to me, his eyes well up. Oh heck. Has he received news of someone's death? I'm not sure I'm qualified for this.

"The Blissful Beauty launch, Gaby," he says, the words croaky. "The venue's gone bust. We can't do it there. And my assistant has been ringing everywhere in London. There's nowhere else, and it has to be that date. Caitlin's schedule doesn't allow for anything else. We're at the beginning of July. We'll find nowhere in London at such short notice."

"When is the launch meant to be?" I ask.

"August the fifteenth."

Now, why does that ring a bell? August the fifteenth… I glance at Dexter, his face still panic-stricken, and then it hits me. A glimmer of an idea starts and gathers pace, growing bigger and more outlandish as I carry on thinking. My heartbeat quickens. Dare I suggest this?

"Dexter," I say, "um, why don't you make the launch of Blissful Beauty so totally different from any other make-up launch there has ever been journalists and influencers talk about it for years to come?"

He went with it. I leave the chalet half an hour later dazed, astonished at what I've just pulled off. Jolene wanted something different and more exciting for this year's Lochalshie Highland Games. She's got it. This summer's Lochalshie Highland Games will feature not only carnival rides, £1,000 for the best tosser of the caber, a re-enactment of the Battle of Stirling Bridge and Psychic Josie to add to the thrills, but the unveiling of a brand new beauty brand and the first ever visit to Scotland by an internationally renowned reality TV star who has more followers on her social media accounts than the population of the country. They will set up a marquee in the village, in-house beauticians and make-up artists will offer free make-overs and samples, and there will be goodie bags a-plenty meaning we are bound to attract people who'd never go near a Highland Game.

I rabbited on and on to Dexter about how difference was the key here. Journalists and influencers were bored with your bog-standard launch, I said to him, marvelling at how confident and knowledgeable I sounded. They didn't want to go to yet another glitzy hotel in London where women handed out goodie bags and hashtags, and someone stood up and gave a talk about this amazing skin cream or that revolutionary mascara.

No, no we Millennials needed our hyper experiences. An event wasn't special unless it was standout bonkers. And what could be madder than a venue and an event three million miles away from your usual location for such things? That it would be a challenge to get to was part of the deal. Blissful Beauty would provide tickets, flights and overnight stays for the top beauty writers, but everyone else would flock there anyway, desperate not to miss out on this one-off occasion. And everyone wanted to meet Caitlin, right? When I first mooted the idea, Dexter had kept up his 'can't be happenings' and no, nos. But after a while, he'd quietened, and his face did that rapid change thing again. I made suggestions, and he kept adding to them, telling me how he'd run the social media campaign for it. Caitlin, he promised me, loved doing things people didn't expect. She'd be overjoyed.

Trying to picture one of the world's most glamorous women in the middle of Lochalshie proved too much for my imagination, but, hey. Dexter declared the idea super-awesome amazing.

This would mean a lot of work for the games committee, but I knew Jolene was up to the task. I wandered over to my car and pulled my phone out to text her. Perhaps it would be better to keep the exact nature of the new attraction for this year's Highland Games quiet until I'd spoken to her in person.

"Gaby!" Dexter emerges from his chalet, the smart business suit back in place and shoes on his feet. "Take me to Lochalshie. I must see the place."

He insists I drive, claiming the narrow roads and death-wish of the local drivers and motorcyclists terrify him and that he'll get a taxi back afterwards. In the car, he continues to run ideas by me. In one, Caitlin roars up the village in a Blissful Beauty branded speed boat and in another, she makes over all the winning competitors in the games, women and men. The 21st century skin care and make-up company, Dexter tells me solemnly, is open to all and you ignore the trans community and its desire to spend money on make-up at your peril. I nod along, excited and nervous about what I've done. Still, when I ask how many people he thinks the launch will attract, the reply should mollify any objections the committee might raise. Caitlin goes everywhere with an entourage of thirty-odd. The list of essential journalists and influencers totals more than seventy, the hangers-on who come along to any event where PR agencies seek bulk numbers to make a launch look more important add up to one hundred, and Caitlin's loyal fans who will travel anywhere to see her number one hundred. Factor in another three or four hundred people in the surrounding area who won't be able to resist such glamour and we're looking at an extra seven hundred or so people. More, even. Blimey. The village will need to do some serious preparation.

As we get nearer to Lochalshie, the nerves kick in. I'm eager for Dexter to see the place at its best, and I squirm in my seat willing the sun to break out from the cloud cover and scatter glitter dust on the surface of the loch and the houses that surround it. I have to force myself to concentrate on the road as I keep sending beseeching glances upwards, begging it to come out. We pass the village sign, and the miracle I wanted happens—the sun shows its face. Dexter stares out of the window, abandoning the series of email messages he's been battering out on his phone. This isn't the usual pale sun I'm used to by now in this part of the world. It's a proper golden globe, and only one or two fluffy white clouds mark the skies. The water sparkles and gleams in the sunlight and the mismatched paint on the houses along the front adds to the colour. Even the top of the hills and mountains that surround the loch are visible. I park in the village square and offer to give Dexter a tour of the place, show him where the games take place so he can visualise his marquee. He gets out of the car and I hear a curse as appalling as the language he used earlier. I dash around to his side and see he's just stepped into a pile of horse manure. Oops. Lochalshie being a small place, normal practice is for Laney Haggerty of the nearby riding school to take one of her ponies for a trot up and down the high street on a Monday morning.

"Sorry about that," I yelp, and hurry him to the side of the road and the grass. "Wipe it back and forth a few times. It'll be fine!"

Equilibrium recovered, we set off toward Jack's house. It's right in front of the field they use for the games every year. I've never looked at it that closely before, but as we draw nearer, I realise it's smaller than I remembered. How will another marquee fit in here along with the beer tent and the essential fiercely contested home bakes sale marquee? Dexter marches up and down it a few times, stopping from time to time to put his hands over his eyes, stare into the distance and wipe his feet on the grass vigorously.

"Is it okay?" I ask. "Do you think you'll be able to do it here?"

His eyes shine when he turns to me. "Oh yes! The whole point will be exclusivity. And we'll put pop-up stalls all over the place, along with a mobile beauty van. That hotel back there—do you think they could host a reception?"

"Yes," I say, answering on their behalf. Let's hope the owner has the sense to charge the company five times his usual rate.

"Take me to the place," he says, and we set off back in the direction we came. Just as Jack's house comes into view, the minibus pulls up, and he gets out. The bus is empty, and I expect he's about to head off and pick up the latest group from either Edinburgh or Glasgow airport. The front door opens, and he jumps down, cat-like on his feet.

"Hello Gaby," he says, the eyes doing one of those up and down confrontational things with Dexter.

Ooh.

"This is Dexter. Dexter, Jack. He runs minibus tours of Scotland for visitors. Dexter's the marketing manager for one of the clients I work for."

A half-hearted handshake follows. It crosses my mind that if these two resemble Jamie Fraser and Jack Randall in the Outlander series, it is only fitting that any meeting lacks enthusiasm. I think about commenting on it, then decide if Jack already hates those comparisons, he won't welcome this one.

"Dexter's here to scope the place for—ouch!"

Ah yes. The stamp on my foot there was no doubt a reminder that these plans are in the early stages.

All of a sudden, Jack grabs Dexter by the lapels of his expensive suit jacket so that the two of them are eyeball to eyeball.

"Did you hurt Gaby?" he growls, and the unworthy part of me cheers. Yes! I shouldn't react this way, but it's *thrilling* when two men appear to fight over you.

Dexter plants his hands on Jack's and throws them off, brushing off his lapels as thoroughly as possible. I jump in with a "no, no I'm fine" before this turns nasty. Plus, I can't have Dexter rejecting Lochalshie as his venue of choice for the launch of Blissful Beauty in the UK, if he only remembers it as the place where he was beaten up. "We're going to the Lochside Welcome, Jack!" I say, my voice too bright. "To see if they'll take a booking. Would you like to come?"

"No." He closes his eyes for a second or so. "Sorry about that. I'm a bit sensitive to men assaulting women. Something that happened a few years ago."

My mind boggles, trying to fill in all the blanks. As explanations go, it's typical male—lacking detail. Nosey and crass as I often am, I know now is not the time to ask all the questions those two statements stirred up. And it was big of him to admit what he did in front of Dexter and me. Dexter reaches out a hand. "Hey, man. No harm done. As Gaby says, I'm looking to do something here in the summer. Something big. You do tours, right?"

Jack nods warily.

"Great!" Dexter gives him a back slap I suspect takes their newfound friendship too far down the familiarity pathway. "I'll be in touch! Hey, has anyone ever told you that you look like that guy," he turns to me snapping his fingers. "You know, Gaby. I bet you watch it. The one who plays… I can't remember his name."

As one, Jack and I exchange an eye meet. I snap my fingers. "You're so right, Dexter! He's the spit of Jon Snow in Game of Thrones, isn't he?"

I watch Dexter's face wrinkle in confusion before deciding I must be right. "Jon Snow! Kit Harington! Totally. Love that show. Season seven was epic."

As we wander off, Lochside Welcome bound, I sense a man smiling as he watches us leave, and when I lift a hand behind my back to give him a thumbs-up, I know he does it back.

CHAPTER 15

"So, he jumped in on this Dexter guy when he stamped on your foot?"

Two days later and I'm at Jack's house working, ahem, and Katya wants me to go over again what happened when Jack met Dexter. We've mulled over the explanation between us, Katya muttering darkly that domestic abuse is no laughing matter. I agree and try to hold back from jumping in with a 'what-a-hero-for-sticking-up-for-women' comment. I'm reminded once more that I am supposed to be on the Convince Jack Kirsty is His Ideal Woman mission.

When I tell this to Katya, she bursts out laughing. "Seriously? You fell for that?"

She stops laughing, however, when I tell her about Donnie, the picture man who offered thousands of pounds for that picture of Kirsty that Jack turned down.

"Mmm," she says, and I'm disappointed when she comes up with nothing else, such as a plausible reason he keeps the picture because it matches his decor. "They deserve each other, stampy foot incident aside. Mean and moody meets whatever she is. I mean, last week she—"

She coughs. "Never mind," and I puzzle at it. What did Kirsty do last week and what does my friend know about it? Still, if she has a weird secret to keep, so do I—something I haven't told my friend.

Dexter and I walked to the Lochside Welcome after leaving Jack, where Ashley the manager was all too keen to discuss possible could-not-be-named celebrity appearance that might take place on August 15. He listed off all the spirits they stocked, eager to prove their cocktail range could compete with any London venue. If a sophisticated crowd needed champagne, he had vintage, loads of the stuff. The bottles ended up ancient by default and no-one ever drank it in Lochalshie. The Wi-Fi reception in the Lochside Welcome was perfect too, thanks to a wee cash handout no questions asked with the mast folks, so the folks who needed to update their Instagram accounts etc., needn't worry.

"Sorry about that, Gaby," he said as I stared at him. I'm in the property right next to the Lochside Welcome, and they get perfect signal/Wi-Fi connection, whereas Kirsty's house is a blackout zone. Dexter nodded along to everything, throwing in the usual 'awesome's' amazing's' and 'fantastic's' before insisting on a guided tour of the whole place. He took lots of photos and issued a steady stream of commands I realised sounded so familiar because I was so used to them. The public bar area was 'beyond beautiful atmospheric'. If, a teeny-tiny suggestion here, Ashley cleared out all the old furniture and ordered in new stuff in colours that matched Blissful Beauty branding. The bar with its modern gin and vodka optics were so authentic they made Dexter want to stand in front of it for hours and stare at its brilliance, but Ashley might want to consider spirits and whiskies that used a particular colour palette, so it matched Blissful Beauty, and replace the lot?

By the end, Ashley wore the same glazed expression I recognised from my first meeting with Dexter. I whispered, "remember the money" in his ear, and when Dexter asked how much he needed to put down as a deposit at the end, Ashley glanced at me, swallowed hard and said, "You get the hotel exclusively for the day and night. £25,000 upfront. Another £50,000 the day before the event takes place and £25,000 afterwards. Not including the two glasses of champagne per guest and the handmade pizzas."

"Okay," Dexter said, and Ashley's panicked look told me he regretted not asking for more. Still, if he added twenty-five percent to all his bar charges, he'd soon make it up. Even with that mark-up, it was still half the price of what Londoners were used to paying.

Dexter then insisted on buying us both lunch. His request for a vegan pizza didn't faze Ashley, who presented him with one ten minutes later. He'd decorated the cheese-free dish with a sprig of rocket, olives and artichoke hearts, and served the accompanying chips with a home-made tomato ketchup instead of garlic dip. He was about to tuck in when I remembered what it said on the menu—*Chips cooked the proper way in beef dripping!* "Sorry," I said, whisking the bowl away from him. "You can't eat them because Ashley fries them in animal fat." Hashtag sorrynotsorry. The Lochside Welcome's chips were something else, though Dexter might not appreciate the spectacle of me cramming handfuls in my mouth the way Jack had. But his eyes as he watched me dip them into the garlic mayo had a mesmerised quality to them. His gaze focussed on my throat too, keeping track of every chip as it moved from plate to fingers to my stomach.

Meal finished and further orders issued to Ashley about all the things he needed to do to make his 'super-cute hotel' even cuter, I offered to drive Dexter back to Ardlui crossing my fingers behind my back he'd say no. He shook his head. "No, I can get a taxi. I've got a business account with Uber." I hadn't reckoned he'd find one nearby, but his app showed there were two cars in the vicinity. Ten minutes later, we heard the driver sound his horn outside.

"Gaby, this has been incredible. The launch will have people talking about it for months, it's so out there. Thanks for the idea."

I nodded, and hoped Melissa would be so pleased with me, she'd award me a bonus or a hefty pay rise. A

Volvo estate pulled up beside the hotel, and the driver wound his window down.

"Are you ready to go, pal? If I can get you back to Ardlui by two, I can nab all the jobs in the east before Joe Alexander gets anywhere near the area."

To my astonishment, Dexter threw his arms around me. "I'm gonna be kinda busy the next few months, but I'd love to take you out properly and feed you more fries when this is all over. What do you say?"

He couldn't see my face as it was muffled up against his armpit; a bonus as my expression was aghast rather than flattered. The next bit took me by surprise too, as he let me go and swooped in before I could stop him, planting a kiss on my lips.

"Ciao, baby!" And with that, he was in the back of the car, giving me a cheery wave as it headed south-east towards Ardlui.

Stunned, I turned away, planning to head back along the road to Jack's house where I planned to carry on with my dual jobs of designing Blissful Beauty's website and bringing the Lochalshie village one up to scratch.

"Gaby, Gaby!"

Argh and double argh. Across the street, her face the perfect picture of curiosity mingled with delight was Mhari, dressed in her pharmacy uniform. She must have been on her lunch hour, and it was my bad luck that the end of it had coincided with Dexter and I leaving the hotel. Yet another thing for her to be the first to tell the WhatsApp group about.

"Who's he, Gaby? That your new boyfriend then? An American! D'ye suppose he'll move up here too?"

"A man I work for. No and no. It's just natural Yankee friendliness. Hugging and kissing people they barely know is standard, and they could teach us closed-off Brits a thing or two," I said.

"Aye, aye?" Mhari asked, her eyes widening and mouth rounding into an 'o'. "Looked awfy friendly to me."

The too-familiar ping sound of WhatsApp messages going back and forth sounded, no doubt three hundred villagers contributing their opinions to the latest developments in my life. Jack's mini-bus passed us, Mhari raising a hand to wave at him and then staring after it, her face creased up in a frown.

"Well, that wasnae friendly. Didnae even wave back. What d'ye think's the matter with him?"

I turned to watch the bus make its way out of the village. "Got out of bed the wrong side. Again."

I headed to Jolene and Stewart's cottage on the street behind the main road to share the good news about the Blissful Beauty launch. Her eyes rounded in wonder. "That's sweet as!" she exclaimed. "For real, Gaby? Caitlin too? Oh boy oh boy oh boy. The committee will hit the roof with excitement. Mind you, I'll need to tell them who Caitlin is. None of them will have heard of her."

I'm not one to stereotype the older generation and what they do or do not know, but it is eons since the rest of the committee bar Jack waved goodbye to their 21st birthday. And most of them favour the tartan/tweed/

wellie approach to dressing. Make-up doesn't darken their doors either.

"Are you sure?" I asked. "I think Blissful Beauty will take the whole place over. The Highland Games won't get half as much attention."

"Who cares? Most of the committee find it an effort to organise the thing every year. If some other company wants to come in and take over, so much the better. We'd better tell everyone in the village to get their homes on Airbnb as soon as, seeing as there'll be heaps of people needing an overnight stay."

She fiddled with her phone, thumbs moving over the screen at double fast rate. If that was the Lochalshie WhatsApp group told, she might as well have put a gigantic ad on the front page of Google, Facebook and Amazon, 'Caitlin to visit remote Scottish village August 15'. Dexter told me Caitlin's agent would confirm nothing, but orchestrated leaks were all part of a successful launch campaign and if word of her whereabouts came from the village itself, even better.

I say goodbye to Katya now, reflecting how right she was about Jack's mean and moodiness, and wonder afresh why I kept quiet about the Dexter Incident. As I open one of the web pages I'm working on for Blissful Beauty, I imagine how a 'date' with its marketing manager might go. Personal Dexter would be too like work Dexter— how could he not be? I'd turn up for our 'date'— and I know it would be in some hipster venue so achingly cool it was bound to make me feel inadequate—dressed in my best gear courtesy of the Dating Guru's recommendations for first date outfits. He'd take one look at me, tell me I looked beyond awesome amazing, and then suggest next time a different pair of shoes might work. And what about jeans that were black not blue, and so on and so forth until he'd recommended a complete outfit change.

My wretched mind then fiddles around with the scenario. Instead of Dexter waiting for me in a hipster bar, Jack picks me up in his mini-bus, drives us to a tiny hotel miles away, lifts me in his arms and carries me across the threshold, not bothering to check us in and whisking me upstairs where he…

Oof. Not only cliched, Gaby, Katya barks at my overactive imagination. *But you've made the bloke superhuman too. In your world, are there many men who can carry someone for so long?* I squawk back at her that the first photo we'd ever seen of him was one where he'd just won the caber toss competition, which made him a contender for such feats. And although I am still to find out what that tossing a caber is, it must equal strength, right? In defiance, my mind returns to the fantasy adding a log fire in the hotel's bedroom and a sheepskin rug where we are just about to discover if it is as soft and fluffy as it looks when the man himself walks in, stony-faced once more.

Expression hastily changed from dreamy to work face, I call out, "Jack! Don't usually see you at this time of the day?"

True, the mini-bus tour days means he returns at 9pm most nights, and I'd assumed when I'd seen him earlier he'd been on his way to Glasgow or Edinburgh to pick up another bus-load of tourists.

"Emergency," he says, scrolling through his phone. "My tour guide's sick, so I've got no-one to do the commentary to tomorrow's tour."

Jack designed the tours and drives people about, but he doesn't do the commentary as it is considered too dangerous. A driver needs to keep all his attention on the road. His usual guide is an old guy called Sam, described as 'knowing every single thing there is to know about Scotland, and who considers it his duty to ensure anyone who isn't Scottish knows its history inside out'. Beautiful as Scottish scenery is, without Sam's running commentary a tour won't be half as entertaining.

As he looks at his phone, Jack's forehead creases. He goes into the kitchen to make a call, and I hear him telling someone not to worry. He hadn't expected them to be able to cover it at such short notice. He returns to the living room, running his hand back and forth over his head.

"What about Stewart?," I say. "He likes to talk, and he knows a lot of stuff."

He looks up at that, one eyebrow doing its best sardonic wiggle thing. "What do you reckon that will do for my TripAdvisor ratings, Gaby?"

Fair enough. Inflicting Stewart on a captive audience would turn the visitors' trip into the holiday from hell.

"Mhari?" I try, and he smiles, the upturn to his lips lifting the heaviness from his eyes.

"Mhari thinks Bonnie Prince Charlie is a pub in the next village. The people who come on my trips are looking for someone who knows a bit more about Scottish history.

"Um…" he says, "Er… would you do it?"

"Me!" I say, "I'm…"

… a fast learner. And history was my favourite subject at school after art.

"And you're a qualified first aider," he says. "I am too, but I've never done more than treat insect bites and grazed knees. You can do the Heimlich manoeuvre. I can give you a book to mug up on Scottish history and point you to some useful pages on Wikipedia. I'll fill in the gaps. I know Sam's spiel off by heart.

"Please, Gaby."

Ooh, it's that last plea that seals the deal. Spending time with Jack—and the precious two hours we'll have in the bus alone before we pick up and drop off the visitors—is too hard to resist. That I'll need to spend my evening learning eight hundred years or so of history seems a small price to pay. And there's the unofficial day off work. I've slaved away on the Blissful Beauty stuff for what feels like an eternity. I decide I deserve it.

"Okay. If you're sure," I say, and he gives me one of those dazzling smiles. "Thanks, Gaby. That's brilliant. We're off to Doune Castle tomorrow, and I've got a book on the castle's history."

He disappears upstairs and returns with it. To my relief, it's not that thick a tome.

"I'll pick you up tomorrow morning at seven am outside your house?" he adds, and leans across to ruffle my hair, warm hands encountering what I hope is still clean hair.

"Thanks again, Gaby."

I sail out of the house.

CHAPTER 16

The next morning, I'm up at the crack of dawn having tossed and turned most of the night through wacky dreams.

In one, I led visitors through the castle dressed as an 18th century woman who looked like Claire Randall, while Jack stood in the ramparts wearing a kilt, waving a sword around and warning us to go nowhere near the Standing Stones outside. In another, the castle crumbled around us and Jack pounced on top of me to save me from falling bits of masonry. I was just enjoying the feeling of his weight crushing me and wondering if that was what I thought it was when Little Ms Mena woke me up with a loud yowl, fed up of having to wait so long for her breakfast.

Jack gave me one of his branded Highland Tours tee shirts to wear, though because he had only spare ones to fit Sam, it is far too big. I need to belt it around the waist, and I do the whole make-up so light it looks like you're not wearing anything wondering afresh on why it takes twice as long as when you trowel it on.

The bus pulls up just before 7am, and Jack throws the door open. "Jump in. The tee shirt looks much better on you than it does on Sam."

Belted up, I run through everything I found out about Doune Castle during last night's impromptu history lesson. "Historians think the original was built in the thirteenth century, though the present-day version sprung up in the fourteenth, built by the Duke of Albany, who also ended up as the regent of Scotland, though his son came to a nasty end of the headless variety. The castle later became the property of the Earls of Moray, and it saw military action in the 17th and 18th centuries, the latter during the Jacobite risings," I rattle off, delighted I've remembered it all.

"Fantastic," Jack nods. "My guide book is an old one, but it might interest you to know that latterly, the castle's been used for the filming of Outlander."

"What!" the exclamation far too loud for a confined space.

That special grin lights up his face, making his eyes sparkle and his skin gleam. "I thought you might like that. 'Course, I never play on the fact I look a teeny bit like Sam Heughan when I take visitors there." At that, he winks. *Stop that*, my inner conscience yells at him. When your blasted eyelid closes, your other eye and the rest of your face does this thing where it appears to invite me to a private party. *Jack, you've got an ex you're not over so please keep your winks to yourself.* My conscience says this all fiercely. My subconscious begs him to wink at me again—and this time slowly, a lazy drop of the eyelid and lashes, a tiny lift of the outside corner of his mouth and the slight puckering of lips that transfix my attention, wondering what they would feel like on mine.

As we are in friendly mode, I risk a personal question. "Sorry to be so nosey, but why don't you and the doctor have the same surname?"

The air changes. I've made a mistake. The arms and shoulders that hang over the steering wheel tense up. If I flicked them with my Doune Castle guidebook, they might shatter. Then, he lets out a sigh, and the muscles of his upper body relax. "My mum left my father when I was six," he says. "He used to beat her up. I don't remember most of it, but I do remember shouting and screaming. She remarried twelve years ago. A guy called Ranald McLatchie, who owns a big farm a few miles west of here. As you might have realised, leaving my father was the best thing my mum ever did. She trained as a GP and has never looked back."

It's hard to imagine anyone cowing the good doctor, but I ought to remember domestic violence victims are all different. The doctor escaped and prospered; a story with a happy ending though that might not have been the case.

"And you," he says, "seeing as we're getting to know each other, why did you break up with your fiancé? Were you together a long time?"

Interest in me. A positive sigh, right? I give him the abbreviated version, gratified when he laughs at the helium balloon bit and adds that he's always wanted to do that too. We've arrived at the pick-up point for today's tour, and I realise Jack's questioning of me allowed him to avoid having to answer anything more himself. Neat.

"Gaby! So great to see you!"

No sooner am I out of the bus when I'm embraced in a massive hug. "When we saw it was to Doune Castle, John Junior here and I could not resist." Darcy, America's most enthusiastic Scottish fan export, has turned up, kitted out in Wellington boots, a fur gilet and a thick waterproof overcoat. She also waves a pair of sunglasses. Scottish weather, she tells me, is not as reliable as Arizona's. It's best to come prepared for anything.

Thanks to Jack's quick tutorial, I know a lot about Doune Castle's recent history as a filming location. Darcy, John Junior and the eight other avid Outlander fans listen as I relate what bits of the castle the film crew used and how they built an entire 18th-century style village in its grounds. Then, Darcy takes over as she and the other visitors discuss Outlander Book 1 scene by scene, and give their considered opinions on all the actors who play the characters in the series. This takes us all the way to the castle where the sweeping drive-way and long approach finally silence Darcy. The group squeals with excitement, however, as they recognise the spot where they re-created the old Highland village.

Much to my relief, everyone opts to pay extra for the audio tour, meaning I don't need to remember any other castle facts. They switch their headsets on and faces light up. Sam Heughan did the voice over, Jack tells me, so all the Outlander fans will delight at having him talk in their ears.

"Do you want a look around?" Jack says as they all head off, heads tipped back to stare at the stone walls that tower over us. How can I resist? My own little tour of the castle accompanied by Jamie Fraser. "Only if you call me Sassenach?" I say, and he nudges me. "As if. Come on then. You might recognise the kitchen."

I do, though I'm disappointed to discover the crew recreated it in a studio rather than filming it at the location. Jack's a brilliant guide. He points out things of interest but doesn't bombard you with information. And he keeps us away from the visitors we've brought here, moving us in and out of rooms just as they leave or arrive. At the top level, we can see for miles around—trees, water and the nearby village. "I bet lots of people have tried to paint this," I say, and he nods. "Not easy, capturing all the different shades of green."

He rests his forearms on the wall, and I admire the way the sun catches the brightness of his hair and sets his profile sharply against the sky behind it. "You're right by the way. I need to go down the Outlander route with the tours. I advertised this one as Doune Castle where Outlander was filmed, and it sold out in minutes. Would you design me some Outlander stuff for my website? I'm happy to pay for it."

I bite back my immediate response, "No charge! I'd do ANYTHING for you, Jack!" That's one job I don't mind doing for free, but it'll sound unprofessional and too much like I fancy him if I offer to waive the fees.

"You two are so adorable," Darcy has found us, and she waves her phone. "I gotta get a picture of you both. I swear it's Jamie and Claire come to life. Throw your arms around her Jack. We might as well make this seem like the real thing."

I mutter feeble (pretend) protests, but Jack is game. I will Darcy's phone to break, so she needs to yell for John Junior to bring the back-up phone; anything to prolong the heavenliness. Jack's got one of those rock-hard bodies—the one I gave him in my imagination. But it's warm and comforting at the same time. He drapes his arms around my shoulders, and his head rests next to mine. I wouldn't need to twist that far for my lips to be within kissing distance. Darcy takes plenty of photos, but it's all over too soon. Jack releases me and tells the group they must get back to the bus if they're to make the next stop on the agenda in time.

"What's your number, Gaby?" Darcy asks as we make our way back towards the bus. "I'll send you one of the pictures, the one I've just put on my Facebook page. Ten people have asked me already if I've just met Jamie and

Claire! I didn't think you looked like her, but other people obviously do."

When Jack drops them off for a late lunch at the coffee shop in Deanston, I sneak a glance at the picture on my phone, blowing it up, so the screen shows only our faces. Wow. The big grin Jack wears might just be for the camera, but it lights up his eyes too. The similarity to Claire Randall, or the actress who plays her anyway, isn't that obvious apart from me having curly brown hair and light-coloured eyes too but if Darcy's Facebook friends only saw a small version of this on her news feed, maybe they'd take me for her.

Everyone agrees the day was a great success when we drop them off at five pm. And Darcy promises by the time she's told all her three and a half thousand Facebook friends what an incredible experience Highland Tours provides, Jack will be booked out from now until 2050. "If God spares him," John Junior adds, the first time I've heard him speak. He says the words solemnly, but his eyes dance. A dry sense of humour is probably a necessity if you live with Darcy.

Tourists dropped off at the hotel, Jack and I have another thirty minutes alone together. I rack my brains, trying to think of either questions that don't sound too nosey or stuff that make me sound witty and fun. I'm still dying to find out the whole Kirsty story, but it's probably out of bounds.

"How's the cat sitting going?" he asks. "Must be a huge relief not to be sneezing every time she comes near you.

Kirsty used to let Mena sleep in the bed. She'd plonk herself on my chest and not move. Kirsty thought it was cute. She was always taking pictures of me in bed, Mena on top of me and posting them on Instagram. The pictures made me look like I loved myself. The villagers thought they were hilarious. And they ripped the piss out of me."

I battle conflicting emotions—the sharp pierce of jealousy when he puts 'Kirsty', 'bed' and him in the same sentence, and elation when he admits Kirsty's pictures of man and cat drove him mad. Not a mistake I would make, I promise myself. I'd be far too excited by the prospect of having him all to myself to want to share it with the world.

(Though perhaps I'd take one picture to show Katya. Best friend status and all.)

"Little Ms Mena is fine," I say, "especially now I've discovered what cat food she likes. It's the most expensive cat food you can buy, but much cheaper than smoked salmon and organic chicken breast." We have about five miles to cover until the Lochalshie sign comes into view. Can I segue the Mena chat into Kirsty questions?

"I'm sorry you and Kirsty broke up," I say, fingers crossed behind my back for such a blatant lie. "She seems such a lovely person." Toes crossed too.

"Are you," he says, eyes on the road in front. Statement or question? Words that say 'I'm sorry too' or 'I couldn't care less'? "I don't know if…"

"Yes, yes," I jump in and the words babble up, nonsense and rubbish. "So kind to want to help people all over the world find love, even when your own heart is broken into smithereens." Did I really say that? "And then there's the new blog too, where everyone will find out the best ways to get a commitment—"

I have said far too much. The bus slams to a sudden halt outside Kirsty's house.

"A new blog?" he asks, his voice incredulous. "What's it called?"

"Ah, I don't know. I've probably got it wrong. Could be a blog about home decor. I mean, judging by this house she's an expert in how to do that well. Home decor blogs are all the rage at the moment. After diet blogs. That could be the perfect combination, couldn't it? How to use wall-papering and paint to help you lose weight, so you get slim and fit at the same time as upping the value of your house three times or whatever. I should suggest that to her."

I trail off, aware I've lost my audience. He might as well be drumming his fingers on the steering wheel, the message 'hurry up and get out of my bus' loud and clear.

I unclip the seat belt and open the door. His face remains staring at the road ahead.

"Um, thanks, Jack. I enjoyed today. If you want me to help out again…?"

He stirs himself. "You did a great job. Really helped me out. Thanks, Gaby."

And with that, he drives off leaving me with the sinking realisation that the Katya voice that sounded in my head just there shouting at me to stop talking was too late. Rearrange these three words, Gaby, into a sentence that sums up what you've just done. Blew. I. It.

Inside the house, Mena comes running. "Hello, little Scrumptious!" I haven't referred to myself as 'Mummy' yet, but it's only a matter of time. She and I can curl up on the sofa once more to watch Outlander Series 3 again, and I can tell her having an unrequited crush on a TV star is much easier on your day-to-day well-being than having one on a real-life person.

The phone rings as soon I as I finish feeding Mena. Kirsty, and I hear her sharp intake of breath when I say I've spent the day on a bus tour with Jack. I'd better not mention his reaction to the blog news so spare me further sighs.

"You were the guide tour for him?" she says, her voice rising to a pitch at the end, and I squirm.

"Yes, but only because it was an emergency."

"But this is counter to my plans," she declares indignantly. "Did you talk about me? Mention the bad boy billionaire?"

"Yes. He looked sad." Oops, Gaby. Not one lie but two. I just couldn't bring myself to say anything. Distraction needed.

"Did you see those pictures I posted of Mena online?" Part of the deal with the cat sitting service is that you upload pictures on the website so owners can check in with their pets. I've discovered the truth of the old saying, never work with children or animals but Mena finally obliged me yesterday by a) looking super cute, and

b) staying still long enough for me to get a good picture. Then, I managed a short film of her jumping up as I dangled bits of chicken over her.

"Mmm-hmm. I hope that was organic chicken. Anyway, the brilliant news is that part one of my plan has worked—the ten steps to commitment process I plan to trademark and publish on my website."

Part one is that pictures of Kirsty and the bad boy billionaire are all over the internet. They don't touch, but he shoots her adoring looks in a lot of the shots.

"Um, don't you like the bad boy billionaire?" I ask. It seems an obvious solution.

"That's not the point. Anyway, please can you make sure you have the pictures on your screen the next time you're in his house, and he's there too? And can you get me Dr McLatchie's phone number? Jack listens to his mother, so the next stage is for me to cultivate that relationship again and she'll start dropping my name into conversations with him."

I put the phone down a few minutes later, dazed. Somehow, I've been bamboozled into agreeing to do everything Kirsty asked for. But plans and processes don't work if you're trying to get someone to date, or re-date, you, do they? As ever, that painting appears in front of me, the colours shimmering and Kirsty's eyes pinned on me. No-one who's been offered as much as five and a half thousand pounds for a painting keeps it if it doesn't mean a great deal to them.

CHAPTER 17

As instructed, I have Instagram open the next time Jack walks into the house while I am working. Kirsty and the bad boy billionaire exchange plenty of smouldering looks, fingers creeping towards each other on tables and heads tilted to touch. Jack's eyes narrow as soon as he sees them and I click out, trying to make it seem like a coincidence I was on the site when he came in.

"You follow Kirsty?" he asks, and I nod, telling him it's for Mena's sake so I can tell her what her owner is doing and let Kirsty see pictures—most of which get far more likes and comments than anything else on my feed. He sighs, and his hand goes to his head, rubbing the top. Blast, blast, double blast. For all I thought bad boy billionaire photos were a dumb idea, Kirsty is Christina the Dating Guru. She knows what she's doing.

Resolution two, I chant to myself. Throw Yourself into Your New Job. I pull up the new Highland Tours Outlander Experience website I've been working on to show him. Jack sent me a list of where he planned to take tourists and what the tour comprised. I spent a few hours with a pen and paper sketching an outline of what it might be like, and voila… here it is, almost ready.

He looks at it. "What do you need me to do? Write about the tours?"

I nod. "The thing is… I think you also need to take advantage of your similarity to Sam Heughan and front this campaign."

He jangles his keys and regards me warily. "And?"

"A photo shoot," I say, watching as he groans and closes his eyes. "In the full get-up, so that as soon as people land on the site, they see Jamie Fraser, aka you."

"I was afraid you'd say that. Isn't it dishonest?"

"No, because there will be a caption clearly stating your name." What I don't add is that it doesn't matter. People zone in on pictures and skim the text. First impressions will be a tour that is led by actual Jamie Fraser or the actor who plays him, anyway.

"I know a terrific photographer in Glasgow," I add. "Christy, a woman who's worked with me on the Blissful Beauty account. She could get pictures of you when you're in Glasgow tomorrow kicking your heels waiting for your tourists to finish at the People's Palace, and she could Photoshop the images of you onto a Glencoe backdrop or something."

He agrees after only one further protest, and I phone Christy to arrange the photo shoot for tomorrow, not letting onto Jack that I'd checked out her availability beforehand.

She phones me the next day. "Gaby, if I wasn't a deliriously happily married woman, I don't know how I'd have kept my hands off this guy. I will have to keep most the pics for my portfolio so I can drool—I mean, show them to clients and impress them."

When I see them, I'm blown away. Future clients will admire the sharp focus, and the seamless Photoshop use where you couldn't tell the pictures had been taken in a studio and not in the wilds of Scotland. As for how Jack looks… Most of the time, people are much better looking in real life than they are in photos. Photography flattens eyes and mouths, and liveliness is a big part of what makes us appealing and interesting.

These photos though. Christy can do magical things with a camera, and that includes capturing a person's essence or aura. The red-headed man with his arms folded and wearing a warm, welcoming begs you to join his tour. I defy anyone to pass up that invitation. When my screen times out because I've stared at the pictures too long, I know Christy has done an excellent job at the same time as not over-flattering the guy.

I keep the website to a few pages. At some point, Jack plans to merge or re-do his existing website. In the meantime, Stewart has set up a basic WordPress site, done some research on Google Analytics to suggest keywords to use, and set up five pages—a landing page, an 'about us', about the tour and some info relating to the filming of Outlander in Scotland. I left it to Jack to fill in the information himself and adjusted the template with boxes, images and formatting.

"What do you think?" I say to him when he returns on Tuesday night, flicking through the pages one by one and trying not to hover too long on the landing page as I do when I'm on my own. "Your website is ready to go."

Apart from grimacing at the large image of himself on the landing page, Jack nods his head. "It's good, Gaby. Thanks."

I deflate at the comment. Good? Flippin' fan-dabby-dozy would be a better word, but then I'm not working with Dexter. And wouldn't I rather have a 'good' from Jack and no alterations, than three million 'awe-somely amazings' from Dexter, along with an extensive list of everything that needs to be changed?

"Send me an invoice," he says, "and I'll get it paid right away. Then all I need to do is wait for the orders flood in, right? As Darcy said, I could end up booked till 2050 should the Lord spare me."

Don't wink at me, I order, while the other part of my brain wills him to, anyway. When he does, the slow, lazy sweep of it does unhealthy things to my pulse.

After he signs off the work I've done on the website, I don't see Jack for two days, but he drops by later that week. He gives me a quick hello before heading off to pick up the latest group from their trip to Callendar. My heart starts its disobedient fluttering thing as soon as I hear him at the door. It goes into overdrive when he smiles at me right away, the usual wariness absent.

"Hey," he sketches me a wave. "What are you working on today?"

I point at the screen and the updated Lochalshie web pages, and he leans in to study it more closely. "Steady, Gaby," my mind warns. The swoop in brought him close enough for our faces to be side by side and that heavenly scent of him—pine and warm skin—all around me.

"Looks good, Gaby-sketch."

The nickname is new, and as imaginative titles go, it isn't up there with the best, but I love it anyway seeing as it comes from him and no-one else calls me that. He stands up straight again and ruffles my hair, a habit I wouldn't tolerate from anyone else. I'd found an article on the Dating Guru's website the other day which said hair ruffling was a no-no along with silly nicknames. It was the thing guys did to girls they felt brotherly and not 'brothely' towards. Blame Katya for that terrible phrase.

"Do you want a coffee and some shortbread, Gaby-sketch?" he calls from the kitchen and I shout back a 'yes'. When I let myself in earlier, I'd been able to smell baking and had so far held back, a heroic triumph of willpower.

"How are the tour bookings for next year's Outlander tours going?" I call through.

No answer. He comes through a few minutes later bearing two steaming mugs of coffee and a plate of short-bread.

"Ah. Nothing yet from the website."

He sets the coffee down next to me and takes the arm-chair opposite.

I'm flabbergasted. What on earth doesn't appeal to people about the Highland Tours authentic Outlander experience?

I waffle about how it is early days, and the site is bound to take off soon, what with the fancy stuff Stewart has put in place and Darcy's one-woman efforts to spread the word via that photo of the two of us at Doune Castle.

But two days later and the situation is the same. Not one booking has come in through the new website. I'm taking it personally. The Outlander tour idea was mine. It took Jack a while to come round to it, but when he did, he wanted me to design the pages for him. And he's already paid me, a transaction that was excruciatingly embar-rassing as I hate taking money from people I know.

The tickets sale failure offends my professionalism too. I know that websites don't get found just because they're pretty. Stewart's magic should have brought people to the site, so why weren't they booking up? Had I judged this wrongly? They looked at the pages, decided the design was so dull, Jack's tours must be boring or unexciting and left straight away? I can't ask my colleagues at Bespoke Design what they think as the job was what plumbers and decorators call a 'homer', in other words done with-out the knowledge of your primary employer, and cash in hand. If Melissa got wind of it, her continued tolerance for my remote working would grind to a halt.

The following day, I ask again when I bump into Jack as I'm leaving his house for the day. Despite it being 8pm, it still feels like broad daylight, the advantage the locals tell me of being that bit closer to the North Pole than England at this time of year. The artist in me admires the way the sun touches Jack's hair, all rippling, bright gleams of red. He's wearing aviator sunglasses too, whipping them off to talk to me apologising for being that kind of poser. He can wear them all day if he wants; they're perfect for his face shape sitting right on his cheekbones and emphasising their slant.

"Nope, sorry," he shakes his head. "I have had no bookings through the website. But Kirsty's been in touch. She's promised to spread the word among her London friends."

Oh, double drat, blast and curses. Where does this fit into the 'hooking a commitment-phobe' plan? Might it be step four: *make yourself indispensable to him*? Kirsty's a social media star. She knows all the tricks to get a person or website noticed, and she has six-figure followers on all her platforms. Business will fly in. Jack will fall at her feet. *Thanks, Kirsty! How did I not notice how useful you are as well as being drop-dead gorgeous?* They'll be engaged in a month at this rate.

Disturbing film footage plays in my head—Jack and Kirsty sit on The One Show's sofa opposite Alex Jones and the farmer guy whose name no-one ever remembers.

"So, Jack!" Alex trills, everyone in the audience noticing she has to tear her eyes from Jack. "You and Kirsty split briefly earlier this year, didn't you?"

Jack can't help himself, jumping in to answer the question. "Yes. I was stupid and blind. I didn't realise how awesome and amazing Kirsty is." (He's morphed into Dexter in this scenario.)

"And Kirsty," Alex's dulcet Welsh tones continue. "You used a 10-step process to get Jack to commit to you, didn't you?"

Kirsty holds up her left hand, waggling her fingers and facing the camera, expression triumphant. On her fourth finger is a diamond ring that re-writes the definition of bling it's so big and shiny. "Yes, I did, and if your viewers sign up for my online course, they too can find the man of their dreams!"

"… but I'm not sure if—Gaby?"

I snap back to the present, relieved to escape The One Show fantasy. Jack stares at me, eyes creased in puzzlement.

"Are you okay, Gaby-sketch? You went pale there."

"Fine, fine," I mutter, "anyway, gotta go. Mena to feed and all that."

I dart off, desperate to escape before I make a fool of myself (again). Brain to speech engagement isn't my top skill. The longer I stay staring at those cheekbones, the likelier I am to beg him to let me lick them or something.

See? Safer to retreat.

CHAPTER 18

As it often does, the loch calls to me—*walk alongside me and your mood will change.* Guaranteed.

A rare evening—the wind has dropped and the waters are glassily still, apart from the small dog who keeps running in and out of the loch just in front of the Lochside Welcome. He spots me and dashes over, little legs carrying him much quicker than you'd expert from a wee, overweight terrier. As soon as he's in front of me, furious shaking coats my light-coloured jeans in dirty water. Thanks, Scottie.

"Sorry aboot that, Gaby," Stewart says. When the loch whispered to me, promising relaxation and calm, she said nothing about Stewart. Ah well. Coding Websites Part 352 coming up…

"Aye, so a lot o' people think ye cannae eat porridge in the summer but…"

Argh. It's the porridge monologue instead. I settle in for the duration, fixing my eyes at the buoy in the middle of the loch that bobs gently on the surface. In breath, one two three, out breath one two three four.

"Some folks say if ye eat enough porridge, the midges keep away too, because they dinnae like…"

I turn up my face to catch the sun's rays and let Stewart's words wash over me.

"So Jack was sayin' there's no' been any bookings through his website yet. But I was looking—Scottie!"

The yell pulls me out of my trance. Stewart runs towards the water. I rest my hand on my head and search the scene for Scottie, who's nowhere in sight. I belt after Stewart, and we stop at the loch edge and scour the waters.

"There!" I yell. In the distance, a small white head bobs, disappears from view briefly and re-surfaces.

"Scottie, Scottie!" The two of us scream as hard as we can, trying to encourage the little dog to use his strength to battle the current and swim back to us. Behind us, the drinkers in the Lochside Welcome add their shouts. Despite the encouragement, he gets no closer, the effort of keeping his little head above water too much.

"I cannae swim," Stewart bleats, wild-eyed and red-faced, and I spot the beginnings of tears in his eyes. "What am I going to do?"

"Ashley's got a dinghy. You could use that," Some helpful soul calls out behind us. "Mind, it's got a hole in it."

I blow out a deep breath. At school, I was a champion swimmer. I even represented Norfolk a few times. But that was when I was fit, exercise having fallen by the wayside when I left school. I was also swimming in large, heated indoor pools and one hundred percent sure of what was under my feet. I stare at the water and see stones, swimming wriggly things and jellyfish. Urgh.

The greater good, Gaby. I take off my trainers, hand Stewart my bag, breathe in and out as deeply as I can, and wade in.

The shock of the water hits me at once. It's so cold my fingers and toes numb. The ground beneath sinks away quickly and I'm forced to swim—a good thing as now I don't need to worry about sharp stones underfoot. I take a few seconds to work out which direction to go but then Scottie's little white head appears and I sum up all my years of five am training and plough through the water to reach him.

When I get there, he barks at me feebly, and I swear his tail wags underwater. But how am I going to get him back to the shore? It comes to me. Those five am training sessions included a lot of backstroke sessions. As a front crawl competitor, that wasn't my discipline, but our coach made us do everything and emphasised the backstroke because it was so good for building core strength and engaging the upper back muscles.

"Scottie," I say through chattering teeth, "please be as good as gold and go along with what I do, right?"

He barks, and I assume agreement turning from my doggie paddle beside him and pulling him on top of me. It's far from ideal. Those backstroke sessions didn't involve carrying a weight. Stewart has slipped his dog too many slices of pizza under the tables at the Lochside Welcome, but after a little wriggling around, Scottie settles back against me. I use alternate arms and as much leg strength as I can muster to propel us both back to the shores.

By the time we reach the shallows, we are both shaking so much you can almost hear our bones rattling. I clutch the dog to me and stumble out, spitting out mouthfuls of loch water. The sun's still out, but it does nothing to warm me up.

Stewart races towards me. We have gathered a small crowd as well as the Lochside Welcome drinkers who line the fence at the back and give me a round of applause.

I hand over Scottie and Stewart pulls the dog towards him. "Ye bad wee dog! I've telt ye before about running off. C'mon. Let's get you home and dried off."

He only just remembers to look back as he hurries away. "Thanks Gaby! Awfy obliged to ye. Again."

Ashley shouts out I can have a pint for free if I want.

A pint? It'll freeze rock-hard the moment it makes contact with my lips. My fingers are blue with cold.

"N-n-no, th-th-thanks. I'll j-j-just get back to the h-h-house."

"Here, have this." Jack materialises beside me, armed with a thick, dark green coloured woollen blanket he must have fetched from his house. He throws it around me, pulling it close so I'm encased from head to toe. It smells of him and I wonder if he sleeps in it, the thought making me tingle.

He takes out a small hip flask. "Take a mouthful or two of this."

"I don't like whisky," I squawk, but he tells me to drink it, anyway. I obey, and fire hits the back of my throat. It's followed by a warmth that seeps through my body and stops the bone rattling.

Mhari, one of the evening drinkers, wanders over to join us.

"I havenae swam in the loch for years! It's Baltic in there. But fair play to you, Gaby. I got it all on film. D'ye want to see it?"

She flashes her phone in front of my face. I close my eyes. The adrenaline, the cold and the whiskey have combined to make me shaky on my feet, and I start to sway.

Jack grabs hold of my arm. "Come on, I'll take you home," he says. "I'll call my mum out to take a look at you."

I don't know if I can put one foot in front of the other, and I wish he'd sweep me up in his arms and take me back to the house. Even if it is a silly romantic cliché. I settle for stumbling after him and when he notices, he slows down and wraps an arm around me. If only that didn't feel so amazing. I can't work out if it's the blanket or him I can smell, that heady mix of pine, skin and whatever deodorant or aftershave he wears.

My hands shake too much to put the key in the door lock, but Jack still has his spare key, and he opens the door and bustles me in. Thanks to the large windows at the front of the house, the all-day sunshine has turned the living room into a greenhouse, all-enveloping warmth. I sway on my feet, and Jack takes my arms and lowers me into the depths of the armchair near the window, allowing soft cushioning to envelop me. Behind me, I hear him opening and shutting doors in the kitchen and he returns minutes later with a steaming mug.

"Hot chocolate," he says. "I should have given you that first, rather than the whisky. My mum will be here in ten minutes."

Sadly, it's more like five minutes. When she opens the door and bustles in, I've not even finished my hot chocolate. Off-duty, I had the doctor down as a tweed and mum jeans wearer, but she's dressed in a 50s style dress and make-up that would do Marilyn Monroe proud. And she's mastered the Victory Rolls, a hairstyle I've tried and failed hundreds of times.

"Gaby, Gaby! I hear you're the hero of the day jumping in after that daft dog. I've interrupted my Ceroc practise for this."

I murmur apologies, and she tells me not to be daft as she checks my pulse. The doctor makes me take my shoes off so she can inspect my feet. The cold might have numbed them so much, she says, I might not have noticed stepping on sharp stones or glass. And I'll have damaged tendons and given myself the sort of injury it takes weeks to recover from. I stare at her open-mouthed, working through the implications of a foot injury that leaves me immobile.

"I think Gaby would have noticed that, Mum," Jack says. "Or I'd have spotted the bleeding when she came out of the water."

"Aye, ye'd think that, Jack," the doctor says as she bends to take my feet in her hands. "But I know these things are often overlooked, what wi' all the excitement. Years ago, a young man cut his foot on a rock at the far side of the loch, and it bled out so badly, he ended up needing an amputation. I was on my holidays at the time, so I missed it. Mair's the pity."

My feet, thankfully, survive the inspection. Jack hands me another hot chocolate, this time accompanied by two pieces of that delicious shortbread he keeps in his house. I remember my manners enough to say thanks and ask where he gets it from. I should stock up on it for the house. Or maybe not. I'd never be able to stick to just one or two bits and those lucky 'eat anything you like and not put on weight' genes might decide it's a test too far.

"He makes it himself," the doctor says, pulling herself to her feet having decided I'm tickety-boo and only in need of old-fashioned rest and recovery. She breaks one of my bits in half and eats it. "No' bad, Jack son. Almost as good as the stuff Ranald makes. You'll beat him in the annual village bake-off competition yet."

I find myself open-mouthed once more. He wins tossing the caber competitions at the Highland Games, runs tours for people, and he cooks? Is there no end to this man's talents? One of those pesky fantasies I'm prone to, decides to take up yet more head space. In this one, Jack and I are in a candle-lit kitchen. He's dressed in a black tee shirt and jeans, bare-footed, and he stands at the hob stirring something garlicky and delicious, turning to look over his shoulder at me. I'm sat at the table doing nothing apart from waiting for my dinner. Your ideal boy-girl scenario, hmm?

Dr McLatchie says she needs to get back to her Ceroc class seeing as they're in the final practice before the big competition next week. She warns me I'll be tired and ache-y over the next few days and I should watch out for any nasty rashes or a sudden rise in body temperature, just in case I've got e.coli poisoning or Weil's disease which could lead to... I don't catch the last few words as there's the sound of someone being hurried out of the house quicker than they expected.

Jack comes back in the room, takes the seat opposite me and smiles. Smiles are transformational, I decide, the light, warmth and excitement they add to a face and the way they make you crave more of them. If getting more of them means jumping into the loch every other day, I just might do it. Might, and only if Jack wraps me up in a blanket and a hug every time.

He takes the mug out of my hand, and our fingers touch briefly. If only I felt more energetic, I might have made more of that.

"I haven't been in that loch for years either," he says. "That took serious guts. I've never seen anything so... You look shattered, Gaby. Why don't you take a nap? I'll keep an eye out for any sudden rashes."

Another smile. Okay, there might be other ways to get smiles that don't involve perishingly cold loch dips. Working out what I might do to get them—stock up on jokes, consult the Dating Guru's forums—is the last thing I think of before sleep overwhelms me.

When I wake up, the light has gone and the view from the window dark as coal. Even the lights from the nearby Lochside Welcome off, which must mean it's after midnight. Someone, Jack, I presume, has covered me with a duvet as well as the blanket and I'm toasty. Mena has settled herself on my lap, and she miaows a hello at me. "Jack!" I call out, my voice croaky. I spot a note on the coffee table next to me and burrow out a hand from my duvet-blanket cocoon.

"*Gaby, sorry but I've had to go out to pick out the next lot of tourists as they're on an early flight. Hope you are feeling better. Jack.*"

Blast him. He might have cancelled his tourists. I mean, what if Weil's disease had kicked in and all my organs had shrivelled up and failed? "What do you think, Mena? I could have DIED, and it would be all his..."

Mena stops licking her front paw and stares at me. "Oh, okay then. You're right. He stayed for a while, made sure I was okay and then headed off because if he left those tourists stranded at the airport, they'd complain to all and sundry. And he might lose his business and income."

I turn the note over. "PS—if you start feeling ill at any point, phone me anytime. I can turn back. I've asked my mum to stick her head in tomorrow morning too."

Oops. Always read the other side of a note. Equilibrium restored, making my way upstairs feels like it would be too much of an effort, and Mena looks too comfortable to disturb. I fall asleep again, the phrase 'phone me anytime' repeating over and over as I do.

CHAPTER 19

Jack's tourists must be one of those groups who do the full tour experience, as I don't see him for the next few days.

It doesn't take long for the warm bubble to burst. The blissfulness of being wrapped up in a blanket, force-fed hot chocolate and then the note that said, *phone me anytime*—all that loveliness trickles away when I don't hear from him.

"He might have sent me a text," I fume—to Katya this time, rather than Mena as I needed an actual response instead of a made-up one. "Seeing as I might have DIED."

"Stop speaking in capitals," she says. "And exaggerating."

I grumble, but I suppose it's true. Paranoia has set in too. What if, please no, Jack witnessed me snoring, mumbling in my sleep or dribbling? Ryan told me I sometimes do all three when in repose. It's mortifying. Christina the Dating Guru and her love self-help rival Jess McCann shake their heads in sorrow. I am a lost cause on the find a boyfriend 'quick and easy, guaranteed' front.

"What about Kirsty?" Katya asks. "I thought you were on a mission to reunite her with Jack?"

Ah. That. Hadn't I done my best, mentioning her the odd time, making sure Jack saw the photos online of her with the bad boy billionaire? (Real name—Christo Griseus, true I promise.) She'd also enacted Step 3 or whatever number it was of her ten-step plan by spreading the word of his Outlander-themed tours far and wide. She's on her own as far as I'm concerned. When I say that, Katya utters a fervent "Good!"

I ask if she's seen the Scottie rescue video, the one Mhari uploaded to the Lochalshie website without asking me first.

"No, I haven't had a chance I've been working so hard. I'll look now."

"Don't bother," I say. "It's very boring."

The day after the dog rescue, Jolene and Stewart popped in, Stewart once more bearing flowers nicked from the village's car park displays, though Jolene produced a box of chocolates so big it'll take me until Christmas to finish them. (In theory.)

Stewart sounded a thousand times more grateful to me for rescuing his dog than when I'd saved him from choking to death, going on and on about Scottie being the love of his life after his Jolene. The Jolene bit thrown in only after she nudged him so hard in his ribs he yelped.

"The brilliant thing is, though," Jolene said, "that video Mhari uploaded on the Lochalshie website of you rescuing Scottie has gone viral."

Stewart nodded. "Aye, Scottie looks his best. I've already had aw these folks getting in touch with me asking if he's still got all his tackle because they want to breed their—"

Jolene shot him a death stare and he shut up. "Anyway, we've had tonnes of enquiries about the Highland Games. Place will be flooded with people, eh?"

Gosh. As well as all the Caitlin fans coming for the Blissful Beauty launch. I didn't get to see the video until the next day, as the reception in Kirsty's house wouldn't allow Jolene to show it to me on her phone.

When I eventually saw it working at Jack's house the next day, it horrified me. Scottie might have looked like a female dog's dream come true, and hyper-cute as he tucked his little head in my arms and wagged his tail like mad when reunited with his owner. I, on the other hand, resembled a drowned rat. Not surprising as I'd just emerged from freezing cold water. My hair was stuck flat to my head, never a flattering look, and my face bright red.

Worst of all, thanks to the chill factor, my nipples were clearly visible through my top. Plenty of people had jumped online to comment on that, and I now have a new nickname—Nora Nipples, something I've always wanted to be called. Not. Is the wardrobe malfunction the reason the blasted video went viral, rather than my dog-rescuing heroics? My heart sank all the more when I realised Jack must have got an eyeful too. He was first on the scene when I came out of the water. The thought turns me hot and cold.

If Scottie's rescuer been Kirsty, she would be the goddess Venus in that classical painting, rising from the water stood on a shell, nymph-like and graceful, blonde hair tumbling down her back, one hand clutching Scottie to her torso to hide her nipples. And stop them getting a flash of dark hair that might reveal her as a bottle, rather than natural blonde when collar and cuffs don't match.

Ooh, catty, Mena (by now the voice of my conscience) murmurs.

Anyway, when Friday arrives and there's still no sign of Jack and no text message—*sorry, Gaby! Been in the mountains. No reception. Frantically, insanely, bonkers worried about you*—I pounce on Jolene's invite. We need to discuss the Highland Games and Blissful Beauty launch. August the fifteenth is now only eight days away. Why don't we meet in the Lochside Welcome, she suggests?

Jolene jumps to her feet as soon as I enter the hotel, its bar and beer garden packed as usual. "Let's sit outside," she says. "It's warm and light enough." And it is, the waters lap gently against the shores as the sun drops in the sky, tinting the surrounding area warm orange and pink.

Jolene's phone explodes with beep-beeps as soon as we get outside, and she switches it to silent. "I'll get us drinks," she says and returns minutes later with a jug of Pimms and lemonade she promises me isn't that alcoholic.

The discussion doesn't take long. The website popularity shows plenty of people plan to come to the games. Every villager with any sense has put their house on Airbnb, Psychic Josie agreed to attend even though the committee knocked back most of the demands she made, and the Battle of Stirling Bridge is to be re-enacted. By kids, using plastic swords so it should be injury and risk-free. We both raise our eyes at that and hope for the best.

Strangers pack the Lochside Welcome's beer garden, an unusual occurrence. Even at the height of summer, few non-locals are hardy enough to sit out here in the evening. I'm with the non-locals, but the Pimms seems... terribly warming. Jolene, a woman who grew up in much sunnier climes, strips off her hoodie so that all she has on is a Broderie Anglaise camisole top, the thin shoulder straps emphasising impressive shoulders.

"Gosh, aren't you freezing?" I say, an exact impression of my nanna whenever I visit her in anything less than a vest, shirt, jumper, jacket, scarf and gloves.

Jolene shakes her head. "Coldness is for pussies, no offence to Mena, eh?"

"No offence taken," I say on my pussy's behalf. That cat has superior seeking out hot spot qualities anyway.

"Dexter," Jolene continues, "the marketing guy who's in charge of the Blissful Beauty launch, did he come and visit the place last month? A hunky American guy?" she asks.

Oof, a too-rapid subject change I'm half-way down my Pimms and lemonade (very drinkable) and the urge to confide hits me. Katya isn't here, which sucks, and I like Mhari, but… As friends go, anything you tell her will be shared far and wide. Plus, she'll upload an unflattering video of you online without asking your permission.

"Um, yes," I say, wondering what she knows already.

"And he kissed you, eh?"

That 'eh' thing again. New Zealanders might always sound as if they are asking questions when that's not the case, but this definitely isn't a question. The WhatsApp group told Jolene as soon as the kiss happened. I'll stake a hundred pounds on that.

"Yes," I say. "He's asked me out. Once the launch is over."

Jolene twists in her seat to lean back, elbows on the table and facing the setting sun. I join her, doing my best not to shiver.

"Sweet," she says. "You should get yourself out there again. Get back on the dating horse, eh, and ride it—"

"Jolene! Please." I'm on my second Pimms and lemonade, and the next few words rush out of me before I can stop them. "Um, what was the deal with Kirsty and Jack?" I cross my fingers, hoping Jolene doesn't do pillow talk with Stewart. He fits the Mhari school of discretion,

220

and it will be all around the village in an instant I asked pointed questions about Jack.

"Kirsty always wanted Jack," Jolene helps herself to more Pimms and lemonade. "From the moment she moved to Lochalshie."

"She's not local, then?" I'd assumed she was Lochalshie born and bred.

"No, Edinburgh. She moved here not long after her dad died. He left her a lot of money, and she bought that pile." She tips her head to the house. Funny how no-one in the village likes Kirsty's house. "As soon as she set eyes on Jack, she decided she wanted him. Stewart and I didn't like her very much. The Lochside Welcome wasn't good enough for her."

How not to endear yourself to the locals. "Why do you think he hooked up with her?"

Jolene shrugs. "You've seen what she looks like. What do you think?"

How disappointing. But as I spend my time drooling over Jack because he's ridiculously easy on the eyes, I can't blame him for doing the same with a woman.

"And the split?" I say, praying it will be for something unforgivable such as attempting to murder his mother when she diagnosed Kirsty with advanced syphilis (or something) rather than just being not suited, a point of view Kirsty is currently doing her best to reverse.

"Ah, now there's a story," she says. "Kirsty was always posting up pictures—hang on, what about Dexter? And

221

eh, why do you want to know so much about Jack and Kirsty?"

Definitely a New Zealander asking a question this time. Darn it. I've almost finished my second 'not that alcoholic at all, Gaby!' Pimms. I should have known better than to trust someone who dates Stewart to judge what counts as head-spinning and inhibition lowering. Stewart's not the only one who regards the Lochside Welcome as his second home. I open my mouth, about to confess all when some remnant of sense kicks in.

"I'm not interested in anyone," I say. "I'm far too busy with my work, and I'm still recovering from a split. Ryan was the love of my life, and I was with him for ten years. Broke my heart into smithereens and everything."

Jolene turns and raises one eyebrow. "Yeah? I thought you managed that by your fourth day here. You know, when Dr McLatchie handed you the keys to her son's house."

Heat flames my face. Does this mean that my unrequited crush on Jack has been obvious to one and all? Yikes. I imagine the villagers remarking on it to Jack and him screwing his face up in disgust. "*Gaby? Nice girl, but seriously? I mean, look at my past record. The painting I have of Kirsty? Case closed. Also the Nora Nipples? Urgh.*"

I've got to get out of here. I gulp the last of the second Pimms and jump to my feet, a movement hindered as I forget we're sitting at a bench. The table traps my legs, and I fly backwards, pulling the table and Jolene with me, and we land in an undignified heap on the ground.

Jolene's reflexes, one hundred times better than mine, shoot her hand so that it darts out to stop the side of the table landing on our abdomens and chopping us in half.

"I'm so sorry," I say. The crash and the yells we both let out have attracted attention. A group of hill-walkers amble over, trying and failing to hide their amusement.

"All right gels?" the first asks. "Was this you doing your bit to show us that the Scottish heavy drinking stereotype is unjustified?" At that, he and his wretched Cockney friends burst into gales of laughter.

"Neither of us is Scottish," Jolene pushes off the table and sending it flying, a move that wipes the grins from the hill-walkers' faces as they follow its progress as it sails across the beer garden and land at the water's edge. "And you now owe us a drink seeing as we've provided you with free entertainment." The men nod hastily, doubtless worrying what might happen if they refuse.

She stands up, brushing dirt and soil from her trousers and extends a hand to me. "I don't want another drink," I whisper as I get to my feet.

"I'll drink yours," she whispers back. "Then we will talk about Dexter. And Jack. And what you're going to do about them."

CHAPTER 20

After one more glass of Pimms—despite Jolene's promise she would drink mine, she foisted it on me—the Dexter kiss is all I admit to. Jolene's on the Lochalshie WhatsApp group. Jack "seems like a decent chap", I utter the words through pursed lips and know my nanna would be proud of me. 'Decent chap' was high praise in the 1960s but tells you nothing. I don't say, 'hot' or use the phrase, "I wouldn't push him out of bed for farting", which is Katya's ultimate compliment.

"There was that photo," Jolene adds, "the one Kirsty put up. Well, she put up tonnes of her and Jack, eh? But Jack's dead-beat pa tracked him down when he saw the pics. Thought Jack was some kind of celebrity and turned up in the village.

"Lochalshie doesn't welcome wife beaters," she adds darkly, "and Jack hated being part of a celebrity couple when it resulted in cockroaches crawling out of the woodwork."

This is all too fascinating and a very revealing insight into the man who takes up too much space in my head. No wonder he hated Kirsty uploading pictures of them so much. Unfortunately, the hill-walker who'd considered himself the soul of wit with his question about Scottish stereotypes decides he fancies his chances with Jolene. He sidles up to her, and she turns to face him, grin in place. It's my cue to leave.

On the way out, I spot Stewart at the bar.

"Gaby!" he exclaims, startling Scottie who'd been sleeping at his feet and who barks at me. I like to think it's a 'thanks for rescuing me the other week' woof. "Have ye seen ma Jolene?"

I shrug. "No." His girlfriend probably isn't interested in the hill-walkers, but her eyes had lit up when Mr Thinks Himself So Witty sidled up to her. I put it down to the window shopping thing women who've been in long-term relationships like to do from time to time. If she has any sense, she'll let the hill-walker talk his (merino wool hill-walking) socks off, and then retreat, buoyed up by enough flattery and attention to last three months.

Back in the house, I feed Mena some left-over ham she goes mad for and phone Katya. Thanks to the Blissful Beauty launch and all those Instagrammers who will need to post updates, Dexter has had words with people in high up places. The phone reception and Wi-Fi now works everywhere. Three months after moving to

Lochalshie, I can finally phone my friend while sitting on the couch in the house. It crosses my mind I could transfer my iMac so I could work here, but I park that thought. Besides, traipsing back through the village with all that heavy hardware would be tedious.

Right?

"Katya! How are you!"

"Have you been drinking?"

I (almost) never lie to my best friend, though I'm often guilty of omission. I press the phone harder to my ear and tap the cushion on my leg to encourage Mena to jump up and join me.

"No. I mean yes, a tiny bit," I say. "I phoned you for a catch-up. Jack, Dexter, tonight. Is that okay? And also to repeat the question—when, when, when are you coming to visit me?"

Awkward silence. It stretches out one, two, three seconds too long.

"So busy," she mutters. "Can't take time off. That's what freelancing is like, isn't it?"

"No," I say. Freelancing allows flexibility you don't get with a nine-to-five job. Is it the Blissful Beauty stuff that's taking up all her time, or what about the ghost-writing book job, I ask? I hear breath drawn in. I've hit the truth.

"The book job, then!"

I've badgered her for weeks about it, tell me, Katya, speculating wildly on who she's ghost writing for. I ran through various celebrities and reality TV stars—even bloomin' Caitlin of Blissful Beauty—asking if that was on

227

whose behalf she was writing and coming up with wacky titles for their autobiographies.

"If I ever tell you I'm considering ghostwriting for someone again, please break my fingers. Honestly, pain in the digits is preferable to pains in the neck, arse and everything else this wretched job has turned into. I've been sitting in front of my laptop for so long now, I'm square-eyed, and my shoulders are stuck up around my ears. I have to write using this celebrity's voice, and she insists on exclamation marks everywhere, even though I hate them and they have no place in a non-fiction book, especially one that's meant to be taken seriously."

"Katya," I say. "I will never allow you to ghostwrite again."

I tell her the plans for the Blissful Beauty launch and about Dexter and his suggestion we hook up post event.

"NO! Did you get the capital letters there? I'm worried you might think I'm kidding around. I decided when you finished with Ryan, thank all the heavens and stars, that I'd vet any prospective boyfriend of yours from now on."

"You did?" Mena hears the startled sound to my voice and tips her little head up to look at me. I stroke her under the chin and she purrs.

"Gosh, is that the cat? I can hear her from here. Yes, Gaby. I did an incredible job of holding back my opinion of Mr Douche-bag for years, but I vowed I wouldn't let my best friend make such a momentous mistake ever again."

How? How did she hold back?

"A guy who puts you in a schedule is a no-no. He's a workaholic too, by the sounds of it. And I've spoken to him. He'd critique your girlfriend abilities. Do you really want that?"

Well, that chimes in with what I feared.

"What was it Bridget Jones said," I say. "I'm going to end up dying alone and being eaten by an Alsatian. Or Mena, though I'm probably not good enough for this fussy puss."

There's a sigh at her end. "Far, far better alone than with the wrong person, I promise."

Heartfelt advice. My best friend has had many short relationships over the years. Her long list of do's don'ts mean that sooner or later whoever she is dating does one of the don'ts and ends up an ex toot suite. Katya is always telling me a woman has plenty to find a keeper, and she enjoys singledom. She's a thousand times better at it than I am.

"What about Jack? That photo of you and him together was cute. You could always ask him out. Women can do that nowadays. They've been allowed to for a while, thanks to feminism."

I (almost) never lie to my best friend. "No. Too much like hard work."

Mena looks at me. She knows a lie when she hears it. Or perhaps this phone conversation thing diverts too much of my attention when I should settle myself in the optimal position for a cat to settle in your lap and purr her head off. Car lights flash past, reflected from the front window that faces the high street. One set of them looks mini-bus shaped, the lights flashing as if they laugh at me and my lies.

To distract myself and Katya, I tell her about the Outlander trips website and how no-one has booked through the site.

"Hang on. Let me look at it," she says. "If Jack wrote the text, maybe he hasn't made it exciting enough to attract people. I'm the words expert around here."

There's a minute's pause. "Er, what did you say the URL was?"

I repeat it, and she tells me there is no sign of it. Website not found.

"He knows how to publish a WordPress site, doesn't he?"

Duh. I forgot one of Melissa's sacred rules about clients. Never assume they know anything. It's better to patronise people than to think your own knowledge is also theirs. No doubt, Jack looked at the site I'd hidden behind a password, said it was fine and thought that was that. He wouldn't have known to disable the password. No wonder the flaming bookings haven't flooded in. It's not visible.

Bothered as I am about the man who doesn't care enough to phone me and check I'm still alive, at least I designed a great website capable of generating bookings—or it will as soon as Jack presses 'publish'. I'm tempted to drop the phone and run to his house, "Jack, Jack switch my iMac on. Let's get this thing live." But it's eleven o'clock at night. Nine more hours of the world not knowing about Outlander tours won't make that much difference.

"I advise you to go after Jack with every weapon in your arsenal. Do you need me to list them?" I might have known I couldn't distract Katya for long, but the last list ended up on Twitter and resulted in the implosion of my relationship. I should steer clear of anything list-related again when it comes to my love life. My friend, however, disagrees and promises me she will detail every single thing amazing about me and send it through.

The promise makes me tearful, though I sense Katya roll her eyes when I tell her she is the best friend a girl ever had the fortune to stumble upon and the universe should also know her stupendous, delightful, remarkable, amazing qualities, like seriously.

"Is that so? And by the way, you 're hilarious after too many Pimms. But I will visit soon, promise! Mhari and Jolene sound like threats to my Gaby's best friend status, and it's time for me to eyeball the competition and warn them off."

That makes me laugh so hard Mena jumps off my lap in disgust, appalled that I've disrupted her comfort.

"Bye, Katya," I say, vastly cheered up.

"Ciao, Gaby. And remember, Jack McAllan is yours for the taking. Go forth and conquer, girlfriend."

The doorbell wakes me far too early the next morning. Despite everything swirling around in my head—the website, Kirsty and Jack, the futility of Jack and me—the three Pimms worked their magic, and I was asleep as soon as my head hit the pillow.

Mena jumps from the pillow next to me and yowls. "Too right, Mena," I groan, throwing back the covers and wondering who on earth is as uncivilised to call on a Saturday at nine am. Last night, I decided removing my clothes before going to bed was a challenge too far, so a quick once-over with a brush to tame the fingers stuck in an electric socket effect, and I'm a quarter presentable.

The bell goes again, someone leaning too hard on it and I tell whoever to hang on, forgetting for the moment that Kirsty's super-fancy house includes soundproof insulation.

I swing the door open. "Okay, okay I'm—Ryan! Good grief! What time did you leave the house?"

CHAPTER 21

Seriously, Gaby? Your ex-boyfriend and week-long fiancé is standing at the door, and all you can think to ask is a query about the details of his journey?

Ryan blinks and then grins, whipping a massive bunch of flowers from behind his back. He's chosen all my favourites—Carnations, Alstroemeria and Gypsophila—and the flowers cover about half of his body. This is one super expensive Interflora purchase. I take them from him and stare at the man I used to see every day, who now seems like a total stranger. He doesn't work in this setting. I'm too used to seeing… other men in this place and Ryan's neat appearance is out of sorts here. He is thinner than he was too but it suits him.

Across the street I spot Mhari on her way to work, her mouth rounded in an 'o' and her attention half on the scene before her and half on the phone. Terrific. Another update to the Lochalshie WhatsApp group.

"Um, come in," I say, anxious to get him off the doorstep before Mhari wanders over to join us and introduce herself.

Mena sees the flowers and Ryan, and hisses, arching her back. Her fur stands on end, making her twice the usual size. "Woah," Ryan stares at her. "What a horrible animal!"

"Shush!" I put a finger to my lips, afraid Mena will overhear and be hurt. Besides, I am a changed woman. Mena, the cat I used to nickname Little Ms Mean, captured my heart some weeks ago and I'm now a paid-up member of the crazy cat lady club. I busy myself switching the kettle and feeding Mena. Ryan puts the flowers on the table in the kitchen and moves about the house, speculating on its price. I pour boiling water into mugs and panic. I've forgotten what Ryan, the man I lived with for years, takes in his coffee.

Milk. Of course. And I've none, seeing as I don't. I hand the mug over anyway, and he grimaces and then resets his face to the devoted ex-boyfriend visiting estranged ex-girlfriend expression.

"Do you want a seat?" I ask, deciding to show off Kirsty's house's best feature—the chairs in the living room that allow you a perfect view of the loch. It's a beautiful morning, the sun high in the sky already and although clouds take up two third of the sky, they are the white fluffy kind and not the too-usual dark-tinted ones that signal rain isn't far away. A gentle breeze ripples the surface of the loch, and we watch birds crest and dive the waves.

As a salesman, Ryan isn't short of words most of the time, but I see him put his coffee down and twist his hands together. Perhaps the seven-hour drive up here wasn't enough time to rehearse whatever he wanted to say. "Gaby, I—" he begins at the same time as I jump in with a 'how are you' inquiry and another apology for the pros and cons list Katya posted online. It was that, or I would ask what time he left the house again. I'm interested. Ryan hates early mornings.

"It's been a funny few months," he says. "Not having you in the flat. I've missed you. A lot, it turns out."

Here's the weird thing about Ryan. He's a car salesman, albeit part-time as in a small family business you do all sorts, and therefore he ought to have the gift of the gab. If you can charm people enough to persuade them to splash out tens of thousands of pounds on a heap of rusty metal, doesn't it go without saying you're able to speak the words of love and want without difficulty? Not so with Ryan. His proposal had the feel of someone who'd asked Google 'how do you ask your girlfriend to marry you', and he and I rarely bothered exchanging of 'I love you's'. I thought that was because we didn't need to say it or that we weren't saps, but since then I wondered if we didn't say it because it didn't apply. Habit's a hard thing to break and me being with Ryan was comfortable, easy and routine. When you've been with each other since school, you can't picture what adulthood without someone by your side is like. I found out it wasn't half as bad as I'd once feared.

He turns his hands up. They tremble, which touches me. Or he might just be shaky after a long journey and an early start. "Do you want something to eat?" I jump to my feet. Cooking will serve as a distraction from a conversation I'm not sure I want to have. He nods and then stands too. "Though I could do it? I'm a dab hand at scrambled eggs these days."

My face must show shock.

"When you left, I realised how much I'd taken you for granted."

He opens my fridge and takes out eggs and a packet of smoked salmon. When I shake my head at that and say it's Mena's, he manages to keep the incredulity to a minimum. And he's as good as his word. The scrambled eggs he presents me with a few minutes later on top of toasted sour-dough are fluffy and perfectly seasoned. Last night's Pimms have left me ferociously hungry, and I put away my helping in double quick time. When Ryan pushes aside his half-finished plate, I take it from him and wolf that down too.

"Kayleigh," I say. "Can you explain that?" Fortified with vast amounts of protein and carbs, I can ask this question. When I say the name, I remember something my mum used to say when I was a teenager: never ask questions you don't want to know the answer to. My body doesn't tense up when I ask about Kayleigh, which means… well, whatever he replies won't bother me. I also remember a Katya point made to me when she was ghostwriting a guide to detection skills for new members of the CID at Norfolk Constabulary. Bullet points listed the signs to watch out for when someone lies to you. Too much eye contact was one as the person tries to convince you they are trustworthy and for men, they often keep their feet entirely still. I'm on eye and foot watch.

Ryan looks away, the light catching him in profile. Once upon a time, I knew that face as well as my own, and now Jack's profile keeps imposing itself on top of Ryan's features. I have to blink to get rid of it and concentrate on my erstwhile boyfriend whose feet tap out an agitated rhythm.

"A mistake," he says. "I thought I was missing out because we'd been together since we were teenagers. And she threw herself at—"

He breaks off as I glare at him. As excuses go, the ol' 'forgive me my male genes, m'lud. I couldn't help myself' is at the top there with the dog ate my homework one.

The doorbell sounds again. Dear heaven. This is my morning for shocks or should I say surprises? The woman at the door throws her arms around me, and I'm pushed up close to a heavily scented body in impeccable clothing. Behind me, Mena yowls—a different miaow than her usual one, and the woman steps back and claps her hands delightedly.

"Mena sweet-pea! I knew you'd be torn in tiny pieces when I left you!"

The fabled Dating Guru then, and every bit as gorgeous as she looks on film and in photos close up, though I can't help thinking the painting Jack has wildly flatters her. She's taller than me, Jack's height, I'd say, and her hair thick and glossy, styled in an 'I woke up like this' way, but one I suspect takes an hour with a heavy-duty hair-drier and straightening irons. Wide blue eyes framed with thick lashes sweep me from top to bottom. I sense the assessment makes her let out a giant sigh of relief.

Mena stays behind me. Perhaps she finds it hard to forgive those who abandon her and I give her a silent cheer. Ryan has moved into the hallway too, and the woman notices him behind me.

"Gaby!" she says, "I didn't want to let myself in in case you were entertaining. And you are." More relief this time and a double helping of delight. I'm not sure of the etiquette here when someone returns to the house and the cat they wanted you to look after. Do you offer them a cup of tea and then make it, even though they know where the kettle and mugs are kept? And the place is a tip too. As the weeks have gone by, I've gone back to slob standards. The house isn't dirty, but I've left clothes lying around upstairs, empty mugs, glasses and plates in the kitchen and magazines and books all over the living room floor. The agency brings in a professional cleaning company at the end of the cat sitting contract, and I've started to rely too much on it

"Er, come in," I say. "I was just about to tidy up. What brings you back then?"

Kirsty walks past me, a tinkle of a laugh. If she objects to the state of the place, she says nothing though her eyes sweep the place and she purses her lips. "Oh, a surprise! A lovely one for Jack and one for you!" I pull the door shut and spot Mhari once more. This must be her morning coffee break. I'm tempted to ask her to join us. Mhari shakes her head furiously and uses her forefinger to score across her throat, rounding her mouth into an emphatic 'no, no!' at me. Flippin' heck. Is Kirsty a serial killer in disguise? I shut the door. Kirsty seems to be on first-name terms with Ryan. She greets him with a "Hello again! I told you this would be brilliant, and I was right, wasn't I?"

I do a double take at that. What does she mean? The three of us stand in the living room, me all too conscious that the carpet in there hasn't been vacuumed for a while. Kirsty glances out the window and remarks how much she has missed the still beauty of the place and its peace. She moves a magazine from one chair, pointedly holding it between thumb and forefinger, and places it on the coffee table before sitting down. I take that as my cue to do so too as does Ryan.

"So, does someone want to tell me what's going on?" I ask. I've positioned myself so I can watch them, and I rack my brains for the rest of Katya's signs of a liar.

"Well," Kirsty says, "So brilliant I found Ryan here! I decided I'm not much of a Dating Guru if I can't help my friends out, right?"

What friends? Oh. She means me. I shift my stare to Ryan. I'd thought the seven-hour car journey was on his own initiative. He shuffles in his chair.

"And what could be better than organising a little re-union for two people who are meant to be together! We flew up here on the red-eye from London this morning. Such devotion on Ryan's part!" She claps her hands once more, and I wrinkle my brow and think, *not as devoted as driving himself all the way up here from Norfolk.* "As you might imagine, my job makes me very sentimental. It broke my heart that so many miles separated you and poor Ryan, and you were unable to resolve your differences!"

"But what about Kayleigh!" I burst out, and Ryan's eyes flit away from mine.

"He can explain that," Kirsty says, nodding her head graciously at him. "Tell Gaby what you told me, Ryan."

"Kayleigh made a play for me, and I held off for weeks. And I felt sorry for her. She's a carer, you know. Her mum has multiple sclerosis and two other kids. Kayleigh has to look after them as well. She's the sole earner so I couldn't say no—I mean sack her. She came in everyday, all the way from Cromer. On the bus too, even though that fare is £3.50 each way, and then poor Kayleigh needing to go to the supermarket on the corner as soon as they drop their prices on the sandwiches so she can buy a half-price lunch."

Ryan mumbles on. "It was that stupid 'the grass is always greener on the other side' thing, but when I got to the other side, I found the grass was brown and dried up, nothing like as rich and succulent as it was on my side of the—"

My jaw drops open. I've never been compared to grass, and if I'm lucky enough to lead a long, long life may it never ever happen again.

Kirsty's eyes, when I turn in her direction, are glassy. "Isn't that so beautiful?" she asks. "I wish I'd filmed it! If I uploaded it onto the Dating Guru website, seven hundred women would have proposed to him then and there! Goodness me, you must be the luckiest woman on earth!"

Mena walks back in and leaps onto my lap instead of Kirsty's. I assure Kirsty it must be a temporary thing, her cat's preference for me, and do a dance of joy inside. The little things, right?

"Kayleigh was a one-off, Gaby. I promise. I've regretted it every day. Didn't you see what I did on Facebook?"

Kirsty nods solemnly. "I've seen it. I used that one for a post on my website—the perfect example of a man who's desperate to get you back. You should have seen the comments, Gaby! Everyone agreed with me. I made it anonymous, but all my followers begged the girl to get back with him. Begged, Gaby! A guy—or a girl—is allowed one mistake, don't you think?

"And then there was your list," she adds, her tone stern, "the one that ended up on Twitter. Not nice. Not nice at all!"

Whatever. I need to talk to Ryan alone. The Dating Guru's comments stop me asking what I want to know.

And too many things make no sense to me. How did she find him, for instance? I'm 99 percent sure I never told her Ryan's name. One big alarm bell goes off in my head, another of the points I remembered from Katya's CID guide for new detectives trying to figure out liars. Liars embellish their stories with little bits of this and that to make them sound authentic.

Dring! The doorbell sounds again, making the three of us start. In all the weeks I've lived here, I've never been as popular. Has curiosity got the better of Mhari and she is outside the door, hopping from foot to foot and demanding I let her in so she can check the situation out? Ryan begs me to ignore the bell, but I tell him Lochalshie is a small place and here, neighbourhood relationships count for a lot. Not answering a doorbell is akin to stealing or running rampage through the village with six cans of neon-coloured spray paint and re-decorating all the houses and bus shelters.

Muttering, "I'm coming, I'm coming" at whoever presses the bell again, I'm still saying the words when I open the door.

"You are? I'd never have guessed."

On the one hand, the delightful Jack on my doorstep early in the morning, eyebrow raised and a dirty smirk in place is a welcome sight.

"Gaby, sorry to bother you so early but I wanted to find out how you—"

On the other hand, the circumstances of his first visit here and him desperate to find out how I am couldn't have come at a worse time. Kirsty has lived with cats a long time, all the better to pick up their expert way of quick and silent movement. I'm thrust to the side as a heavily perfumed body pushes past me and flings itself on Jack. His eyes meet mine above her perfectly coiffed head. I search for signs of distress, shock and repulsion, but all I see is puzzlement. The mini-bus is parked outside the house and empty of tourists.

"I'm so excited to see you!" Kirsty doesn't bother lowering her voice. Across the street, I spy Mhari and wonder how many coffee breaks she can squeeze into her working day. She's back to using the slit throat gesture, echoing how I feel now. "Are you off to Doune Castle for another tour?" Kirsty asks. "History's my favourite subject, so I'll be able to help you out. And I've got so much to tell you."

Jack's mouth has opened and closed a few times in what might be a 'rescue me' plea for help. Kirsty turns back and points past me to where Ryan stands in the hallway. "Besides," she says. "We should leave Gaby and Ryan to talk. He travelled all the way from Norfolk to see her. Can you believe it? So romantic!"

She grabs his hand and pulls them both to the mini-bus, leaving me opening and closing my mouth in silent objection. The bus roars off minutes later, heading east and Kirsty's hand held up, fingers waggling goodbye. I fight the urge to return the gesture in a much cruder way.

I blink, remembering that fantasy I had where Jack whisked me away in his mini-bus, and we headed for that luxury hotel in the middle of nowhere. Seems I was the understudy all along. The fantasy's real star is back and about to experience that roaring fire and the soft rug for real. *Oh, heart, thou art well and truly daft, I mutter to myself. The sooner you get over this silly crush, the better for your owner's well-being.*

CHAPTER 22

Mhari watches the bus drive off, her face the picture of comedic dismay. I shut the front door and force my attention back to Ryan.

"Is that Kirsty's ex?" he asks. "The guy she's trying to get back with?"

What other answer is there? "Yes," I say. "Let's get out of here. I'll show you around the village."

It will take all of ten minutes, but it beats sitting in the house. I start at the loch-side and wonder at the tactlessness of the weather, which has decided against reflecting my mood and is instead sunny, dry and whisper it, warm. The dog walkers pass us, various golden retrievers and Labradors tearing ahead in a bid to obliterate the wild bird and duck population.

"I meant it," Ryan says as we stop to watch them, the water lapping at our feet. "About missing you. I threw you out of the house without thinking it through. Then, I got so upset the only way I thought I could get your attention was to make it public. That's why I put all those messages on Facebook. And you never responded. Ten years, Gaby! We can't just throw it away."

I drop to the ground, pulling my knees up to hug them and Ryan seats himself beside me. He tries to snuggle up—the ever-present wind has a way of getting under any gap in your clothes—but stops when I shake my head.

"It was your own decision to come here, was it?" I try. When I thought Ryan had done it all himself—decided to visit me, woken up at silly o'clock to do so and then driven for seven-plus hours—the gesture impressed me. My heart might even have fluttered a little. Knowing he flew up here with Kirsty knocks the shine off. Perhaps he talked her into it, though. Persuaded her she should return and I could give up the cat-sitting gig early.

"Yes," he says, but when I ask, "Sure about that?" he shakes his head.

"Okay, no. The truth is Kirsty got hold of me. Some-one had added a link to that Facebook plea I made to the comments on one of her blogs and she worked out I was your ex and got in touch. She told me she had a plane ticket going spare because her agent wasn't able to come with her to Scotland. A first class flight too, Gaby, they give you—"

"Ryan," I interrupt before I get the details, first-class travel not being something I give two hoots about when I'm trying to work out the sincerity of my ex's claims.

"I know it doesn't sound as good," he says, and I raise my eyebrows at the honesty, "but when she suggested it and how romantic it would be to drop in and surprise you, I thought—"

"Yoo-hoo!"

Never attempt a private conversation in the open in Lochalshie. The mad barking should have alerted me. As we get to our feet, Stewart lumbers into sight. Scottie is off his leash, and he runs around the both of us, yapping his head off. By the time Stewart reaches us, Scottie has gone through his repertoire of tricks—rolling over and playing dead for a few seconds before leaping back to life and wagging his tail in expectation of treats.

"How're ye, Gaby?" Stewart says, sticking his hand out. "Is this your ex, then?"

Ryan takes his hand. "Hoping not to be the ex too much longer."

With a quick aside to Scottie that he is the best wee dog in the world as he does his ninth dead impression, Stewart's forehead creases at that.

"Oh, aye? But whit about the American bloke Dexter? Isn't he waiting a wee bit and then he's going tae take you out for chips, Gaby?"

How, how, how does he know? Two possibilities—Mhari, who wouldn't think anything of installing listening devices all over Lochalshie, so she never misses out on any key bit of gossip. The more likely explanation is that I spilled my guts to blasted Jolene when she force-fed me those three Pimms. Curses on her and curses on Stewart.

"What?" Ryan's replaced his until now 'I'm doing my best to convince you of my sincerity' benevolence with fury, his eyes screwed up, and his mouth pinched. "Who the hell's Dexter? You broke my heart when you left and, now I find you've been carrying on behind my back!"

Stewart holds both hands up. "No, she didnae, big man. She's no' done anything except kiss him, and Mhari says he jumped on her and took her by surprise."

Mhari. I might have known.

"And she wasnae going out wi' you at the time, was she? So you cannae call it carrying on behind your back, can ye?" He folds his arms and eyes Ryan beadily. An unlikely champion, but a nice one.

Ryan holds his hands out. "Er, yeah. Sorry, Gaby. I didn't mean it. It's just… just hard when you've been with someone for so long, and then your life changes just like that. I don't know if I'll ever get used to waking up and not having you beside me."

To my astonishment, Stewart wipes a hand across his eyes. "Gaby," he says. "I like this yin much better than that American bloke. It's awfy romantic!"

It is? Nothing I've seen of Stewart and Jolene's relationship so far convinces me either of them has a close acquaintance with the soppy and sentimental. Still, it makes me look at Ryan afresh. "Do you want lunch?" Ryan asks me. "On me. Wherever is best around here?" He casts an eye in either direction, the absence of anything chain restaurant shaped plain. Ryan loves a cheeky

Nando's and PizzaExpress in that order. So do I, but they don't encourage romance or intimate conversations.

"Over there," Stewart points at the Lochside Welcome. He shows no signs of leaving us on our own either. As the hotel's his second home, this is to be expected and his company saves me from having to talk, my head churning with everything that's happened over the last four hours.

The hotel's busy, the usual Saturday crowd that gathers for boozy brunches and lunches. I get waves that Ryan clocks and realise that I've established myself as an honorary resident, never mind I've only been here for eleven weeks and two days. It's enough to give a girl the warm and fuzzies, though I also note that no-one bothers disguising the huge 'and who's HE?' that appears in comedy speech bubbles above their heads. Ashley waves, halting a conversation he's having with his chef to wander over. I'm his favourite person ever since I stuck Dexter in front of him and Ashley wrangled close to six figures for the Blissful Beauty launch.

"We're trying out a new pizza," he says, "in honour of Caitlin and Blissful Beauty. Would you do me the honour of sampling it?"

By the time we get a table and place our order, Stewart has left us, the attractions of the bar far too tempting. "What's the Caitlin and Blissful Beauty thing?" Ryan asks, and I explain, throwing in the fact that little ol' me thought up the whole idea. Impressive, hmm? The Brit in me who believes it's vulgar to boast and thus can't say any more when Ryan does not pick up on what a huge deal that was.

"I know our relationship grew stale."

I stare at him, shocked. Ryan's like most guys. He'd rather scoop his own eyeballs out than talk about his feelings. Whenever I attempted a 'what do we want from our relationship' chat, he'd clam up at once. The words he says now have the echo of Dating Guru advice. The woman must have spent their entire journey up here coaching him.

"I could change, though. We could go out more. To Norwich. London even. And, um, if you want to live somewhere else, we could do that."

Blimey O'Riley. We are talking about the man who loves his home town so much he has its name tattooed on his back. True. And what would he do about his job? Ryan's worked for his family ever since leaving school at sixteen. I don't think he's got the skills or experience to do anything else. Ryan takes my hand. "Please Gaby," he says. "Can you think about it? Take your time. I've got to go back home tomorrow. And Kirsty's going to give 'em a lift back to the airport. You'd make me the happiest guy in the world if you came with me."

I open my mouth, about to say, "but what about the cat sitting?" and then I remembered Kirsty's reappearance, a clear signal she'd changed her mind about the three-month extension. Her big blog project just needs the last bit of work—presumably where she gets Jack back. I didn't think I'd be able to watch that. It was bad

250

enough wanting someone so badly and not having them. Lochalshie being so tiny, imagine having to bump into the happy couple every day. Kirsty would crow like mad too. If I'm back in Great Yarmouth, I won't need to see any of it, and I can chalk the whole cat-sitting thing down to experience. Or perhaps that's what I'll persuade Ryan to do. Kirsty promised me a glowing reference. We could travel the world together, me working for Melissa and him doing odd mechanic jobs here and there.

Ryan and I had plenty of fun in the ten years together, such as the first time we went on holiday together as eighteen-year-olds or the Christmas we had when we persuaded my mum and Ryan's parents that no, we wouldn't be doing the family duty thing this year because we wanted to spend it alone together. I attempted to make the full four-course Christmas dinner but misjudged how long a turkey takes to defrost and cook, so we ended up ordering takeaway from the local Indian and eating it in front of the telly in our pyjamas. It counts as one of my favourite Christmas's.

The *happiest guy in the world* though. The words don't ring true. If I went onto the Dating Guru's website and searched for things to say to your ex to make her come back, would that line appear there? And there are too many people ear-wigging this conversation. I'm reminded of our engagement, which also happened in a public place. Is it safer to say these things in front of an audience where the recipient feels under pressure to respond positively?

"Ta-da!" Ashley puts the Caitlin/Blissful Beauty pizza in front of us. The topping is pink, the exact shade of the Blissful Beauty logo, and the letters BB made out in grated mozzarella, and silver stars made from goodness only knows. It's closer to a pudding in appearance than a main course and shouldn't be appetising, but it smells heavenly. I lean over it, breathe in freshly baked bread, tomatoes, garlic and cheese and let out a sigh of contentment.

Ryan screws his nose up, then remembers he's supposed to be on his best behaviour. I move in for the kill. "Kayleigh, then? Was she the first?"

I can't see his feet, so I don't know if they are motionless. I'm willing to bet they are because the hands that until now were fiddling around with the salt, pepper, vinegar and tomato sauce have stilled. There's a pause five seconds too long before the automatic denial—*yes, yes., how can you ask that?* Then, he takes my hand, crushing my fingers so I fear for my circulation.

"She was a one-off, Gaby!" A double squeeze of the digits there. "I promise! A mistake I'll regret for the rest of my life. I made mine, you made yours. Anyway, Kirsty said everyone's allowed one mistake, isn't that right?"

One mistake, eh? I rack my brain, and remember another receptionist at the garage a few years ago who was also beautiful and our age. Didn't she resign in a hurry too? And what if it wasn't because her grandmother died suddenly and she was overcome with grief as Ryan told me, but because he'd had a fling with her and ended it when the guilt set in? If I fix my memory on it, before that there was another saleswoman—aged 22—who left after six months because…

… her grandmother had multiple sclerosis and died, and she was overcome with grief.

Wow. Not even different excuses. I hope Ryan's donating money to the charity that supports MS. They flippin' deserve it after the number of times he's taken their name in vain to justify women having to leave the garage's employment. I find myself on their side too. If the garage sacked them, how rotten unfair was that?

"Lisa," I say, holding up my fingers so I can tick off names. "Dannii?"

No reply.

Ashley puts a large bowl of chips wrapped in fake newspaper and wafting malt vinegar between us, and I grin at Ryan. Chips are our nemesis. He ordered them. I didn't therefore the chips are solely, exclusively Ryan's. The last two time I nicked chips off men, they gave in with good grace. I move the bowl towards me, and Ryan yanks it back before remembering himself. He pushes it, begrudgingly, back. I adopt the same beaming smile and dig in, ignoring the tic in his jaw as I bite into and swallow chips number four, five, eight, ten, the last used as a stick to swirl through garlic mayonnaise, scoop up the biggest blob of it and plank it in my mouth.

"Nice pizza," I say once I finish the mouthful. "Honestly, you'll love it."

"There you are!" Every head in the pub turns to the door. Mine is the one whose expression lights up.

"Katya! What a fantastic surprise!" Beside me, there's a grunt of disagreement I ignore. I stand up and fling my arms around my friend, rucksack in one hand and a packet of smoked salmon in the other. "Looks like I got here just in time," she whispers. "I don't like your present company."

"Neither do I," I say, not bothering to lower my voice. "Ryan's going back to Great Yarmouth tomorrow. Without me."

Public announcements oblige you to stick to your word. Especially those that coincide with a lull in the conversation. Ryan slams his hands onto the table and pushes himself to his feet. "Suit yourself, you cow," he says, adding a few more choice terms that send Ashley scuttling over, murmuring that the Lochside Welcome doesn't welcome that kind of language in a family-run hotel and if sir doesn't desist, he'll be forced to call security. Security turns out to be Stewart, who it seems has many talents besides coding and boring for Scotland. He plants himself beside Ashley, arms folded and glare in place. "Aye, aye. Gaby, I think ye would be better off wi' the American after all."

Faint cries of "Hear, hear!" call out behind him, and my friend wears a triumphant grin, eyebrows peaked and laughter not far away.

The pub's occupants mark Ryan's exit with cheers. It's almost enough to make me pity him. Then I remember that the pizza was supposed to be his treat. I ordered a double helping of Ashley's Chocolate Decadence cake for afters too.

"Do you want something to eat?" I ask Katya. If I beg, I'm sure Ashley will reheat the remains of the Blissful Beauty special and rustle us up another bowl of chips.

"Too right," she says, pulling out the chair opposite me. "I have a lot to tell you, starting with a book I've been trying to write.

CHAPTER 23

Ashley said he didn't mind making us another Blissful Beauty special pizza as I'd finished most of the first one, on the house as I'm still the flavour of the month thanks to the launch. He added in an extra bowl of chips as a reward for the entertainment I'd provided via the stand-up row with Ryan, and the two slices of Chocolate Decadence cake were free too. I tell Katya about Ryan and Kirsty's unexpected arrival that morning. She dumps her rucksack on the chair beside her and rustles around it, pulling out tattered sheets of paper stapled together.

"Read that," she says. "And weep. Or laugh. It explains a few things."

I glance up. "Um, this says strictly confidential at the top."

She waves a hand. "Those papers have the look of a template someone downloaded from a business website somewhere. I doubt it would hold up in a court of law. Anyway, having worked with the woman for three months, I'm so sick of her I don't care. Check out the co-signature on the back page."

And this is when it all comes out. Katya, my best friend, is the official ghostwriter for Kirsty, once of this parish.

"I've never met her, and she has no idea who I am," Katya says. "I have to do everything through her blasted agent. The two times I was meant to meet her to discuss the book, the first time she didn't turn up, and I'd travelled all the way to London to meet her. The second time, so many people mobbed her when she arrived at the hotel where we were to meet, she never got to the table I was sitting at. But all the phone calls I've had with her have been awful. She never answers a question directly, and she contradicts herself all the time. Nightmare, nightmare job."

The book title is, wait for it, *How to Hook a Commitment Phobe: Your 10-Step Guide*. The steps she told me about are all official, but it's a book and not a blog. Things you do to hook a guy or a girl and the book when it comes out will benefit three hundred times twenty because Kirsty can prove her method works.

She can, can't she as she outlined the steps she'd take to me. Thanks to the bad boy billionaire, Dr McLatchie dropping Kirsty into conversations with her son all the time as I'm sure she now does, and Kirsty promoting Highland Tours to her online followers, the zillions of them, Jack's weeks off proposing to her, isn't he? I can't offer that kind of influence. Nowhere near it. I'm neither beautiful nor useful; useless personified instead.

My One Show nightmare flashes up again. This time, when Alex Jones asks Kirsty what other women looking for love can do, Kirsty whips the book out, a thick tome wrapped in a glossy dust jacket featuring a picture of the world's most beautiful couple locked in an embrace. "Only £20.99!" she says. "And you can get it on Amazon, Kobo, Apple Books, Nook, Barnes and Noble and everywhere!"

They re-enact the embrace for the camera, and the audience lets out a collective "ahhhh!", though Alex has to step in when it looks as if the kiss might break the dictates of the 9pm watershed.

"Kirsty vanished with Jack earlier this morning," I say, hating the way my voice cracks. "And I haven't seen them since. Maybe they're in a church or a registry office as we speak, staring lovingly at each other and repeating 'I do.'"

Katya, by now on her fifth slice of pizza despite shunning such stuff normally because if it features meat or dairy, it's the devil's food, sits back so she can stare at me. "Is that what you think? They are the most unconvincing couple since Kate Winslet and Leonardo Di Caprio hammed it up on the Titanic. Granted I've never seen Kirsty and Jack together in the flesh, but have you seen all the photos of them online? She's too busy pouting or blowing kisses at the camera, and he looks as if he'd rather be at the dentist's having teeth pulled without an anaesthetic."

I've never checked out the pics of them online, too scared the jealousy would hit me so hard in the guts I'd double up.

"But what if her methods work, you know—"

"First, I don't know. That's why you're telling me. Haven't I drummed that habit out of you yet? Second, get a grip. Do you honestly believe people are daft enough to fall for those stupid steps? If you ask me, there's no such thing as a commitment-phobe—just a person who hasn't met the right lid for their pot. And I can't believe I've just used your nanna's favourite saying."

Neither can I, but I am vastly cheered by Katya's descriptions of the Jack and Kirsty pictures. I go back to their disappearance, and Kirsty's claim Jack has never lasted three months with anyone.

"With any luck, he's dumped her in the middle of nowhere and gone off on his own with his tourists," she says. "And as for the commitment-phobe, may I quote from the font of all wisdom that is your grandmother once more: these things take time. The longest relationship I've ever had was nine weeks, but as soon as I have worked my way through all the duds and met the right guy, I'll be willing to share my little corner of the earth with him. Or her, if that's what it takes."

"That's brilliant!" There is the scrape of a chair pulled up beside us and someone sitting down without waiting for an invitation. "I've always wanted to meet a real, live lesb—"

"Mhari, Katya. Katya, Mhari."

Mhari helps herself to a slice of pizza. "So, ye didnae murder Kirsty like I suggested, Gaby? Naebody here would blame ye. She was always posting selfies and all these icky-sicky ones of her and Jack. Then, there was the one time."

She sighs regretfully. "I shouldnae really say."

Katya rolls her eyes. Like me, she can recognise a blatant cue for us to beg for the info. As the seconds tick by, Mhari sniffs. "Och, I'll tell you anyway. Jack's father came back because he saw the photos online. Tried to weasel his way back into the doctor's affections—"

"Sorry to disappoint," I say. "But Jolene has already told me that story."

Mhari's face falls. She prefers to be the first one with the news. "Well, anyway, your friend's right. No-one's daft enough to fall for Kirsty's stupid advice. She's always telling women to be all tinkly laughy, agree wi' everything he says but hold back on the goodies till he whips a ring out. Why would anyone want tae marry someone when you don't even know what they're like between the—"

Ashley places two plates of the Chocolate Decadence dessert in front of us, cutting Mhari off. Pink icing, the exact colour of the Blissful Beauty branding, holds together five layers of dark sponge, the lot covered in a ganache that sparkles with edible silver glitter. The chef has studded the top of the cake with stars made from white chocolate and piped a perfect BB in whipped cream on the top. We pick up the cake forks in unison, waiting for someone to fire the starter pistol.

I decide against telling Katya and Mhari I've been following the Dating Guru's advice since I came here. They will howl with laughter. And far from eyeballing the friend competition and telling it to back off, Katya has decided she and Mhari are now best buddies. If only so they can join together to mock me.

Katya breaks the cake stand-off, using her tiny fork to scrape off a ginormous helping of cream and chocolate ganache. Mhari and I follow her example, and as smooth, rich cocoa flavoured with hazelnut, vanilla and what might be brandy hits the backs of our throats, it silences us.

"Room for a little one? That's heaps of cake for three people."

Jolene pulls up a chair, armed with another cake fork. "Is this Project Gaby where we sort out this lady's love life between us once and for all?"

"No!" I say, dropping my fork a moment of weakness that allows the three women about me to dive into more cake.

They ignore me anyway.

"Discount Ryan," Katya says. I raise a hand in objection. Isn't the one-time love of my life allowed another chance? My companions make it clear I'm a sap, fool, one hundred percent idiot to entertain such thoughts.

"On the one hand," Jolene holds up her right hand. "We have Dexter, the American. Possible workaholic and also heaps too critical? But easy on the eye, rich and mould-able?"

Mhari and Katya nod solemnly. Given that neither of them has ever met him, I don't know if I should trust this character assessment.

Jolene swaps to her left hand. "On the other, Jack. Mean, moody magnificent. Amazing in a kilt, loyalty as a friend unquestionable."

"Resembles Jamie Fraser."

"Can you keep your voices down," I hiss. "We don't need the whole of Lochalshie to know my business. If they don't already." I shoot a daggers look at Mhari, her hand sneaking towards her phone. "What? I'm photo-ing this for Instagram," she says, pointing at the cake. "Puddings always get millions of likes."

"Mind you add in the hashtag Lochside Welcome!" Ashley shouts across the bar, killing my last remaining hope that our conversation hasn't been audible to all.

Pizza, chips and cake finished, we push our plates away.

"What now?" I say. "Presumably Ryan has gone back to the house, so it is out of bounds and Lochalshie has no cinema or shopping malls for Katya and me to mooch about in."

"They're setting stuff up in the park for the Highland Games," Jolene says. "Let's do that. Get a bit of exercise in and practice for me."

Katya and I agree as it means we are finally about to find out what tossing a caber involves, but Mhari has to go back to work. In the park, the organisers have roped off areas, and we spot tractor tyres, heavy metal balls at-

263

tached to wooden sticks and a stack of piled up wooden logs. Jolene unzips her hoodie and rubs her hands.

"Right. Tyre turning first?"

I've an inkling Jolene is much stronger than your average woman, but Katya and I agree to take her on anyway putting a tenner on us beating her. Two minutes into the race and I know I will be ten pounds poorer by the end of the afternoon. Tyre turning involves flipping the tyre over and over until you reach the end of the park. It turns out that much rubber is too heavy for a soft southern weakling to lift and I break two nails trying to heave the thing up. By the time Jolene reaches the finishing line, I've only turned the wretched thing twice, while Katya is half-way down.

Jolene allows us two minutes' recovery before leading us over to the pile of tapered logs. Tossing cabers means holding one end of a log upright and throwing it, so it turns end over end in front of you. This time, my efforts get the log off the ground—just—but it tips from my hands before I have the chance to throw it, narrowly missing my best friend who is forced to leap out of the way to avoid the same fate that befell the laptop I took to the first Dexter meeting.

Next comes throwing the hammer. The metal balls attached to sticks are supposed to be whirled around in a circle and flung away as hard as you can manage. Mine lands a metre away while Katya and I watch jaws dropped open as Jolene's sails over the field and hits one of the vehicles in the car park, shattering its front window.

She clamps a hand to her mouth, and the three of us run to the damaged car.

"Oh dear," I say. "I think this is Kirsty's hire car—the one she and Ryan got at the airport."

Katya bursts out laughing. "What a shame. Though it would have been much better if they'd both been in it."

"Katya!" I say, mock outraged, but the laughter is infectious. In seconds, the three of us are in hysterics, tears running down our cheeks. Stewart, having heard the noise when he ventured out of the Lochside Welcome to let Scottie stretch his legs, wanders over and joins in. The hammer has blown the window out and is embedded in the front seat. This being Kirsty, her chosen hire car is a BMW. I dread to think what the repair bill will cost, but when I voice the thought, it only makes us laugh harder. "Thousands of pounds!" Jolene yelps. "My nursery school teacher salary will cover that no bother! Stewart, you'll need to cut your daily pint rations down if we're ever to pay this off."

"Whit?! It wasnae me who threw the hammer."

More gales of laughter follow this, but a sudden outraged shriek silences us.

"What have you done to my car?"

Whoops. Jack's minibus has pulled into the car park, and its passenger marches towards us, eyes narrowed and two spots of high colour on her cheeks. My head twists back to the minibus, its other occupant emerging more slowly. If he is angered on Kirsty's behalf, it doesn't show.

265

"Sorry Kirsty, I'll pay for someone to fix it," Jolene says, her words coming out in fits and bursts because she's trying not to laugh.

"You'd better, you stupid, clumsy fu—"

"Kirsty."

Kirsty's head whips around. I guess she didn't realise Jack was so close behind her. The screwed up expression slides off her face and her mouth curls into a big smile that doesn't reach her eyes.

"Jack!" Giggle, giggle, and I bite my lip hard to stop myself sniggering at the tinkly laughy bit Mhari talked about earlier.

"Just a little accident! That's why we have insurance, isn't it?"

If any insurance company fork out for this, I'll eat my hat but Jack digs his phone out of his pocket, moves away from us and has a conversation with someone that consists of 'aye' 'no' and 'ten pm'.

"Lachlan Forrester'll fix it," he says as he returns to us. "Tonight."

Stewart nods. "Aye, Lachlan's the man for the job. He'll make it look brand new. The company will never know."

Kirsty threads an arm through Jack's and pecks him on the cheek. "My hero! It's amazing when a guy comes to your rescue like that, isn't it?"

Stewart nods again. "Aye, Lachlan's a good bloke. You mind last year, Jolene, when we needed to change the number plates on the car after that wee incident on the—"

She stamps hard on his foot, and he shuts up.

"I meant Jack!" Kirsty says, tinkly laughy again. "We'll wait for Lachlan in your house, shall we?"

And with that, she steers him away. I long for him to turn his head back our way and mutter something—*sorry, we're not going to do anything, she's not given me a choice*—but his head stays fixed forward.

"I can't believe that daft git is going back to her," Jolene says. My heart, already in free fall, nosedives to my feet. I wait for Katya to say something, shrug off Jolene's words and give me hope to cling to, but she stays quiet, giving my arm a tiny squeeze I guess she means as consolation. We head back to the house.

By the time we get back there, it's early evening. Ryan, whose lift back to Glasgow airport won't take place until tomorrow morning, has settled himself in front of the TV and he makes a point of turning the volume up when we come in. Katya curls her top lip and makes loud comments about a-holes, idiots and lousy, cheating cads. The open plan nature of the ground floor of Kirsty's house doesn't lend itself to hiding away in other rooms.

We were stuck with him. Thankfully, the two pizzas, extra chips and cake mean neither Katya and I want to eat so we take ourselves upstairs to the spare room, followed by Mena who's decided she'd much rather be in the girl gang than the boy one. I lie on the bed and ask Katya to sort my life out for me. She'd done it once before, getting me out of Great Yarmouth. It looks as if my Lochalshie cat-sitting gig is about to finish and I can't return to my old home. Mena sits herself on my chest and purrs, which makes me tearful.

"Th-th-thing is," I say, "I want to take this little one with me. I lo-lo-love her so much."

"Get a grip," Katya says, though she sticks a hand out to stroke Mena too, her little head butting against her fingers. "There'll be other lovely cats. Why don't you go for somewhere more exotic next time? I found plenty of cat owners in Las Vegas looking for sitters when I checked."

That's what Kirsty promised. She owes me a glowing reference, that's for sure. When Jack goes back to her, she'll be so pleased with herself she'll write anything. Instead of Las Vegas, perhaps I can go to Los Angeles. That will please Melissa, seeing as that is where Blissful Beauty has its official headquarters. I want to be millions of miles away from the perfect couple, and if I never to go on social media or watch The One Show ever again just in case, I can avoid any accidental sightings.

In the end, we both fall asleep early, the food, exercise and fresh air kicking in. My dreams are a terrible mash-up of Jack dressed as Jamie Fraser appearing and disappearing behind the walls of Doune Castle, a blonde woman who giggles too much and hammers that smash through the castle walls while a white Highland terrier barks his head off.

The sunlight streaming in on Sunday morning wakes us, the smell of toast and bacon drifting upstairs.

"I don't s'pose any of that is for us," Katya says, throwing back the duvet and swinging her legs out of bed.

"Nope," I say, "but worth a try."

Up and dressed, we edge our way to the kitchen just in case Ryan has booby-trapped the stairs. To my astonishment, Kirsty perches on one of the high chairs around the kitchen island, her chin in her hands, a move that looks too practised, all the better to display her heart-shaped face to advantage. Ryan moves behind her in the kitchen, making scrambled eggs once more and grilling bacon. He doesn't bother looking around. Kirsty lets out that (annoying) tinkly laugh as soon as she sees us.

"Goodness me! I've no idea why I'm so bright and fresh this morning. And I had hardly any sleep last night! How was your night?" she says, the words directed at me.

"Brilliant," I say. "Catching up with my best friend."

At that, her eyes narrow. "Oh? Didn't you and Ryan…?"

Ryan slams the frying pan down on the chopping board.

"No," I say, careful to make my voice cheerful. "Kayleigh wasn't the first, so yes, Kirsty, I allow everyone one mistake. I draw the line at six though."

The number was a wild guess, but when Ryan doesn't deny the figure, I realise I've hit the spot. Katya starts up about lousy cheating gits once more, but Kirsty says we'll all feel better after tea.

"I'm taking Ryan back to the airport this morning," she says. "I promise you he's a changed man, Gaby. Who could fail to be thrilled by a guy who does something as romantic as that amazing post on Facebook? Everyone on my website swooned at that. You must have a heart of stone!"

She giggles again when she says that and Katya mimes vomiting while Ryan glares at her.

"Well," Kirsty slides off the seat and pats me on the back. "Think carefully, Gaby. Ryan's your best opportunity. You should give it a week, hmm? That isn't much for a guy to ask after ten years, is it?"

I nod automatically, stopping the moment Katya digs me hard in the ribs. It's a huge relief to wave them off in Kirsty's good as brand new BMW half an hour later, Kirsty telling us she needs to return to London for talks with her agent about the personal project she's working on and the latest super-exciting development but she'll be back next weekend. My heart sinks further. That will be the development where she's able to add a personal story to the back of her ruddy *How to Hook a Commitment-Phobe* book, complete with a sickly picture of her and Jack. Urgh.

"Good riddance to bad rubbish," Katya says as we watch the car drive off. "I'm chucking that ghostwriting job. The book's nowhere near finished because she's so useless so I haven't written too much to have to keep going with it. I've also decided I'm going to stay the week as I want to see how the Highland Games turn out. How does that sound?"

I hug her. "It sounds brilliant."

CHAPTER 24

A week later, the village transforms in front of us. Lochalshie's villagers have focussed their efforts on wishing for sunshine or at least a dry day. Whatever they did, and I suspect it meant a deal with the Devil, it has worked and the day of the Highland Games dawns bright and sunny.

We are up almost before the sun rises as there is so much to do. Katya comes with me to meet Dexter, desperate to clap eyes on the man she's done so much writing for. Or rather, wrote the first article, changed it, rewrote it, revised it once more and then returned to her original version, which he finally declared himself happy with. "I want to meet this idiot," she mutters darkly, "so I can see what a fool looks like. And persuade you not to give his offer any headroom. I'm here to save you from yourself."

Katya is still not convinced I am not giving serious consideration to Ryan's offer either.

Already, the village is filling up. When we open the gate to Kirsty's house, cars queue up the whole road heading for the car park, and the games don't start for another four hours. Jamal waves at us both from across the street where he is busy putting out baskets with sun hats and rain ponchos (one must cover all the bases in Scotland). The Blissful Beauty team have given him an end of aisle make-up display, especially for the occasion. As he'd read up on how much Boots charges for an end of aisle display, Jamal named a fat fee when the company approached. He gives us a cheery grin, no doubt expecting a flood of customers. People pack the streets too. Katya and I have to dodge around hundreds of young women, all peering at their phones and talking about where will be the best place to park themselves when Caitlin makes her appearance. Stewart stands at the shores of the loch and yells at Scottie who has tangled himself up around the legs of one woman.

"OMG!" Another of them exclaims, stopping dead in front of Katya and I. "That's Jamie Fraser! Luce, let's get a selfie with him!"

My head jerks instinctively in the direction they run off. I have only seen him in passing since the car park incident last week, though my mind has filled in plenty of torturous imaginations since. *Be still my heart,* I mutter to myself to no avail. It throbs double-time, taken aback by how glorious he looks today. Katya lets out a low whistle I hope he doesn't hear. Today, as he will be manning a stall advertising the Outlander tours, Jack has dressed the part in an authentic 18th-century kilt. They are drab compared to the bright greens, reds and golds you see in modern tartan, but the simplicity of it highlights his beauty I decide. Brown tones drive the eyes upward and show off the gold glints of his hair. You focus on his face and its exquisite, sharp planes and those big brown eyes. And the knees are on show, the bit of his body I'm strangely obsessed with. We watch as Luce and her friend screech to a halt in front of him.

"Can we get a picture with you?" the first one asks, and he rolls his eyes and agrees. Over the tops of their heads, he catches my eye and shakes his head. I guess he knew this was bound to happen today, but it doesn't mean he's comfortable with it. A second later and he smiles at the phone the girls hold up. Katya clutches my arm. "Dear heaven," she breathes. "He's lethal."

I wave at him as we pass, mouthing the words 'good luck!' both for the Highland Games when he will contest the caber toss, and for the tours. Since I explained to him his failure to publish the website I made for him, it's now live and the bookings have flooded in. Today will be the icing on the cake. Thousands of people will walk past a stall manned by someone who looks like Sam Heughan. Or his younger brother as Jack keeps reminding me, promising them tours of places mentioned in the books or that turn up in the TV series. Success guaranteed. He doesn't need my good luck, but I pass it on anyway and hope it makes him think of me fondly.

Dexter is in residence in the Lochside Welcome where the launch is to take place—sort of. His Glaswegian experience had convinced him of the wisdom of not putting your trust in the British weather. He booked the hotel and decided Caitlin could launch her skin care and make-up brand there. If the skies opened on the day, at least she would be warm and dry.

The hotel is unrecognisable. The Blissful Beauty's branding people arrived last night and littered the company's colours and logos everywhere. They have replaced the hotel sign with a Blissful Beauty one, and a long pink and silver carpet stretches out the front. in the grounds, projectors beam Caitlin's face and the Blissful Beauty logo on the walls of the hotel. Organised chaos reigns inside. I wave at Ashley, who stands at the stairs, a glazed look on his face as people bustle about him, lugging furniture and boxes, and shouting orders at each other. Every optic at the bar offers pink gin to match Blissful Beauty's company colours, and pop-ups and decals decorate the whole area. The Blissful Beauty people have even changed the lighting, pink bulbs sending out a soft glow.

Dexter stands in the middle of the room, armed with a clipboard. When he spots us, he signals us over, and I introduce Katya. The next bit astonishes me so much, I'm forced to question everything I thought I knew about life, my best friend and the universe.

"Katya," Dexter says, his tones reverential. "So awesome to meet you at last."

"Dexter," she says, her tone an exact match for his. "Ditto."

I search the words for any trace of sarcasm and find none. They regard each other solemnly, and I work out that Dexter's original offer of a date post event has nosedived to the ground, crashed and burned. The handshaking continues far longer than it should, two people reluctant to stop their contact with each other. I wonder afresh at my nanna's insight—there's a lid for every pot. *Too right, nanna*, I think. It's just that sometimes you'd never put a particular lid with a particular pot. I remind myself of Katya's list of 'dont's' for boyfriends. Dexter probably ticked every one of those boxes, but it looks as if she is about to abandon that list.

When they eventually drop hands, Dexter turns to me. "The website's live, Gaby. We launched it this morning, and it crashed after an hour!"

In theory, this is a bad thing. The back room stuff on a website shouldn't be so feeble a flood of traffic causes it to meltdown. But these days, a website crash is a badge of honour. Take Meghan Markle, for instance. The Markle Sparkle means anything she's worn in the last year from a relatively unknown designer has caused websites to blow up the world over. It says something about your company if you implode, thanks to too many people typing its name into Google. I'm in no doubt that behind-the-scenes tech bods are working their socks off to get that website live again. And meanwhile Dexter can put messages on Blissful Beauty's social media accounts saying, "Sorry everyone! We're experiencing so much traffic at the moment, our website can't cope! We'll have it back up and running as soon as. In the meantime why not sign up for our mailing list, so you don't miss out?"

"Good-o!" I say. "When's Caitlin arriving?"

Dexter tears his eyes from Katya, the move reluctant. He holds his wrist up to check his Apple watch. "Two minutes' time. We cleared the school football field for her helicopter. Do you wanna come and meet her?"

It's a question addressed to both of us in theory when it means just Katya. Much as I love my best friend and want to encourage this burgeoning relationship, the opportunity to meet one of the biggest megastars in the world is too tempting to resist.

"Yes!" I say, "but you two go ahead of me. I want a quick word with Ashley."

I watch them skip out of the room, heads tipped towards each other. I count to thirty and follow them, arriving at the football field as the chopper descends. It too is decorated in pink and silver, a contrast to the two pilots who wear the universal uniform of pilots the world over—shirt, trousers, peaked hat, aviator glasses and stony faces. The blades slowly whirl to a halt, and the door opens. Out jumps the tiniest woman in the world. I'm serious. It's common knowledge that celebrities are always much shorter and thinner in real life than they appear on the screen, but Caitlin must be the universe's smallest person. She bounds over to us, extending a hand.

"Hey! I'm Caitlin," she says and flings her arms around first Dexter, then me and then Katya. Her being so small her arms only come round our waists. I was ready to hate her, but the gesture makes me melt. Then she cements my like for her forever.

"Dexie, you beautiful man you, I need to pee like nothing else. For the love of everything holy, please get me to a toilet before all this liquid explodes out of me."

We hurry her on to the Lochside Welcome, her promising us she's just about desperate enough to squat on the street and let it all out. She exclaims about the beauty of the place and expresses huge disappointment Dexter decided against the thing where a speed boat soared into the loch, did a fancy double turn and deposited Caitlin to walk down the pier. The crowds of people gathered in the streets see us, and there's a collective gasp.

"It's HER!" And they surge forward. Dexter must have expected this and security guards jump into place funnelling us a tunnel to walk through while Caitlin waves and blows kisses to her fans. Inside the hotel, Ashley hurries to meet her, grasping her tiny hands in his massive ones, having to bend in half to do so as she reaches his knees.

"This counts as the most fantastic day of my life," he says, tears in his eyes. "Caitlin's Cool Life is the best thing on TV. It's a dream come true to meet you."

Caitlin kisses his hands, and he sways, overcome. I worry he might faint. "Ashley," she says. "I gotta pee. Where are your toilets?"

He points her toward the toilet and watches her run off. "I'll need to put a sign up," he tells us. "'Caitlin used this toilet.' Imagine the crowds that'll attract."

Caitlin rejoins us minutes later, her expression much calmer. "Boy," she says. "You can't beat a good horse pee, is there? It's better than anything, better than s—"

"Shall I run through the programme for today," Dexter interrupts. "And your speech?"

They move off, though I don't miss the look he shoots Katya, which I interpret as 'I'll hook up with you later if that is okay'. I'm not facing my friend so I can't see what she returns it with. but I'm willing to bet it was agreement. "Well," I say, "I'm gob-smacked. I would never, in a million, billion years, have put you with Dexter. You said he was a workaholic and too critical."

Katya purses her lips. "Yes, well. Perhaps I've changed my mind…"

She blushes, which astonishes me once more. In all the years I've known my best friend, I've never seen her embarrassed. Mainly because she leaves making a fool of oneself to me, and secondly because she is an expert at styling anything out. It's a day for mind-blowing revelations.

I suggest we head to the park and offer our services helping set up the games. Outside, we move against the tide. Everyone else is heading to the Lochside Welcome, and I cross my fingers the games will get enough attention. In the park, the hive of activity makes the Lochside Welcome look tame. People dart here and there, putting up signs, fencing off areas for stalls and stages and cart about strange bits of kit I assume are for the Highland Games bit. The re-enactment of the Battle of Stirling Bridge appears to have started early as groups of kids wearing fake armour bash each other with plastic swords.

Jolene, armed with a clipboard, waves at me, and we ask her what she wants us to do. She points at a small purple tent at the far side of the field. "Can you help Psychic Josie set up?"

"Psychic Josie?" Katya asks as we head over to her tent. "Yes," I say. "She communes with the dead to make predictions about your love life. Wildly successful by all accounts."

"What absolute tosh," Katya says, just as I decide I'm going to ask Psychic Josie if Ryan is telling the truth and if she thinks I should give it another try. Or, and my mind is too afraid to even admit it to myself, I should concentrate my questions on some-some-some-one else.

The tent's interior is as dark as the outer, the entry covered by old-fashioned, brightly coloured door beads that clink together as we enter. An oil distiller burns, wafting out jasmine, lavender and eucalyptus. There's a table against the back, and a woman sits behind it, her face half hidden by a veil that covers her mouth and nose, and a Paisley-patterned scarf on her head. She looks familiar, and I put it down to having seen her on social media somewhere advertising her seminars.

"I sense a non-believer," she says, and Katya bristles beside me.

"Too right, but if daft gullible people want to hand over money for your advice who am I to stand in their way? What do you need doing?"

The veil covers her mouth, but I sense Psychic Josie smile. She points towards boxes. "If you could put the signs up outside, that would be great. And then set up the money box and float. D'ye want me to predict how you and Dexter will work out, love?"

Katya's mouth tightens. She grabs one of the boxes and flounces out. I'm still trying to figure out Psychic Josie's accent. It's part Eastern European, part Scottish. I guess she's a Romanian who has lived here most of her life.

"Shall I do you?" she says to me. "A freebie? The air trembles with the incredible energy coming off you! And the spirits hover, desperate to intervene and stop you making a mistake."

Ooh. "Okay then," I sit down opposite her and she takes my hand, turning it over, so it's palm up.

"Dinnae make mistakes with your love life," she says. I screw my face up. Is that it? I'm not the one claiming psychic powers here, but don't make mistakes with boyfriends is like the advice they give you in horoscopes— far too general to be useful. It could apply to anyone.

"Anything else?" I say, glad I didn't pay for this crap.

"I sense questions. Ask me, and I'll channel them through the spirits. The spirits are never wrong, ye know."

Sod it. I go for the question I really want the answer to.

"Will Jack go back to Kirsty?" The words burst out of me. Psychic Josie is a stranger so she won't know who they are and if she is as good as she says she is, I'll get a proper answer.

"Dear lord, I hope no'!" All traces of the Eastern European accent vanishes, and she pulls the veil down. I groan, horrified. Dr McLatchie. I'll say this for the woman. She has a wide range of interests, what with doctoring, dancing and giving people daft advice about their love lives. She doesn't seem too bothered I've just outed her either.

"That yin," she says, "was no' interested in my son. All she wanted was a good-looking boy on her arm. Mother-ly bias and all that, but ma Jack is an awfy handsome lad. But if I got her a daughter-in-law, I'd leave the country. Mebbe even the continent."

Her eyes narrow and then her mouths rounds into an 'o' of surprise.

"D'ye like Jack, Gaby?"

Spirits indeed! Shouldn't they have revealed that to her already? I say that, and she waves a hand. "Och, I tell people what they want to hear and that makes them hap-py. Ye just use a bit of body language analysis. And social media helps because most folks spill their guts on there. I get everyone to book in advance and check everyone out quickly before they come in to see me. It's awfy easy."

"Don't tell Jack I asked about him and Kirsty!" I beg, and her face drops.

"But wouldn't it be nice if you—"

"NO! I mean it if you do I'll tell everyone here you're a fraud."

Blackmail is a dirty word, but these circumstances are exceptional.

"Spoilsport," she says. "Why d'ye think Jack will get back with Kirsty?"

"She stayed the night the other week and smiled a lot afterwards. And there's that painting," I say. "Why does he keep it? Big Donnie offered him five and a half grand for it, and he knocked it back. I'd have thought the money would come in handy. He must still love her if he hangs onto it."

At that, the doctor bursts out laughing. Hysteria makes her difficult to understand, but eventually I get what she's trying to say.

"He painted it!" Dr McLatchie tells me. "It's far too flattering if you ask me, but he's proud of the picture, and that's why he keeps it. Nothing to do wi' the sitter. He painted all those other pictures in his house too. It's what he likes to do in the winter when he's no' doing the tours."

"But, but," I throw in. "He's never been that keen on me. He didn't even invite me to that party he held way back in June."

The doctor frowns and then smiles. "He did ask ye! He got Jock to do it because he forgot when youse were on the bus. And I can tell you something else. He wasnae pleased when you didn't come. Thought you were being snooty, considering yourself too good for small town parties."

I stare at her, amazed that she still doesn't realise Great Yarmouth is no metropolis and astonished that my thinking for so long has been wrong. For weeks, I was convinced that Jack didn't like me enough to invite me to the legendary annual Lochalshie party, and he'd done so all along. I think back to that night and the conversation I had with Jock. Even now, three months into my Lochalshie residency, I'm no nearer to understanding what he says most of the time. We muddle along with smiles and waves, me saying 'good, good' all the time. But on the night of the party, he said to me, 'Perty tonicht', translation obvious now I think about it. And the word 'McCollin' could just as easily be McAllan.

I'm an idiot, or eejit as they like to say here.

Katya has finished setting up outside, and she wanders back in, brushing her hands against her jeans. "Anything else need doing?" she asks, and Psychic Josie stroke Dr McLatchie whips the veil back over her face and asks again if Katya wants to know about her and Dexter. Katya tightens her lips and shakes her head. I wave an awkward goodbye to Psychic Josie, conscious that I threatened her. And yet she's just told me news that has made this weekend do a one hundred and eighty-degree turn in terms of my happiness levels.

"I think I might find Jack's stall," I say, my tone as casual as I can make it.

It doesn't fool my friend for a second. "Go for it," she says. "Pluck him from Kirsty's grasp as firmly as you can!"

CHAPTER 25

Jack's stall was at the far end of the park where it could capture people leaving the games overwhelmed with a fondness for all things Scottish and inclined to sign up for an authentic Outlander tour.

I headed in its direction, pushing my way past nervous Highland dancers waiting to compete on the stage, kilted men stretching their muscles ahead of hammer throws and caber tossing, and pipers warming up. I recognised a good few of the locals among the dancers, pipers and strong men. This year, the Highland Games had captured everyone's imaginations, and all the villagers wanted to take part.

"But we were so fabulous together, Jack darling!"

Because the park was so noisy and crowded, I was almost at Jack's stall when I heard her. Kirsty had made good on her threat to return then. I'd allowed my hopes to rise when Katya and I hadn't seen her in the house that morning. To make the stall's purpose clear, Jack had parked his minibus next to it so prospective tourers could check out how comfortable it was. The table in front of him featured leaflets and plates of shortbread, the latter being my suggestion. In addition, a full-size cut-out stood at the side of the table, the idea of which had horrified Jack.

"I can't put that up," he said when the order came through from Print Express the week before, his face aghast. "Everyone will think I'm the biggest egotist in the whole of Scotland. I'll never live it down." Egotist wasn't the word he used; something far stronger and easy to imagine the Lochside Welcome punters announcing in jeering tones the next time he dared put his head around the door. I sympathised, but if a man is to succeed, he has to do certain things.

"Too bad," I'd said. "I know a lot more about design and branding than you do and this cut-out will bring 'em in, in droves. And when you need a break from manning the stall, people will still know what the tour guide looks like."

I edge behind the cut-out now, as Jack and Kirsty haven't spotted me. This is a conversation that makes my nerves jangle.

Behind me, one of the warming up pipers decides now is the time to belt out the opening bars to Flower of Scotland. Great. Whatever Jack replies, I can't hear it.

The piper pauses again. Kirsty's profile is visible, though Jack's isn't. She's pulled out all the stops. The temperature isn't that warm, but Kirsty wears a scarlet-coloured sequined kimono dress. The knot at the front low enough to show she isn't wearing a bra, and she's put her hair in two loose French braided pigtails, tiny tendrils framing her face. It must be Dating Guru tip #176—always wear your hair up so he can imagine pulling it loose…

"I've thought a lot about what went wrong," Kirsty continues, her voice a low purr. "We went too fast, too soon. And I know the photos on Instagram were too much. But I wouldn't make that mistake again, and I would…"

The blasted piper starts up again, and the noise drowns out the rest of what she says. It doesn't matter as Jack turns at that moment and I see his face in full. I was hoping for disgust or at the very least dismay, but he wears a huge grin. Those eyes of his sparkle and my stomach squeezes, a combination of nausea and despair. I'm too late.

I stumble away, pushing past the pipers and the dancers, and trying to hold back tears.

"Gaby! I was looking for you."

Jolene does a double take and asks me if anything is wrong. "Wind making my eyes water," I say, plausible as I've yet to spend a single day in Lochalshie when the wind hasn't been close to gale force.

"We need to get the Games started. Caitlin's going to declare them open so can you help me marshal the crowds?"

She points behind her, and I baulk. Crowds is an understatement. Perhaps it's because the place is so small, all you can see is faces—young, old and what looks like every colour and creed. How we are to make our way through, much less stop them surging forward the minute Caitlin appears I do not know. I'll be crushed to death in the rush, though the mood I'm in at the moment means I won't care.

Jolene puts two fingers to her mouth and whistles, a talent I've always wished I had. Minutes later, men appear at her side—the ones I spotted earlier stretching their muscles ready for games. "What d'ye want us to do, Jolene?" the biggest of them asks, a man so massive I have to crick my neck to look up at him. He has biceps bigger than my torso and a broken nose that sends out a clear 'don't mess with me' message. "Get us to the front of the park, Angus," she says, "and help us with crowd control."

Seven of them form a circle around us and move people to the side so we can get through, parting them like Moses did with the Red Sea. We're at the front in no time, and Jolene runs through the plan with me. Caitlin will exit the hotel and make her way down the high street, accompanied by the Lochalshie and District Pipe Band. When she gets to the front of the park, there will be a microphone and podium from where she will announce the games open and cut the ribbon at the gates to the park. At which point even more people than are here already will stream through. The other half will flow back to the Lochside Welcome where the official launch of Blissful Beauty is to take place. I cross my fingers, hoping the entertainment in the park is enough that the crowds don't all disappear back to the hotel.

Jolene holds up a walkie-talkie, and I do a double take. Wouldn't a phone have done the job? But I suspect it makes her feel like a proper events organiser and I hear Dexter's voice. His security team is still battling back the crowds at their end. Hired hands aren't half as good as Lochalshie's strong men who also double up as its rugby team and people not afraid to wade in. The pipes start up at the far end of the village and Jolene gives me a thumbs up. Misery over Jack aside, I match her broad smile. Months of planning and hundreds of emails back and forth are about to pay off. The mass of people in front of us swivels their heads, too hemmed in to be able to turn and watch. The police have done their best to keep people off the road and give the pipers a clear path to the park. I sense their slow movement is because stragglers dart out to take sneak photos of Caitlin.

Jolene and I have no hope of seeing anything. One of our security team stoops over, so his face is level with mine. "Want a lift up tae see?" he asks. I demur, "I'm too heavy." He ignores me and sweeps me up onto his shoulders. A man who routinely pulls a two-tonne truck behind him will not find me a burden. It's almost impossible to see Caitlin, and then I notice a horse and rider in the middle of the pipe band and—

No. My eyes are fooling me, I decide, shaking my head at the same time as the crowds around me cotton on too.

The woman sitting astride the horse and giving out cheery waves appears to be naked, her bits covered only by what must be a long wig that trails down her front. Thousands of phones are held in the air, everyone desperate to catch what is just about to break Twitter and Instagram. Jolene, beside me on the broken-nosed guy's shoulders turns to me. "That wasn't agreed!" she exclaims. "Her manager asked me to get her a horse, seeing as she's so small, and I got her one of Laney Haggerty's ponies from the horse riding school. I dunno if she'll take it back now!"

Anyone still in the park has come out, the rumour spreading quicker than the Lochalshie's WhatsApp group updates. They duck under the ribbon and Jolene and the giants carrying us sway as sheer numbers push past. When Caitlin comes to a halt in front of us, the pipers man and woman-fully keeping their eyes upfront, so they don't ogle her as she slides off the pony. She isn't naked after all, instead wearing one of those nude bodysuits. It is transparent enough, though, to show she has no underwear on and she favours extreme grooming of the lady garden.

The giants lower us to the ground. Angus tries so hard not to stare, Jolene ends up tumbling from his shoulder and landing in a heap on the grass in front of Caitlin. As my giant carrier manages a more graceful disembarkation of his passenger, I step forward. My mind blanks. What do I do? Ask her to open the games while almost naked? It's a family event, and around me, I can see mums and dads with their hands clamped over their children's eyes. Someone thrusts a plaid blanket in my hands, and I step forward without stopping to thank whoever.

"Caitlin," I announce. "It's awfully cold and windy in the park. Let's cover you up."

She grins at me, a woman who knows she's taken advantage big style. "Cute!" I hiss at her as I do my best to fashion a cover-all dress out of a brown blanket. "Bet they'll be booking up months in advance for next year's games," she replies, white-toothed beam not moving a millimetre. "Who knows? I might come back." I roll my eyes, but she's right. As stunts go, this is up there. A non Blissful Beauty branded helicopter circles above us and I wonder which of the TV news channels it represents.

Back on her feet, Jolene hands Caitlin the giant pair of scissors used every year to declare the games open.

"Guys! It's fantastic to be here. As you can see, Blissful Beauty makes skin care and make-up so amazing, you don't need to cover up."

"Ahem," Jolene says, blatant advertising being something else the games committee didn't agree to.

"So, after you've watched the competitions and eaten your fill of haggis, why not treat yourself to a little TLC courtesy of Blissful Beauty? And in the meantime, it is my great honour to cut the ribbon and declare the Lochalshie Highland Games open!"

Oh well. Yes, people will remember the games for years to come. The legendary summer an A-Lister opened the games naked (sort of) and plugged her make-up line to an audience who, in the main, wouldn't recognise one end of a lipstick tube from another.

She cuts the ribbons and the crowds cheer, the sound so loud I'm forced to put my hands over my ears. Dexter appears by my side. "Seriously?" I ask, and he shrugs not quite meeting my eyes. "Caitlin's, um, impetuous," he says and moves her past people where a car awaits to drive her the 800 metres to the hotel. I'm relieved that the crowd splits evenly—half following Caitlin's car, and the rest streaming into the park accompanied by the pipers. It takes ages for the front of the park to clear, its gates unused to groups more substantial than a handful entering at a time. Outside Psychic Josie's tent, a huge queue has formed. And scepticism or no, my friend Katya has taken up the position as bookings taker.

"Expertly done, Gaby sketch," words whisper behind me and I spin around so fast I almost trip.

Jack, I now realise was the mystery blanket provider. He's got previous for it. His minibus carries spare blankets should any of its passengers get too cold, Scotland not being known for its warm weather even in the peak of summer. "I'm in awe of your quick thinking. You promised me you'd help out for an hour or so with the stall? I've got to defend my title as chief caber tosser."

He tilts an eyebrow at that, and the warmth that lit me up when he used my nickname trickles away. I'm just wanted for my usefulness, it seems. Jack's going to vanish with Kirsty, all tendril-haired and red-dressed. Perhaps they will even end up at the Blissful Beauty event, laughingly taking selfies as Caitlin steers them toward that lipstick or this face cream. I don't suppose Jack is bothered about lipstick, but I am open-minded about these things. The all-too-plausible scenario is easy to imagine. It benefits everyone. Kirsty goes back to Jack. Caitlin gets yet more beautiful people on her social media sites. Jack ends up with… well, another go at gorgeous Kirsty and no doubt plenty of eager punters ready to sign up for the authentic Outlander tour.

"Of course," I say. "Let's go."

The park is still so crowded, it takes much longer than it should to push through. When we get to Jack's stall, his cut-out has fallen victim to the winds, despite the sand-bags. I move it upright reflecting that this is the closest I'm going to get to Jack's body ever.

"I need to double check something else as well," Jack says. "I won't be long. Are you okay to stay here while I go? Help yourself to shortbread."

I watch him walk off and snaffle four bits while no-one is watching. Naked stunts aside, the Lochalshie Highland Games Committee can have no complaints. Every stall—from those selling Scottish-related crafts and food and drinks to the ones flogging boat trips and Highland safaris—has groups of people around it. The stage where the Highland dancers perform is crowded and cheers roar from the far side where obscenely muscular men hurl hammers as far as they can. The cheers almost drowns out their grunts—almost but not quite. Plenty of people wander past me carrying small pink and silver bags branded with the Blissful Beauty logo. I will be having a word with Dexter later on. He owes me a freebie bag, and I won't be settling for a sample size nail varnish and a tiny pot of blusher either.

A steady stream of people ask about the tours. I show them the inside of the bus so they can get a feel for its luxury, allow them to take selfies next to cut-out Jack in exchange for their email addresses and a sign-up to the mailing list, and send them away with handfuls of leaflets and bits of shortbread. An hour later and I battle exhaustion; plastering a cheery smile on your face and non-stop sales talk isn't as easy as it looks. I'm relieved when the queue tails off, and people head elsewhere.

I spot Katya, and she forms her hands into a heart and then gives me a thumbs up. I must get her to do one of her pep talks later. "Gabrielle Amelia Richardson—you helped make this year's Lochalshie Highland Games a ginormous success. Ditto the UK launch of Blissful Beauty, its products in the entire hands of Scotland (feels like). You're Melissa's number one employee, laptop accidents aside, and you created not one but two amazing websites for the people here. Plus, you've made great friends. Next time, though, don't fall for the local heart-breaker, and you'll be tickety-boo!"

The boo bit's all that sticks of that imagined lecture, it is too close to what I want to do, boohoo all the way home. I force myself to say the words out loud, reasoning it is advice I read on the Dating Guru's website. She urges you to stand in front of the mirror in the morning and say "You're beautiful, sexy and amazing!" as a way of building your confidence. If I do the same with the career success bit, I will talk myself into happiness.

"Melissa's number one employee," I start with. Then, "Created not one but two fan-dabi-dosy websites for businesses here."

"Fan-dabi-dosy, were they?"

Curses. Jack has once again performed the trick of sneaking up on me. A blush starts, but I hold my ground. "Fan-dabi-dosy indeed. Look at this list of prospective customers I've got you, all thanks to them seeing the website beforehand and the cut-out."

He takes the list from me and his fingers brush mine. I'd hold on to it longer to maintain the contact, but I suspect I'd look silly. As if I haven't already made a fool of myself in front of him countless times already.

"I think it's more to do with you. They saw you standing here and decided you were too gorgeous to leave alone. Plus, they've heard you're a whiz at first aid, and you dive into lochs to save drowning dogs."

"Wh-what?" I splutter, but the words are nectar. He's serious too. I see no trace of mockery or sarcasm there. "Oh, and how did the tossing go, I mean your status as the best tosser... um. The Highland Games."

He pushes his lips together; a gentleman trying not to snort with laughter. "I lost," he said, remarkably cheery. "But mainly I needed to get away because I wanted to ask a few questions," he says. "Katya had a word with me earlier"—when, when, I'll kill her for not warning me—

"about the book she's been writing for a 'client'. She said it was only fair to warn me that someone might no' have pure motives for wanting to get back with me. And not that I didn't believe her, but I thought I'd ask the client herself to be fair."

When he pauses I only allow him two seconds. "Don't stop there! What happened next?"

"I wasn't ever going back to Kirsty," he says. "We're too different. But being used to sell books was the last straw. It helped push me in a direction I have been trying and failing to go for the last month."

"And where might that—"

"Jack! Gaby!"

Stewart, his sense of timing as impeccable as ever, makes his way unsteadily from the beer tent to Jack's stall. Behind him is a large group of people who all look as pie-eyed as he does. If they've been matching him drink for drink, tomorrow they're scheduled to experience the world's worst hangovers.

"I've just been telling the good folks here that this is the best tour of the Highlands and it's run by Jamie Fraser himsel'! They've all come tae sign up!"

CHAPTER 26

We end up stuck at the stall for the rest of the afternoon and into the early evening, the email sign-ups coming in thick and fast.

Every time I try to ask Jack the questions, *what did you need to check, and which direction do you want to go in*, another prospective tourist butts in. "'Scuse me, but do we get to see Castle Leoch on this tour?" or "Do I need to learn Gaelic to understand Jamie?" My customer service skills fly out the window as I am desperate to return to the previous conversation. Beside me, Jack sighs, plasters on a fake smile and replies, *Yes, Castle Leoch otherwise known as Doune Castle IS part of the tour, and no, no Gaelic necessary*. By the time, it gets to seven o'clock, I want to collapse on top of something warm and comfortable. And with someone. I beg fate not to let me be mistaken about what I thought Jack meant.

At last, the crowds drift away. They file out the park and stalls begin to pack up. Cars parked everywhere, the car park, the fields set up for the overflow and the streets rev up engines as too many people attempt to leave at once. I suspect Lochalshie is about to experience a once-in-a-lifetime event—a rush hour and a traffic jam. Stewart returns, more welcome this time as he has Katya and Dr McLatchie with him and they offer to pack up the stall for us.

Katya repeats her thumbs up, and I smile back, happy to forgive her for her prior meddling. She whispers to me that she saw Kirsty in her car earlier having what looked like a furious conversation with someone on her phone. Her agent perhaps—the one she'd promised a brilliant, foolproof guide to hooking a commitment-phobe in just ten steps and the story to prove it.

Jack grabs my hand. "Want to escape?"

I nod at once, exhaustion banished.

"C'mon then," he says, pulling me in the loch's direction. "Let's talk paintings and misunderstandings."

At the far side of the loch, I spot Stewart and Jolene, Scottie doing his wildly exciting diving for ducks thing. I send up a prayer that I won't need to rescue him again. Jolene waves, Stewart doing the same when he turns to see what his girlfriend is doing.

The whole place is adjusting back to normal. When Caitlin and her entourage left two hours ago, the vloggers, bloggers and journalists vanished soon after. I'm glad. They all spent shed-loads of money while they were here which is brilliant. But I've decided I'm a local now, English and not having lived here that long status notwithstanding. I prefer Lochalshie when I look around it and recognise everyone I see. Especially this one, the kilted, red-headed Scot who wants to know why I never bothered finding out the truth about him and Kirsty, the party and the painting from the source.

"You could have asked me," he says, retaking hold of my hand. He could do that a thousand times, I decide, and I'll never tire of it. The wind lifts tiny locks of copper hair and the question's curious, rather than accusing.

"What?" I say. "If you were still in love with a beautiful woman whose painting you clung onto for dear life?"

"I thought you were interested in that American dude," he adds. "Or you were going back to your ex. Mhari kept talking about it, and I didn't want to…"

"You could have asked me." Ditto, hmm?

I tell him about my mother and her belief that you should never ask a question if you don't want to know the answer. He grins and I watch the movement, one I've memorised over the short time we've been together. It starts slowly, a lift to the corners of his mouth as if he's trying it out for size. The uplift settles and then widens until the smile lights up his whole face. It touches his eyes and they sparkle.

"Do you like me, Gaby?"

Oh. Not fair.

I decide he doesn't get it all his way. "I tried asking you a few questions," I say, turning away, so we're not eye to eye any more. Dark clouds hover, the ever-present threat of rain. Who cares? Elements do your worst, I tell the skies. You can rain on me forever more, and I won't care. I am ninety percent sure of what is happening here. Nothing as certain as death or taxes is another of my nanna's sayings hence my ten percent left aside as a cautionary gesture. And the bubble of happiness inside me is impenetrable. "And you were dead rude."

"Was I?" The question expresses genuine surprise and I grin back at him. "Yup, totes. Mean and moody, one hundred percent. I kept thinking to myself, who is this ars—"

At that, he grabs hold of me and does the death move—the tickle you till you beg for mercy one. Arms fasten me to him and fingers dance under my arms and up and down my belly. I'm pressed in so tight it's suffocating. In a good way. I've always been ticklish, and my breath comes in gasps as I beg him to stop. I'll do anything, anything, I say.

"Answer the question then. Do you like me, Gaby?"

He ramps up the tickling.

"You. Are. Okay," I cough out. I remember Katya's ultimate compliment. "I wouldn't push you out of bed for farting."

Noooo… My brain connects with my heart at the same moment and I shake my head. Imagine bringing up flatulence in front of a man who makes you squiggle and squirm. The Dating Guru is aghast, her mouth down-turned in horror. One doesn't throw about the F-Word like that.

"If I tell you that despite your promise, I'm the only guy in the world who never farts, what would you push me out of bed for?" he says. The smirk is back in place.

"Eating toast in there," I say. "Also, cheating on me."

"Writing about me on a website," he says, and I turn at that. His expression is part serious, part spoilt by a grin. "Or telling a publisher you have a foolproof plan for making me propose to you."

We've reached the end of the west side of the loch. From now on, you need to scramble over rocks to reach the sands to continue walking. The sun is setting, and I want to watch it. I flop on the sand, its surface broken by up stones and Jack drops down beside me. He takes out a hip flask and promises me it's only Bailey's and not anything lethal like whisky. Or Pimms. The eyebrows raise at that, and I work out someone must have told him about the sodding falling over in the Lochside Welcome episode. Jolene, probably, the disloyal… Ah. She was Jack's friend first.

I take a gulp of the Bailey's. It's still cold and tastes, as it always does, of melted ice-cream. "I'd never write about you on a website," I say. The skies always look better when you lie on your back. "I wouldn't even change my relationship status on Facebook. And no gushy, loved-up pics of us either."

Jack nudges me. "I might allow you to do that on the odd occasion," he says. "And change your status. Girl-friend of Jack McAllan and a big hands off sign."

O-ho! I was ninety percent certain what was happening, but I allowed some doubt and the confirmation adds oodles more to my happiness levels. I grin back at him. We're both ridiculously pleased with each other and the smiles stay in place just as the first big raindrops splat on us. Three minutes from now and it will be a downpour, but I am reluctant to break the spell. The rain flattens and darkens Jack's hair and each drop rolls down his face, dripping from his eyebrows and down his nose.

"What about your location when you update your status on Facebook?" he says, and the smile vanishes. A serious question then. I'm a stranger here. I'm no longer welcome in Kirsty's house, the contract at an end and solemn promise to help her get back with Jack broken. Wondering if I could persuade her to part permanently with Mena distracts me for a few seconds. I'm a cat lover now, or maybe it's just little Mena who's clawed her way into my heart along with a red-headed Scotsman.

"Ah," I say, "there's a thing. I don't know if I could manage a long-distance relationship."

"I couldn't," he says, not taking his eyes from my face. "And now I've persuaded you I'm not a rude, arrogant git, I've decided I want to spend a lot of time with you."

My phone beeps—a WhatsApp message, I'm about to ignore it, but Jack takes the phone from me and beams. He pushes it back at me. The Lochalshie WhatsApp group, or rather the group's most prolific poster Mhari, has put a message up. Turns out she is looking for a flatmate, having decided at the grand old age of twenty-five, it is time to leave the parental home. I shoot Jack a suspicious look, and he shrugs far too innocently. This smacks of forward planning and the idea delights me, though how on earth Jack and I will keep any detail of our new relationship quiet, I have no idea. And I'll need to persuade Melissa my remote working gig is permanent. Can you imagine the Bespoke Design logo with Great Yarmouth, Lochalshie written at the bottom? It does not have the ring of London, Paris, New York.

But these are all worries for another day. The rain is beginning in earnest now, soaking through our clothes. Jack's tee shirt moulds to his body, outlining the well-defined pectoral muscles.

"The second time I saw you," I say, "I was worried I'd burst in on you while you were in the shower. I'm sorry to say my mind conjured up the image anyway, you naked with just a towel wrapped around your waist. And now I will finally see if my mind got it—"

Gaby, Gaby! Katya shakes her head sorrowfully. No need to go overboard on the keenness or the blatancy.

He raises an eyebrow. "Funnily enough, my mind's done the same thing the last few weeks."

A pause.

"I didn't bother with the towel."

"Perv!" I exclaim, and he laughs. We're going to have such fun. Ryan never laughed at himself.

"Do you plan on lying here in the rain for much longer?" he asks, lying down beside me. He's as wet and cold as I am, but it doesn't matter. I'm only aware of warm skin and the desire to stretch out next to it.

"Just another minute," I say, watching the wind chase the dark clouds from one side to the other. The sun peeks out beneath them, and a rainbow appears, the whole arc of it visible and bright. If Jack moves to the left, his head will appear at the end, his coppery hair my pot of gold.

He moves anyway, propping himself up on one elbow. He lowers his face until it is only centimetres from mine. We lock eyes, green ones saying 'you first', brown ones bouncing the question back, 'no, after you'. Some agreement is reached as we move at the same time and our lips meet. It starts softly, our lips moving against each other and then the intensity builds. His hand goes to my face, gentle movement that belies what our mouths and tongues do. He tastes of Bailey's and mint. My heart flutters furiously against my rib cage, and I feel his do the same thing. The rain has turned into a downpour, and yet neither of us lets its impact bother us, and I'm sheltered from the worst by his body. I open my eyes and meet his, the dark brown turned black and glittering, and inside me, every nerve ending explodes. And this, this is only a kiss and the start of it.

The rain too heavy to ignore any longer, we concede defeat. Jack gets up and holds out a hand to pull me up.

"Come on then," he says, "Let's watch the storm come in from the comfort of my home."

We run towards the village hand in hand, and I turn my head back briefly to the loch, a final glance at its magical beauty and a silent thank you to Lochalshie.

THE END

OTHER BOOKS BY THIS AUTHOR

I have other books—*The Girl Who Swapped, Artists Town* and the non-fiction book, *The Diabetes Diet*, which outlines how to use a low-carb diet to best effect. I also have a book of short stories, *Ten Little Stars*.

I hang out on Twitter, Facebook and Instagram @pinkglitterpubs, and my website is *https://emmabaird.com* You can also sign up for my (infrequent) newsletter at *pinkglitterpubs@gmail.com* I'll attempt to make you smile as often as I can. My cat features frequently (cats rule the internet, right?) so at the very least you'll see your fair share of cute cat pics. And I'll throw in a freebie for you. Wondering what happened when Dr McLatchie met her second husband? The Night We Met sets out the back story and you get to say hello to Jack again albeit a much younger one…

Highland Heart is the follow-up to *Highland Fling*, and I plan to release this in September (2019). Inner voice: *Emma, you bonkers eejit. You're committed now.*

*Here's the blurb for **Highland Heart**:*

*The follow-up to **Highland Fling**, **Highland Heart** is the story of Katya and Dexter—lovers who met at a magical village in the heart of the Scottish Highlands, but who begin to drift apart. She wants him; he wants her but there are thousands of miles between them.*

Meanwhile, there's a new dude in town. Zac is fun, flirtatious and determined to seduce Katya. The trouble is, can she resist? Especially as Dexter seems to be throwing himself into his work as marketing manager for a big reality TV star and her brand-new make-up company on a mission to take over the world.

And what about his relationship with Caitlin, the reality TV star he works for? Is it one hundred percent professional or are those photos that keep popping up in her Instagram feed as innocent as he professes?

*Village shenanigans, an eccentric cast of loveable characters and a catch up with Gaby and Jack of **Highland Fling** fame, **Highland Heart** explores what happens once the honeymoon stage of a relationship wears off.*

Finally, if you liked this book please review it. Reviews help authors like me get found, sell more books and encourage us to keep writing. Writing's a lonely, vulnerable experience. We cherish the flattering reviews and store them up to keep us going. Many thanks!

My other e-books can be found here:

https://books2read.com/tenlittlestars
https://books2read.com/artiststown
https://books2read.com/tgws

THE GRATEFUL THANKS BIT

When I think about the good folks who helped me with this book, I well up. Blimey, I found myself an A-Team for Highland Fling.

Enni Tuomisalo stumbled on my book via Wattpad. She lives in New Zealand, and she's a graphic designer so I couldn't have asked for a more useful beta reader. Thanks to her, I know a lot more about graphic design, New Zealand, Kiwi slang and the Maori people, and it's wonderful knowledge to have. She also designed the beautiful book cover for me, and she writes smart, thought-provoking women's fiction. Why not check her out? *https://yummybookcovers.com*

Eric J Smith is a man of honour. He has struggled his way through two of my books (I'm not his genre of choice). His comments are insightful, useful and proof that he takes beta reading seriously. Eric offers this as a service. If you are a writer, I can't recommend this highly enough. Email: *ericjsmith_2000@yahoo.com*

Kristien Potgieter picked and prodded her way through my book, loving it at the same time as telling me what was wrong and implausible. Again, she offers advice and help to aspiring writers, and I recommend her whole-heartedly. You can find her on Upwork.

Caron Allan lends me a lot of support, championing my writing and adding wise words about indie publishing and the myriad things it involves. Find her and her books at *caronallanfiction.com*

I must give a shout out to NaNoWriMo. For those of you who haven't heard of it, NaNoWriMo is a movement which encourages people to write a book or 50,000 words in a month. Highland Fling came about because of that. You join the group, post your daily word counts to the website and voila—thirty days later, you have a book (ish). The organisation also contributes money and encourages writing programmes for the young. What's not to love?

I owe Diana Gabaldon a shout out too. She's the author of the Outlander novels and the creator of the original Jamie Fraser. If you haven't read the books, I envy you. A wonderful world awaits.

Lochalshie is a made-up village—much easier to write about places if you make them up—but it is loosely based on Arrochar in Argyll & Bute. It's a beautiful place. Visit if you can.

If little Ms Mena inspired you to open your own home to a cat, can I urge you to adopt and not shop? There are cats in shelters everywhere and they all long for a forever home. I've had rescue cats all my adult life and they have brought me tremendous joy.

As I grow older, I'm increasingly conscious of how fortunate I am family-wise. Lovely sisters, a lively mum who has always made us her focus, and a husband who keeps paying the bills while I promise him at some point we *will* do our weekly food shop at Waitrose or Marks and Spencer's instead of Aldi because I make enough money through my book sales.

This book's been an experience—highs, lows, but mostly highs. I hope you enjoyed it.

THE STORY CONTINUES...

*Here's an excerpt from **Highland Heart**, the follow-up to **Highland Fling** and due out in autumn 2019.*

"... hey, what a coincidence! I was about to call you! There's this totally amazing, beyond awesome announcement the Blissful Beauty board made today at work—"

Katya zoned out, mouthing the all-too familiar words to herself. Beyond awesome. Totally amazing. When she'd first met Dexter, she found his hyperbole irritating. Then it became cute and now it had zinged back to making her want to scream. She put the phone on speaker and opened her laptop, deciding to finish a blog she'd been working on for a client. Dexter multi-tasked all the time, anyway. Doubtless while he phoned her he was checking his emails, updating his Outlook calendar and making an appointment with his over-worked hygienist. Those super-white American teeth didn't stay that way by accident.

"So what do you think? Isn't it the most exciting thing ever?"

Whoops. Caught out not listening and with Dexter, the 'most exciting thing ever' could be anything or nothing. The man was an enthusiasm machine. Mind you, Dexter also tempered his enthusiasm with plenty of suggestions. He could declare anything as awesomely amazing and add ten ideas for changes which would make the said thing 'beyond brilliant'.

Katya believed you should use hyperbole sparingly. If a person routinely come out with the words 'amazing', 'fantastic', and 'utterly brilliant', where were they left to go?

She let out a sigh. "Sorry, the phone cut out there. You know what the reception is like in this place." Fine most of the time. The reception excuse was the one everyone used when they pretended the real reason wasn't because they weren't listening. "What were you talking about?"

Go to the bottom of the supportive girlfriend list, she told herself. *And do not leave there until you are a much nicer person.*

He sighed back, or it might have be a harrumph. Had he put her on FaceTime and spotted the lack of attention? In case there was a sneaky tech way of spying on someone she hasn't worked out, she turned her phone face down.

"Blissful Beauty's UK launch was such a success," he said. Work talk once more. "Caitlin wants to conquer Asia and specifically South Korea. South Koreans spend

313

$13 billion on skincare and make-up every year. I mean, man—what potential. It'll be super-amazing if we crack that market."

Katya knew her friends envied her too. Dating the UK-based marketing manager of reality TV star Caitlin Cartier's Blissful Beauty make-up and skincare company did that to girlfriends. "The freebies!" they said, followed by, *"Um, so can you get us that glow serum/sparkle bronzer/lip plumper? I tried online, and it's sold out at the moment."*

Her handbag, propped on the desktop next to the laptop had spilled its contents—said glow serum and lip plumper among them. The bright pink and silver packaging, stars and all, seemed to wink at her—a sign the products themselves realised how desirable they are. Every single twenty-something wanted them in their handbag, beside their bed and tucked away safely in a locked bathroom cabinet.

"So… this weekend?" His enthusiasm quotient ratcheted back down and she tensed.

"I know we were supposed to meet up this weekend, but I gotta work—make a start on what we will promote and where. It's a whole different ballgame, South Korea. We gotta think much smarter than we did for the UK launch, and if I don't get started, some dude in the LA office will wing his or her way in there with beyond awesome plans that blow Caitlin—"

Enough already, to borrow American phraseology.

"You're cancelling."

"No! I'd love for us to meet in London, but it would need to be for one night only? And I'd have to catch a later flight than I planned, and to get away super early on the—"

"It's fine, Dexter. Let's cancel." No-one could accuse Katya Bukowski of not being able to take the hint. A weekend where she spent several uncomfortable hours on an overcrowded coach to get to London from Great Yarmouth, and then another few grabbed hours with a man too distracted to pay her attention?

No. Thank. You. And, *I did not sign up for this.*

Made in the USA
Monee, IL
11 August 2022

11401717R00187